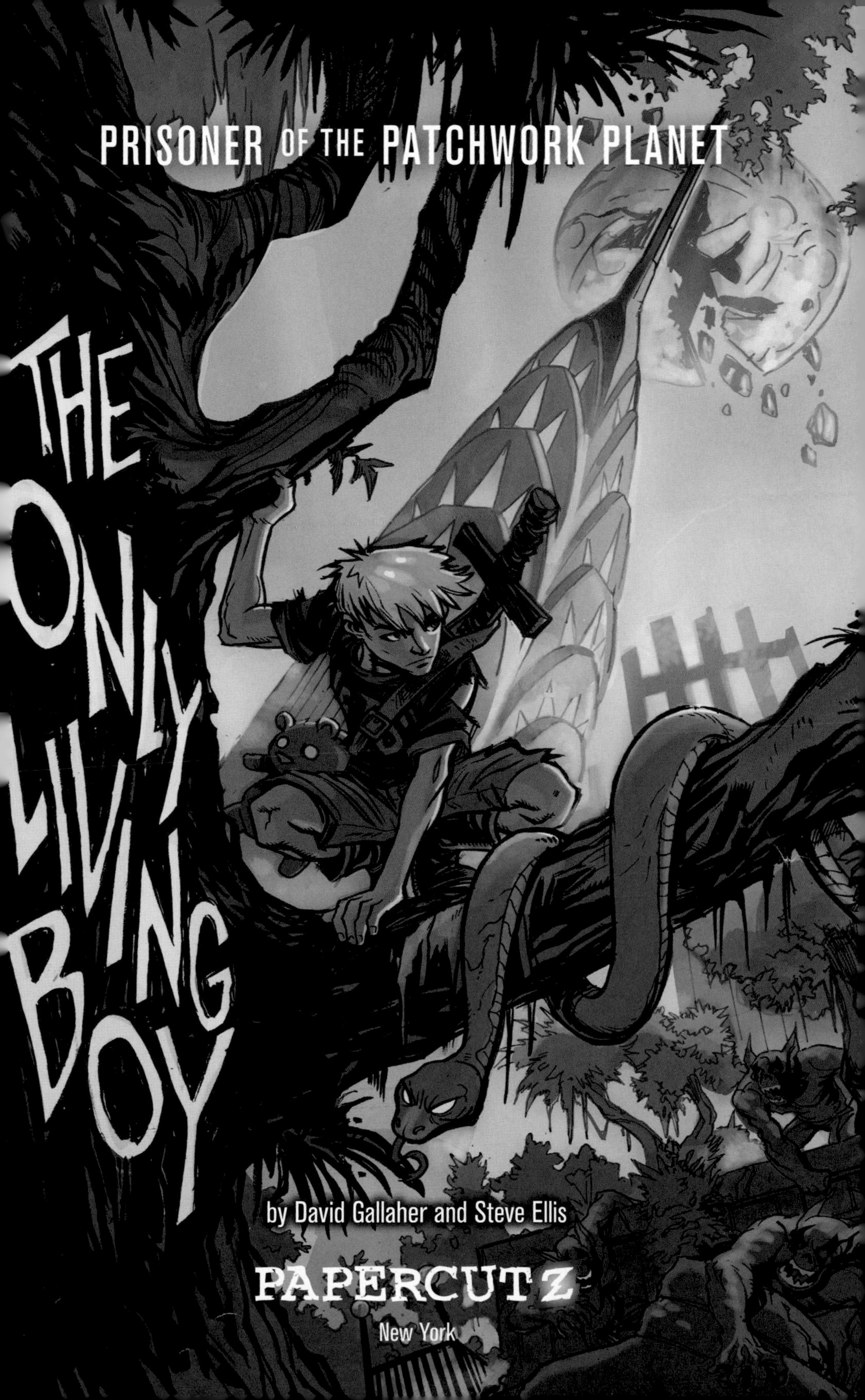

The Only Living Boy

Prisoner of the Patchwork Planet

by David Gallaher and Steve Ellis

PAPERCUTZ
New York

Dedicated to anyone who has felt lost
and longed for greater adventures

THE ONLY LIVING BOY #1 "Prisoner of the Patchwork Planet"

Chapter 1
Writer/Co-Creator: David Gallaher
Artist/Co-Creator: Steve Ellis
Color Flatting: Mike Paar
Lettering: Scott O. Brown, Christy Sawyer

Chapter 2
Writer/Co-Creator: David Gallaher
Artist/Co-Creator: Steve Ellis
Color Flatting: Mike Paar, Ten Van Winkle
Lettering: April Brown, Scott O. Brown, Christy Sawyer

Originally serialized at: www.the-only-living-boy.com

Publication rights for this edition arranged through Papercutz and Hill Nadell Agency.

Papercutz books may be purchased for business or promotional use. For information on
bulk purchases please contact Macmillan Corporate and Premium Sales Department at
(800) 221-7945 x5442.

Production – Dawn Guzzo
Cover Logo – Adam Grano
Production Coordinator – Jeff Whitman
Editor – Carol M. Burrell
Associate Editor – Bethany Bryan
Jim Salicrup
Editor-in-Chief

PB ISBN: 978-1-62991-442-8
HC ISBN: 978-1-62991-443-5

Printed in China July 2016 by Imago
2/F, Blk, 402, Cai Dian Industrial Zone
Huanggang North Road
Futian District, Shenzhen
China

Distributed by Macmillan
Second Papercutz Printing

CHAPTER ONE

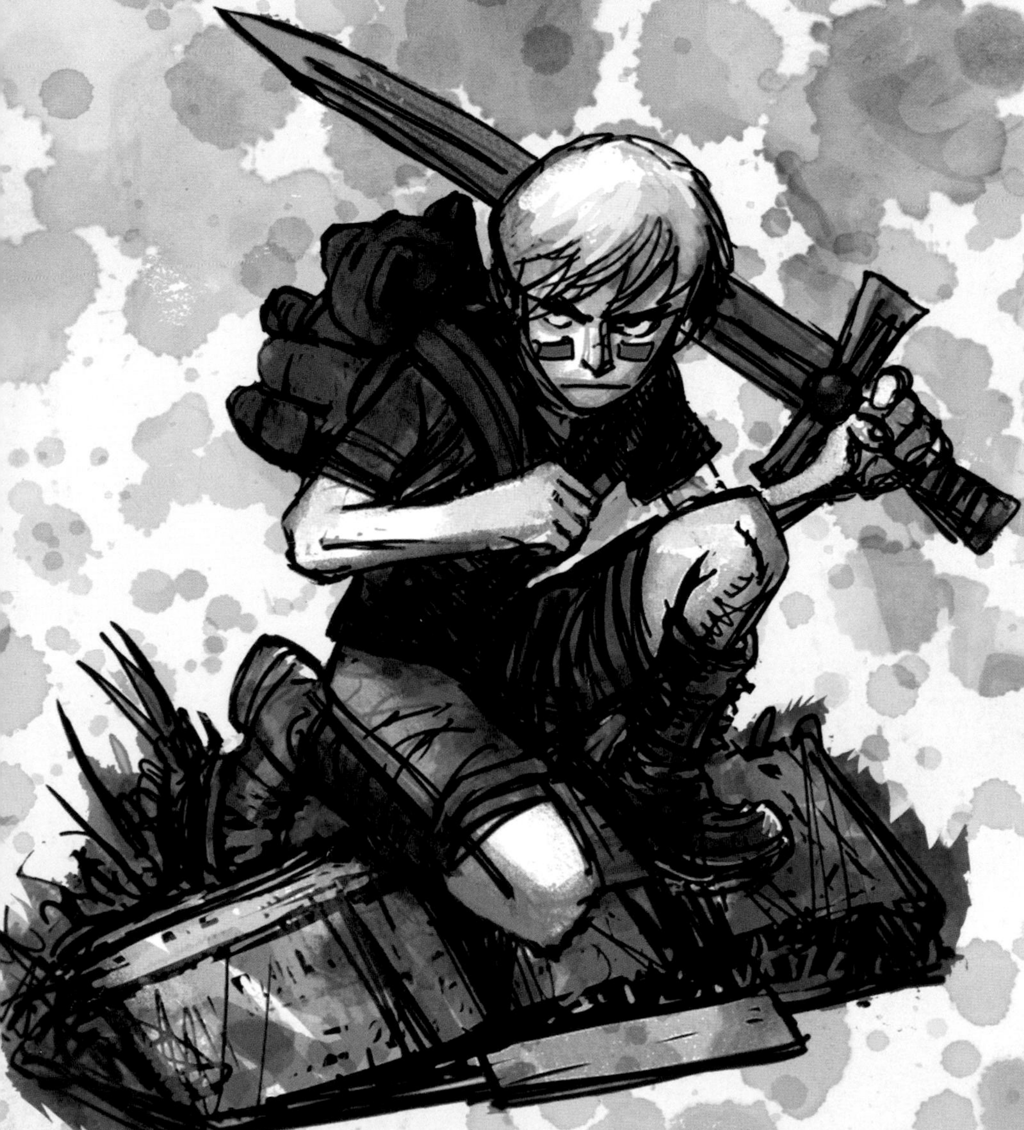

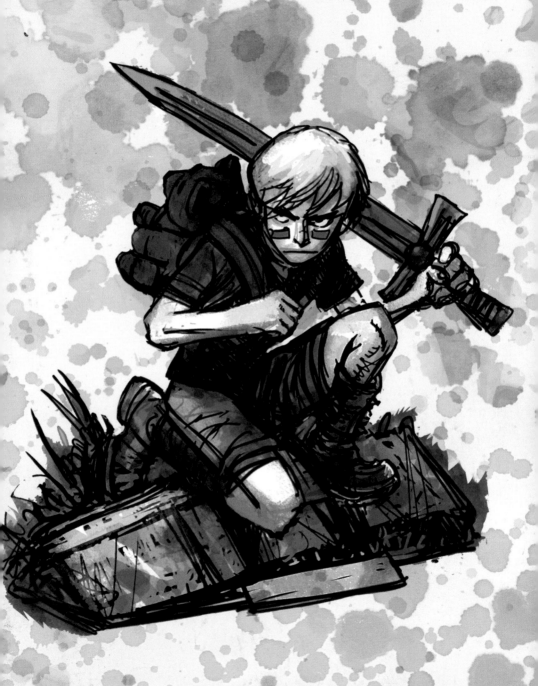

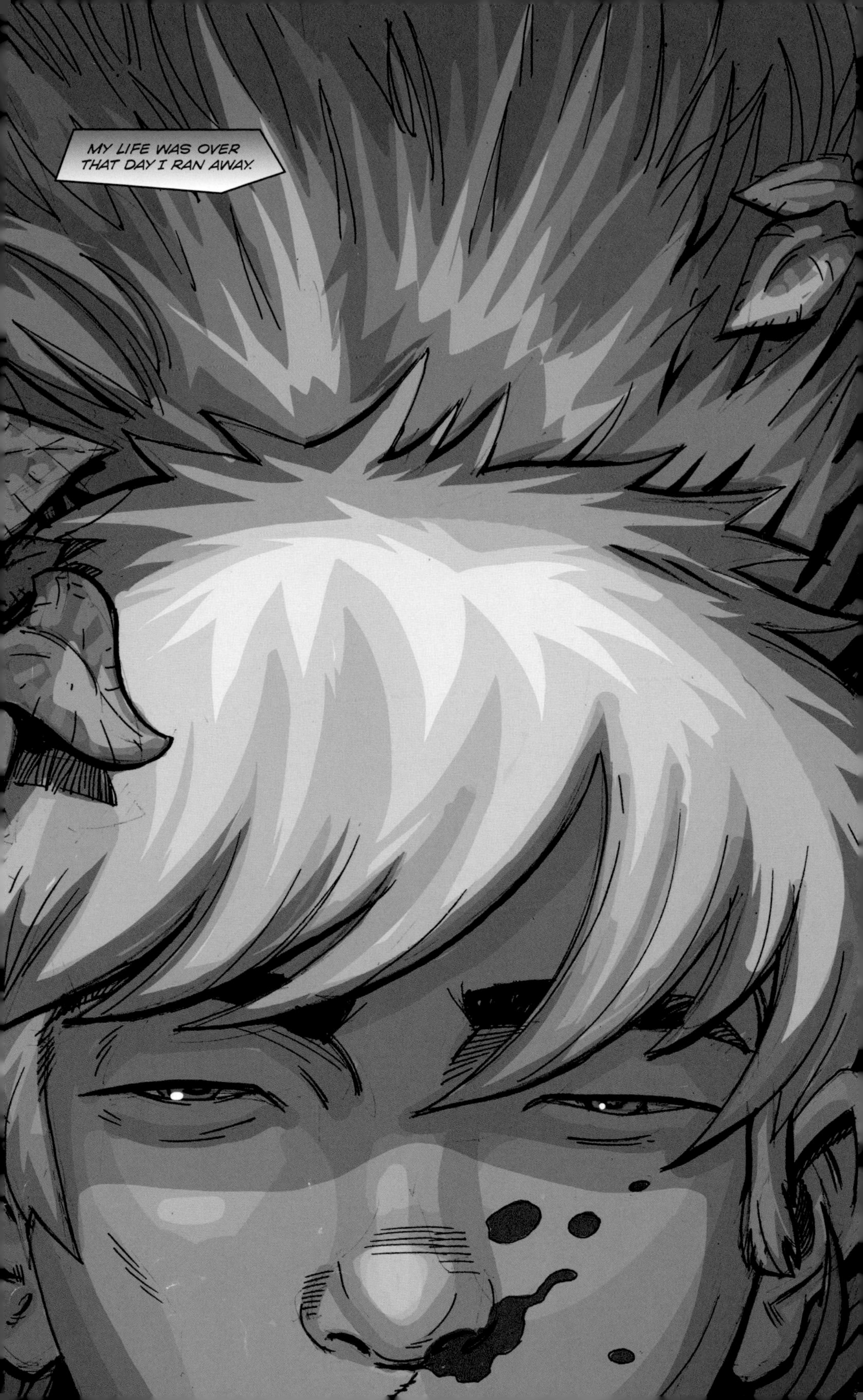
MY LIFE WAS OVER
THAT DAY I RAN AWAY.

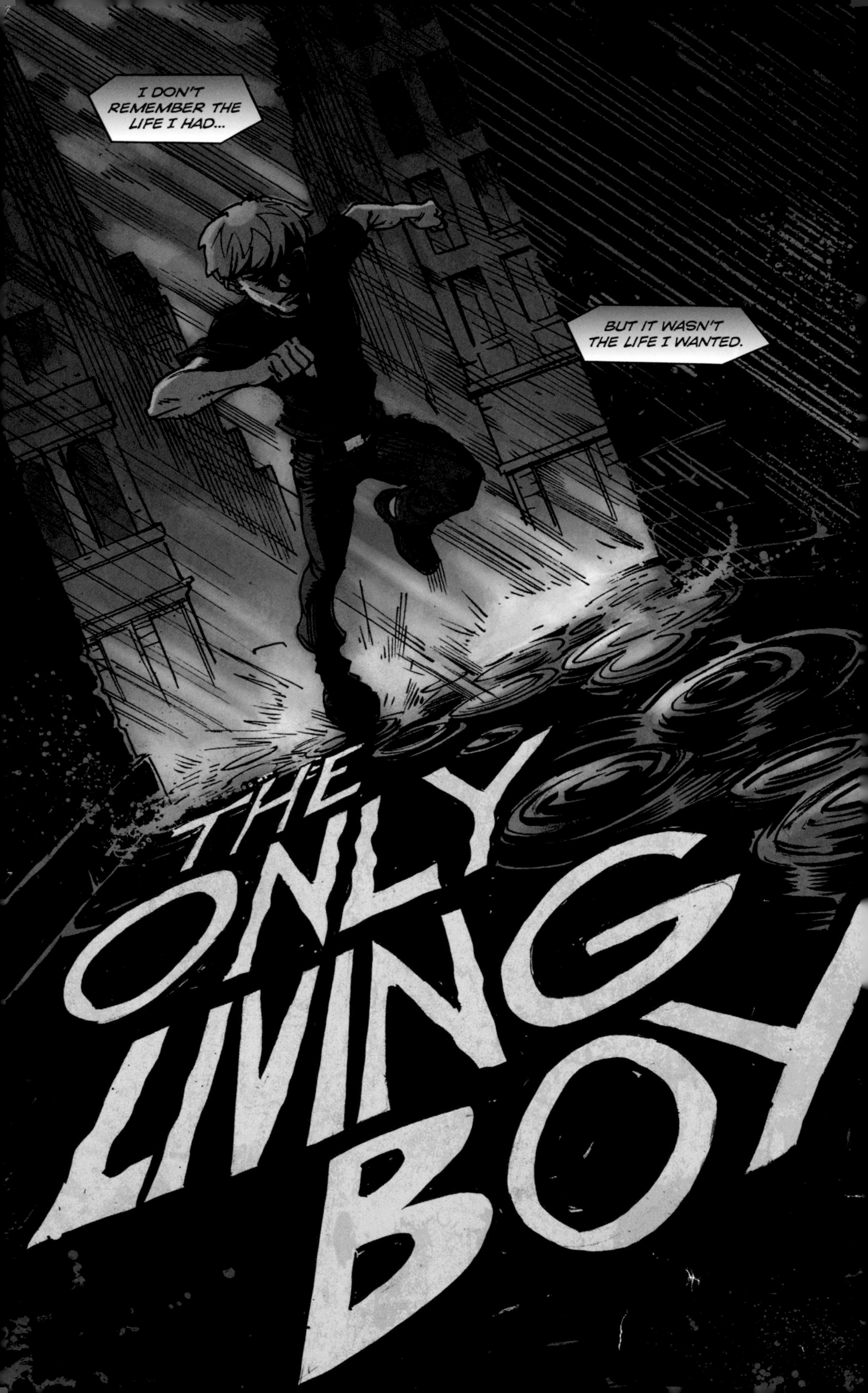
I DON'T REMEMBER THE LIFE I HAD...
BUT IT WASN'T THE LIFE I WANTED.
THE ONLY LIVING BOY

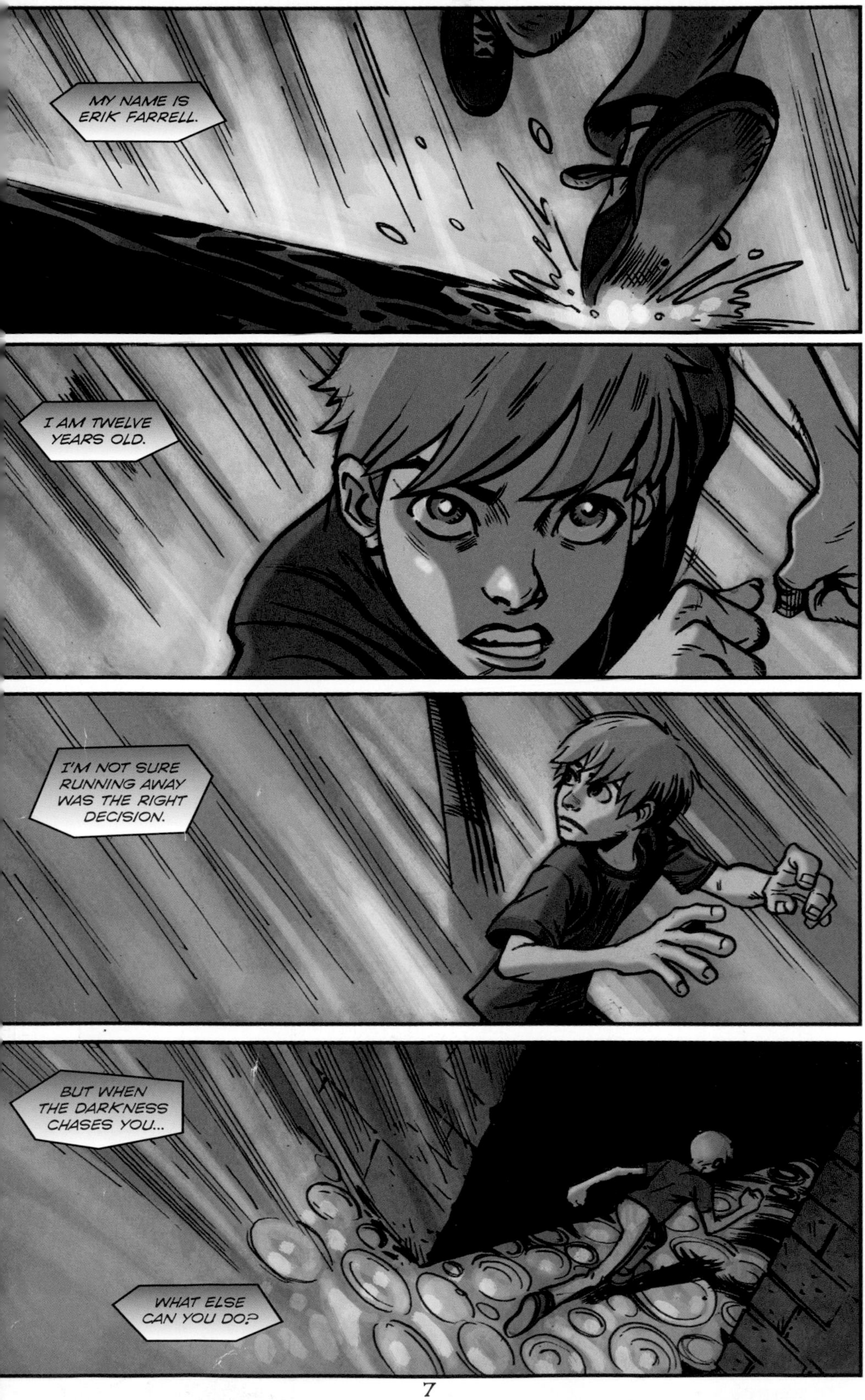
MY NAME IS ERIK FARRELL.
I AM TWELVE YEARS OLD.
I'M NOT SURE RUNNING AWAY WAS THE RIGHT DECISION.
BUT WHEN THE DARKNESS CHASES YOU...
WHAT ELSE CAN YOU DO?

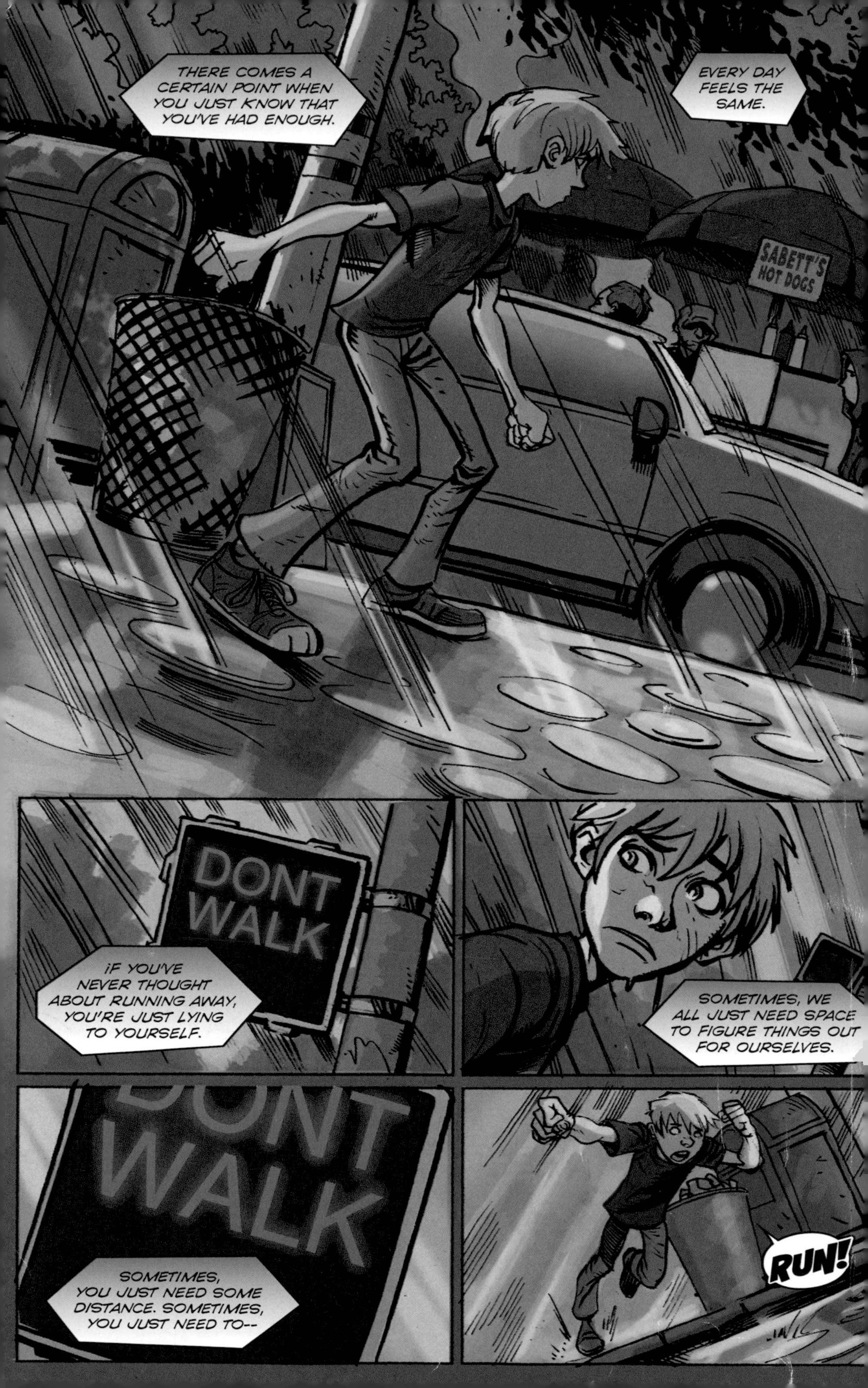
THERE COMES A CERTAIN POINT WHEN YOU JUST KNOW THAT YOU'VE HAD ENOUGH.
EVERY DAY FEELS THE SAME.
SABETT'S HOT DOGS
DONT WALK
iF YOU'VE NEVER THOUGHT ABOUT RUNNING AWAY, YOU'RE JUST LYING TO YOURSELF.
SOMETIMES, WE ALL JUST NEED SPACE TO FIGURE THINGS OUT FOR OURSELVES.
DONT WALK
SOMETIMES, YOU JUST NEED SOME DISTANCE. SOMETIMES, YOU JUST NEED TO--
RUN!

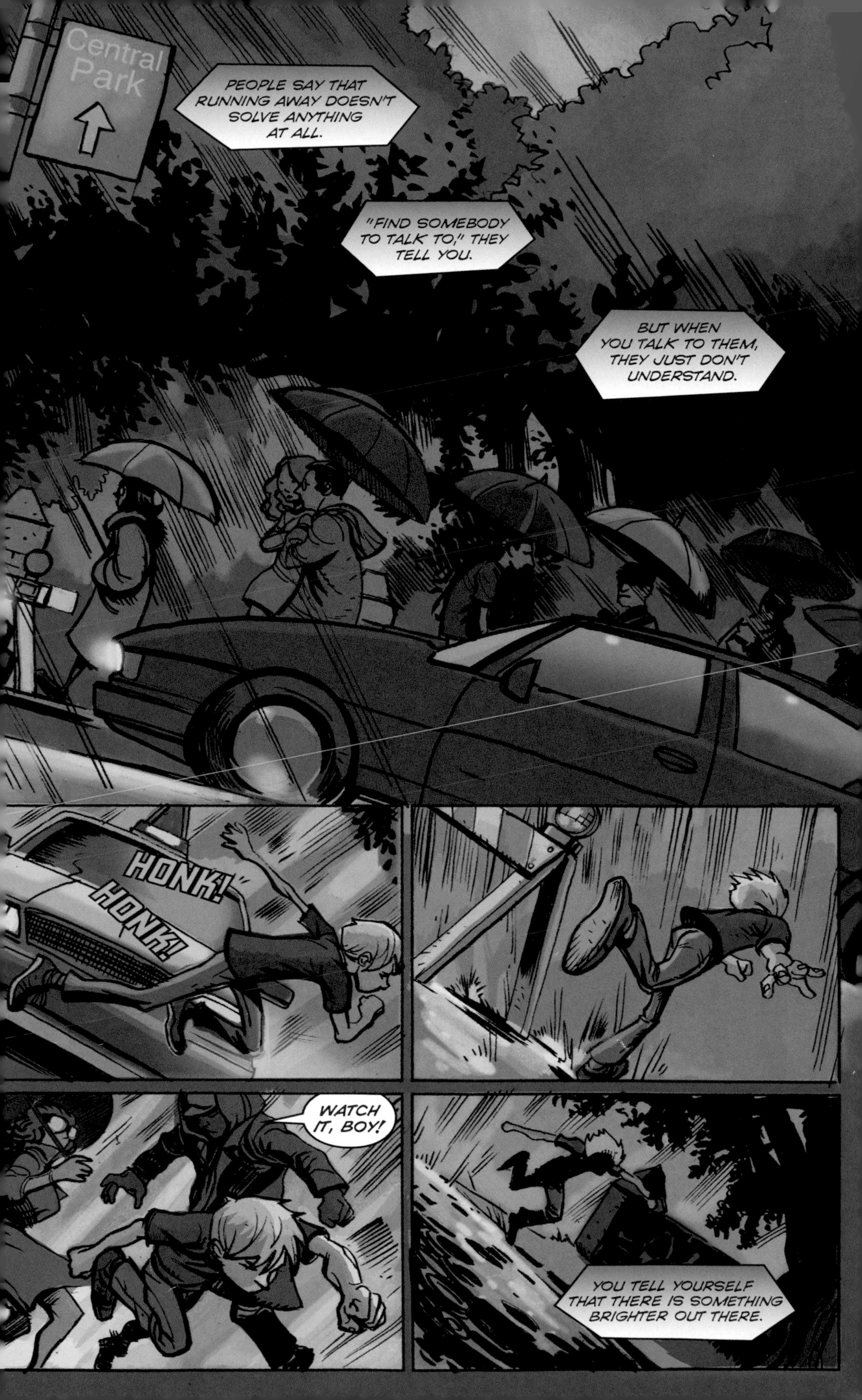
Central Park
PEOPLE SAY THAT RUNNING AWAY DOESN'T SOLVE ANYTHING AT ALL.
"FIND SOMEBODY TO TALK TO," THEY TELL YOU.
BUT WHEN YOU TALK TO THEM, THEY JUST DON'T UNDERSTAND.
HONK! HONK!
WATCH IT, BOY!
YOU TELL YOURSELF THAT THERE IS SOMETHING BRIGHTER OUT THERE.

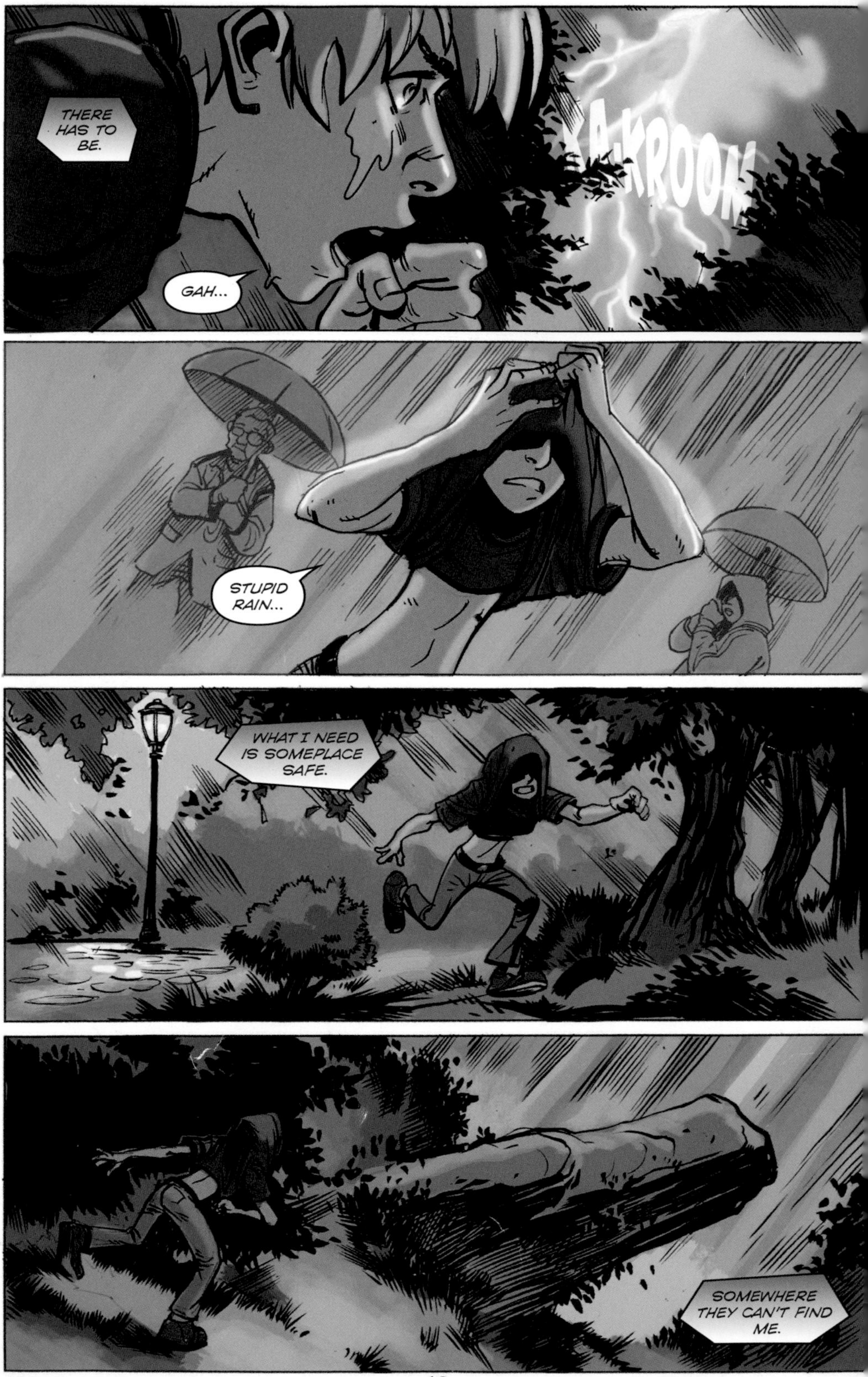
THERE HAS TO BE.
GAH...
KA-KROOM
STUPID RAIN...
WHAT I NEED IS SOMEPLACE SAFE.
SOMEWHERE THEY CAN'T FIND ME.

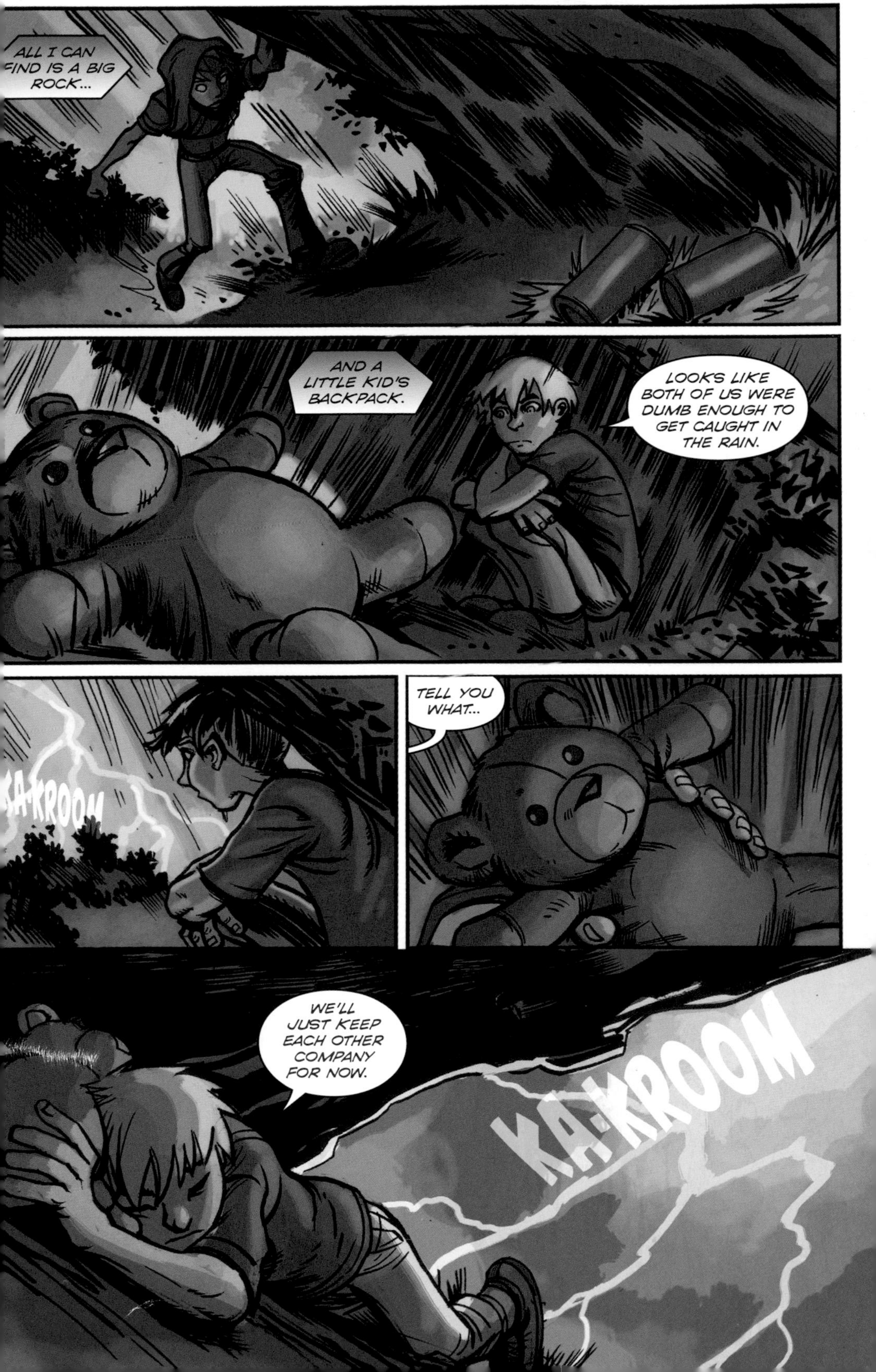
ALL I CAN FIND IS A BIG ROCK...
AND A LITTLE KID'S BACKPACK.
LOOKS LIKE BOTH OF US WERE DUMB ENOUGH TO GET CAUGHT IN THE RAIN.
KA-KROOM
TELL YOU WHAT...
WE'LL JUST KEEP EACH OTHER COMPANY FOR NOW.
KA-KROOM

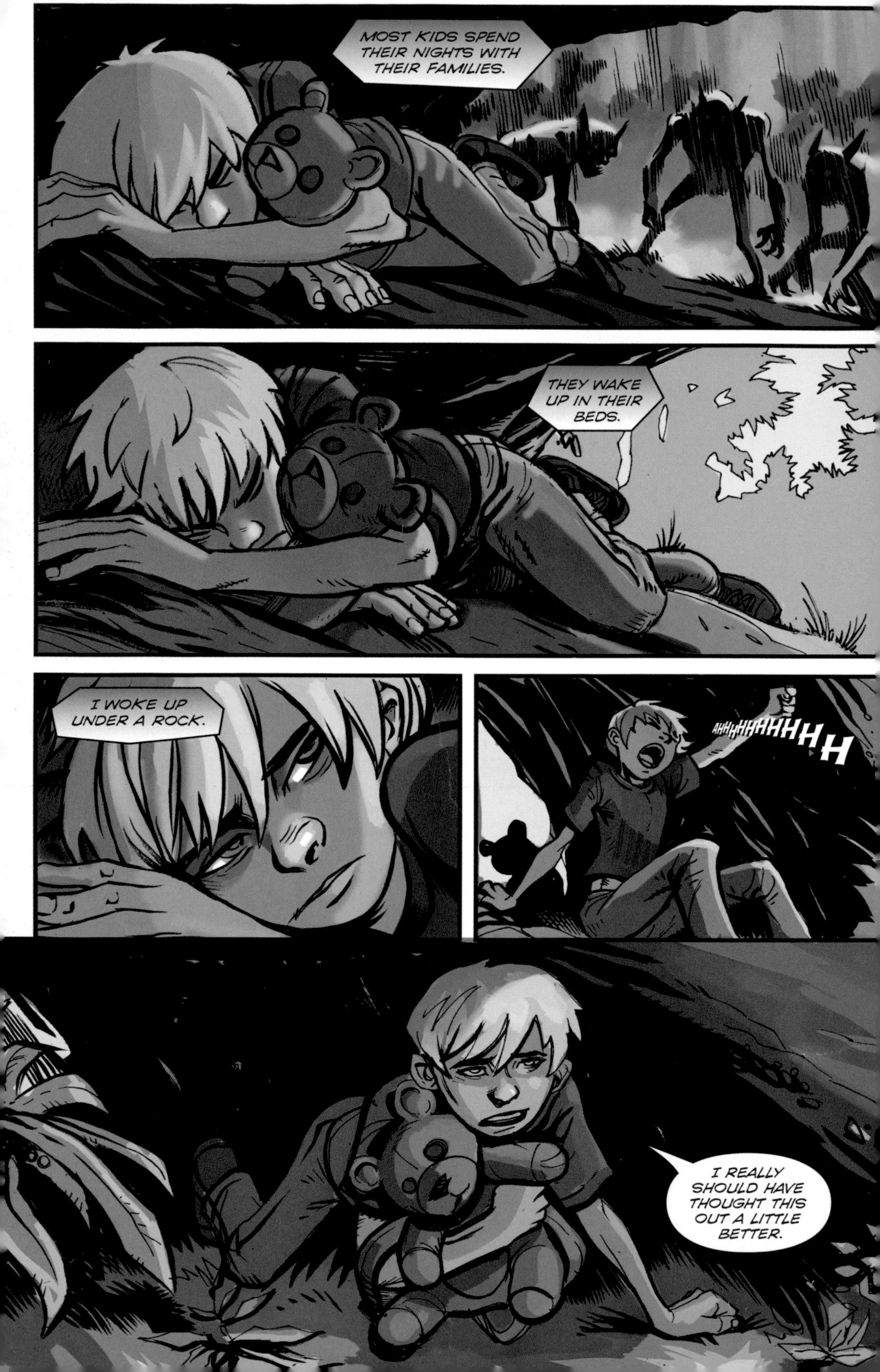
MOST KIDS SPEND THEIR NIGHTS WITH THEIR FAMILIES.
THEY WAKE UP IN THEIR BEDS.
I WOKE UP UNDER A ROCK.
AHHHHHHHHHHH
I REALLY SHOULD HAVE THOUGHT THIS OUT A LITTLE BETTER.

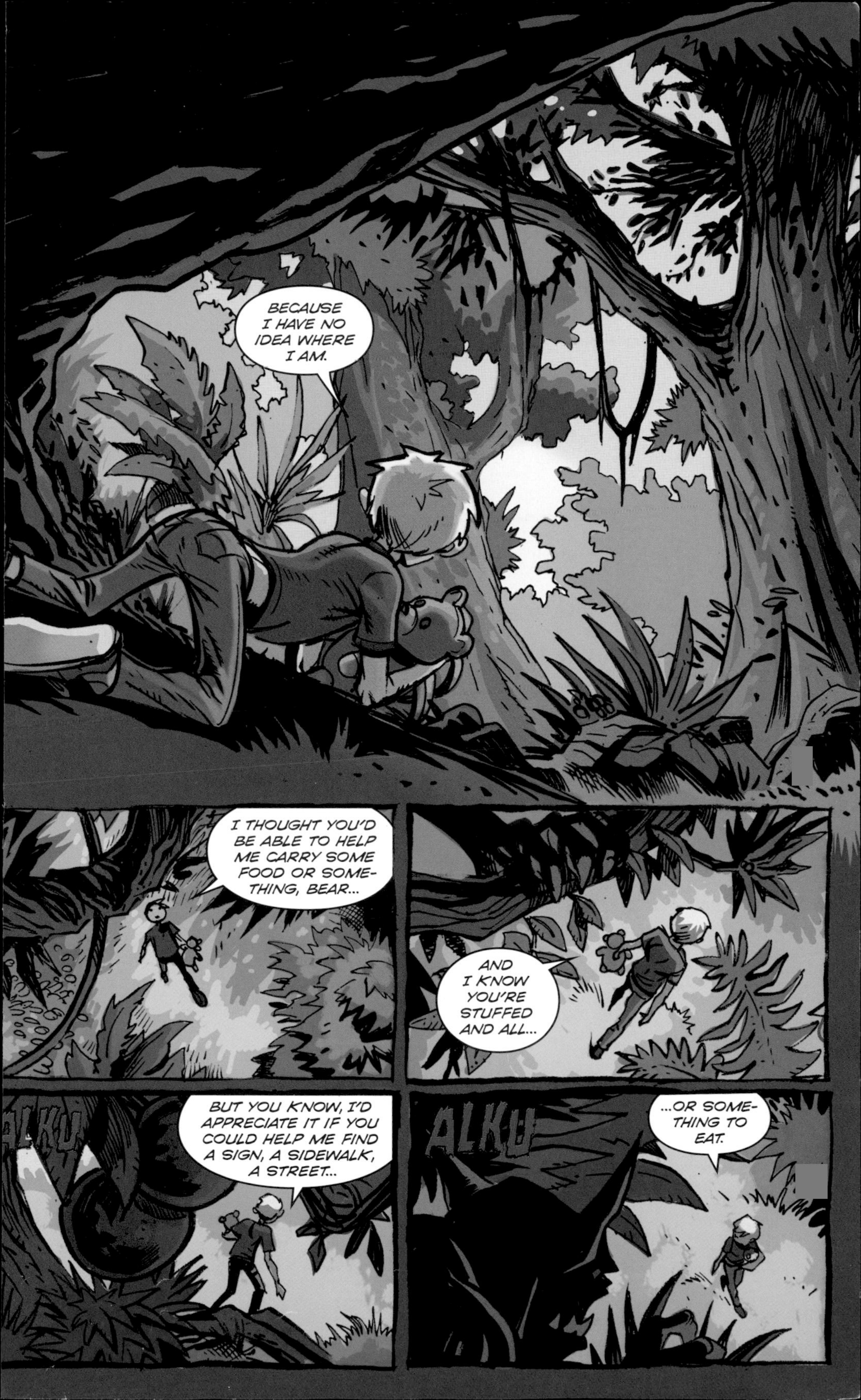
BECAUSE I HAVE NO IDEA WHERE I AM.
I THOUGHT YOU'D BE ABLE TO HELP ME CARRY SOME FOOD OR SOME-THING, BEAR...
AND I KNOW YOU'RE STUFFED AND ALL...
ALKU
BUT YOU KNOW, I'D APPRECIATE IT IF YOU COULD HELP ME FIND A SIGN, A SIDEWALK, A STREET...
ALKU
...OR SOME-THING TO EAT.

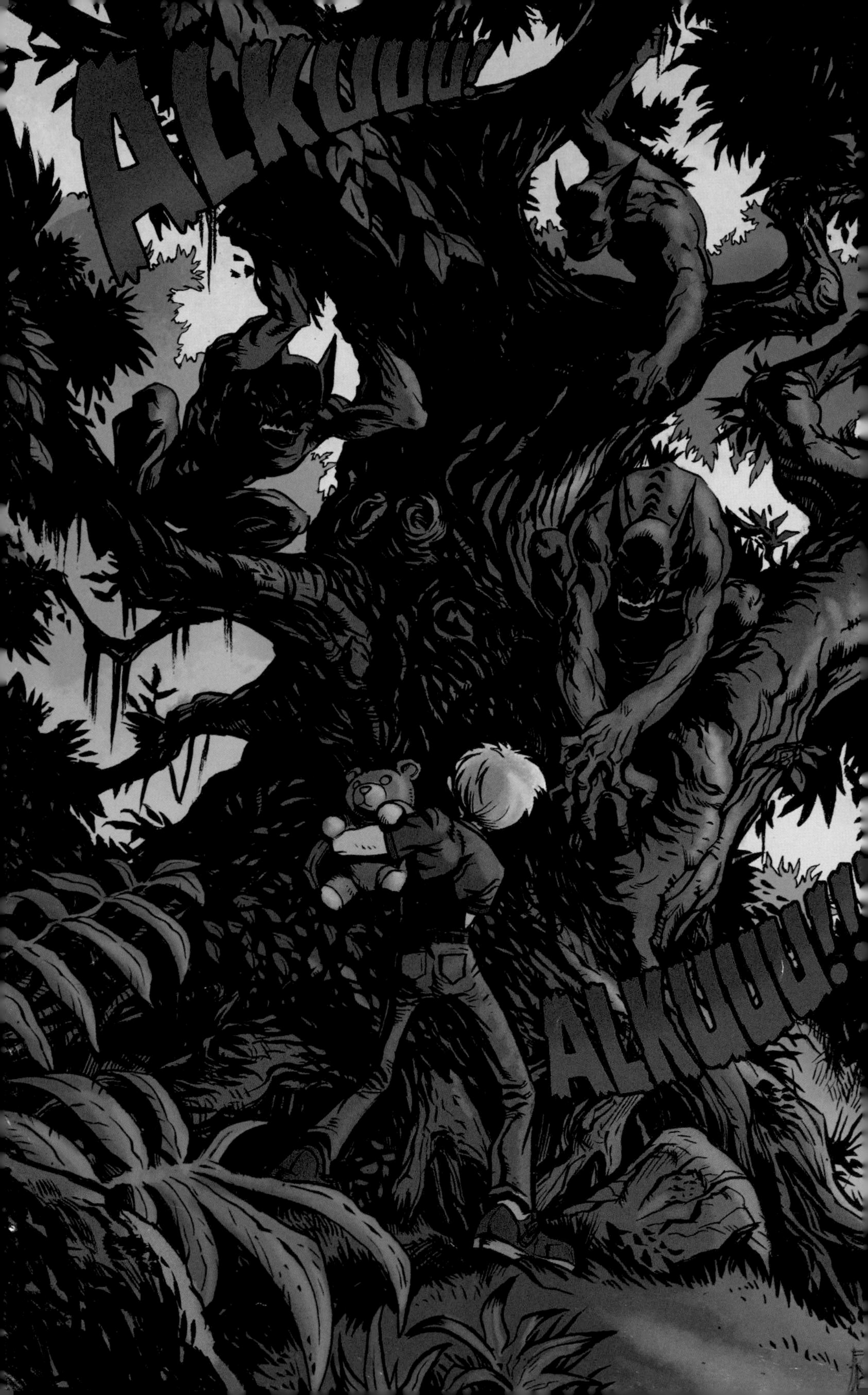
ALKUUU!
ALKUUU!!

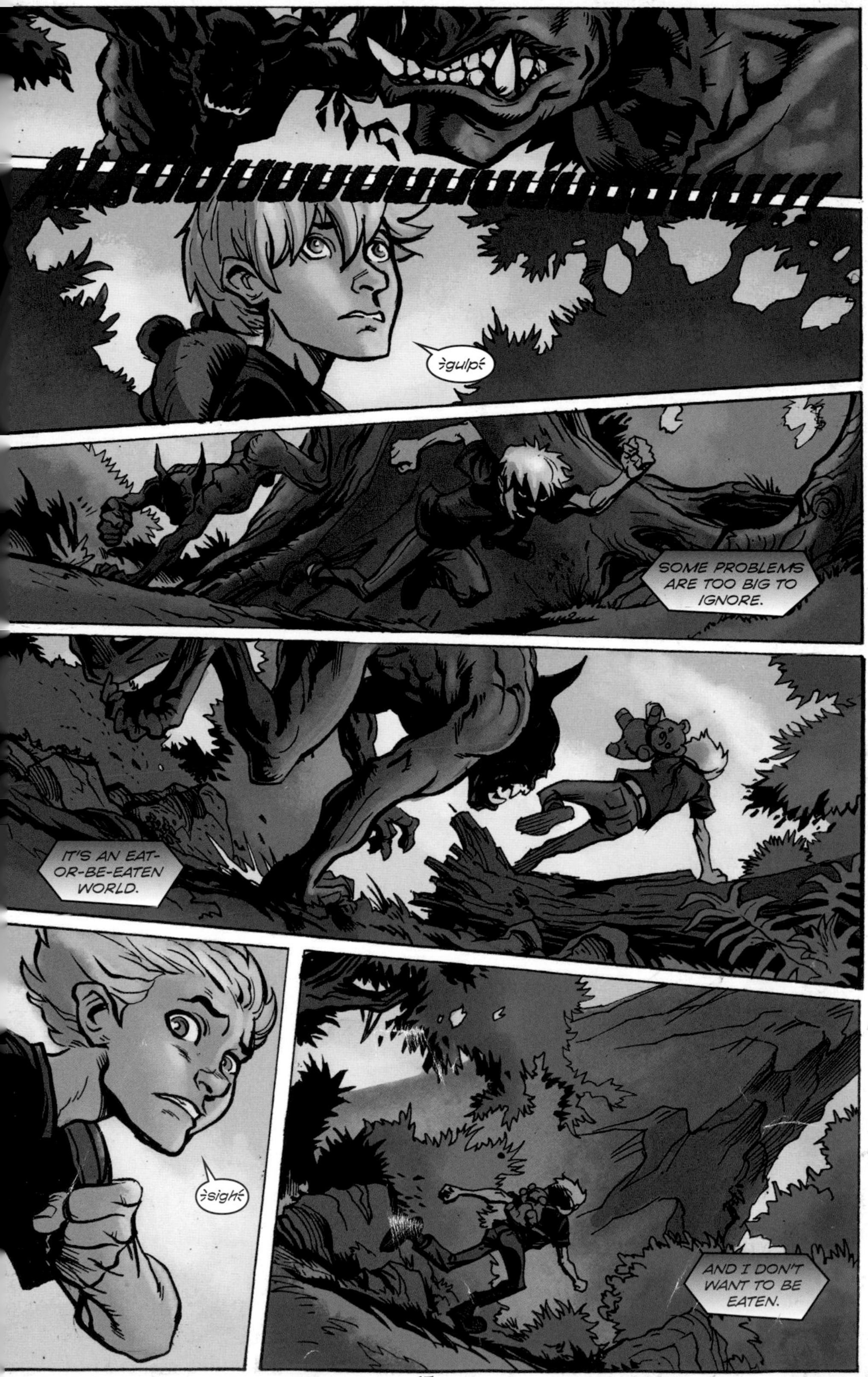

gulp
SOME PROBLEMS ARE TOO BIG TO IGNORE.
IT'S AN EAT-OR-BE-EATEN WORLD.
sigh
AND I DON'T WANT TO BE EATEN.

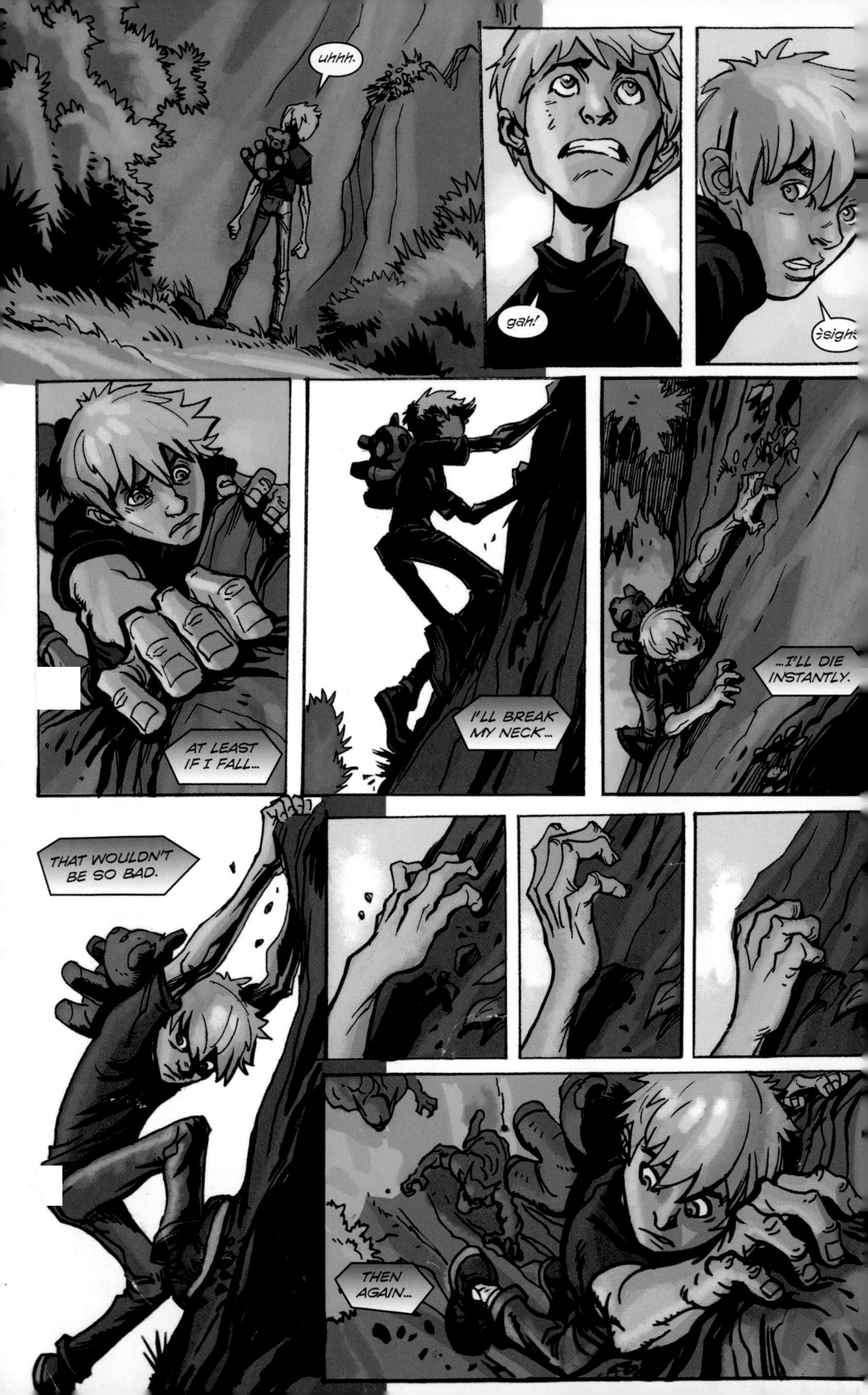
uhhh.
gah!
;sigh;
AT LEAST IF I FALL...
I'LL BREAK MY NECK...
...I'LL DIE INSTANTLY.
THAT WOULDN'T BE SO BAD.
THEN AGAIN...

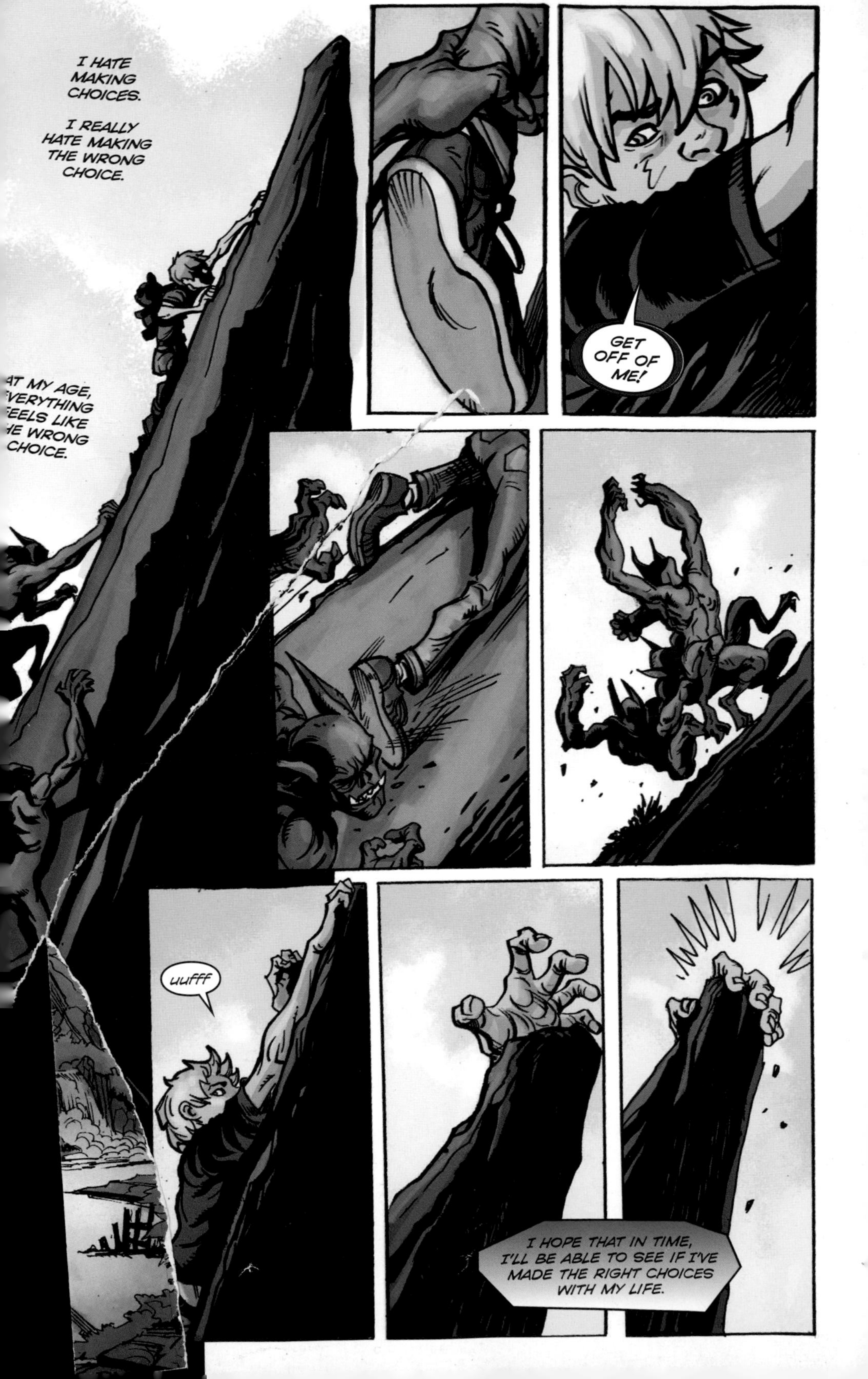
I HATE MAKING CHOICES.
I REALLY HATE MAKING THE WRONG CHOICE.
AT MY AGE, EVERYTHING FEELS LIKE THE WRONG CHOICE.
GET OFF OF ME!
uufff
I HOPE THAT IN TIME, I'LL BE ABLE TO SEE IF I'VE MADE THE RIGHT CHOICES WITH MY LIFE.

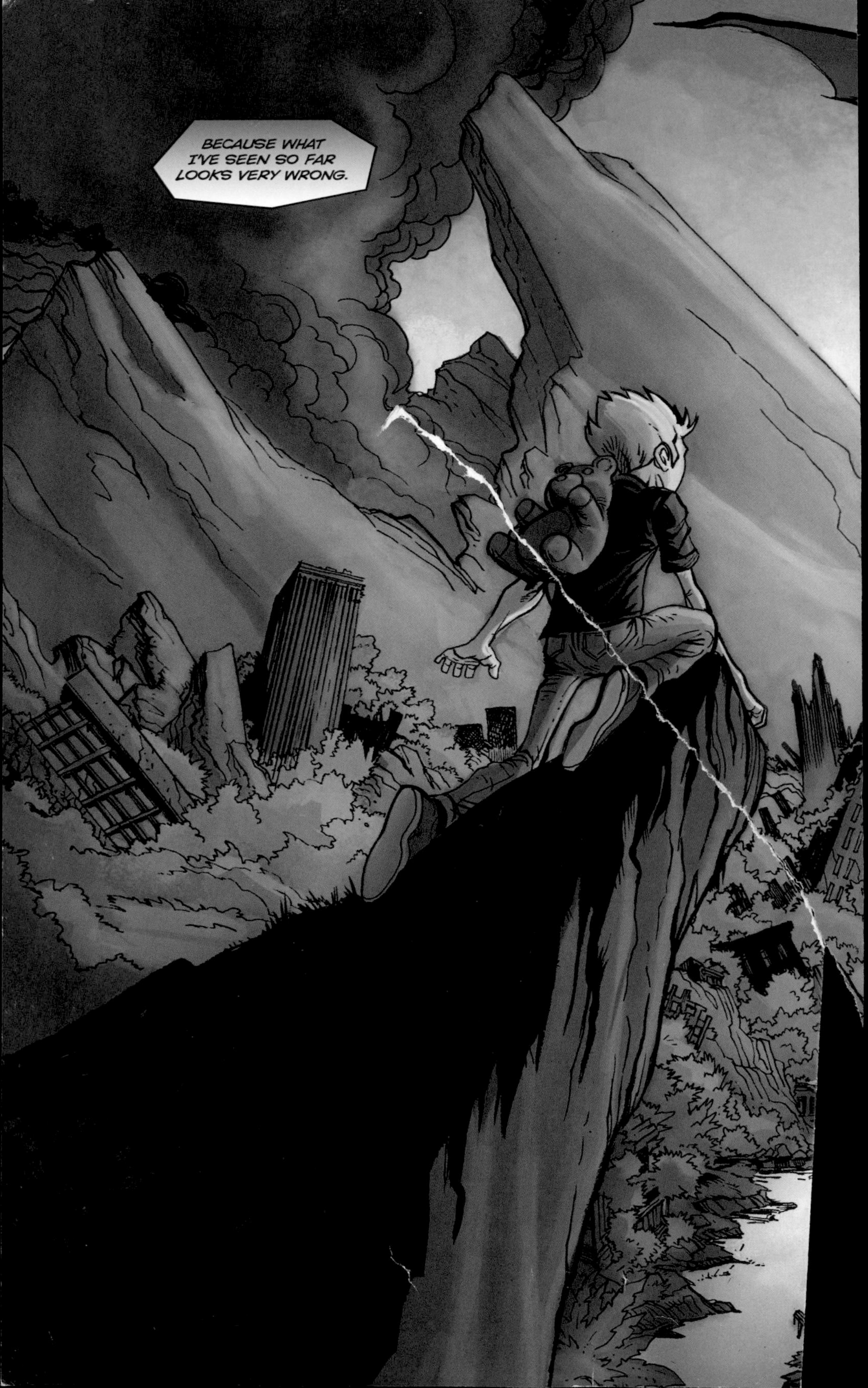
BECAUSE WHAT I'VE SEEN SO FAR LOOKS VERY WRONG.

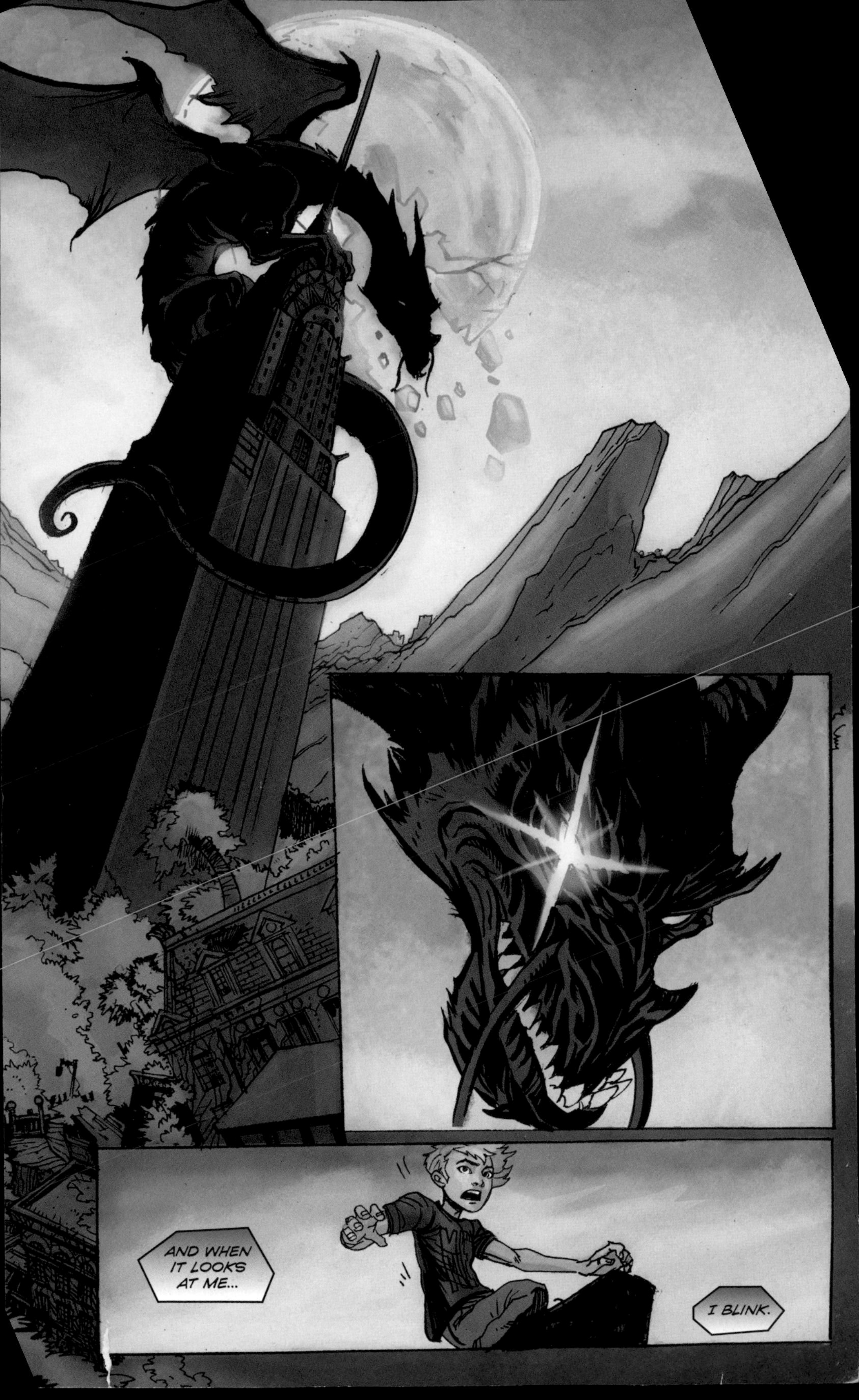
AND WHEN IT LOOKS AT ME...
I BLINK.

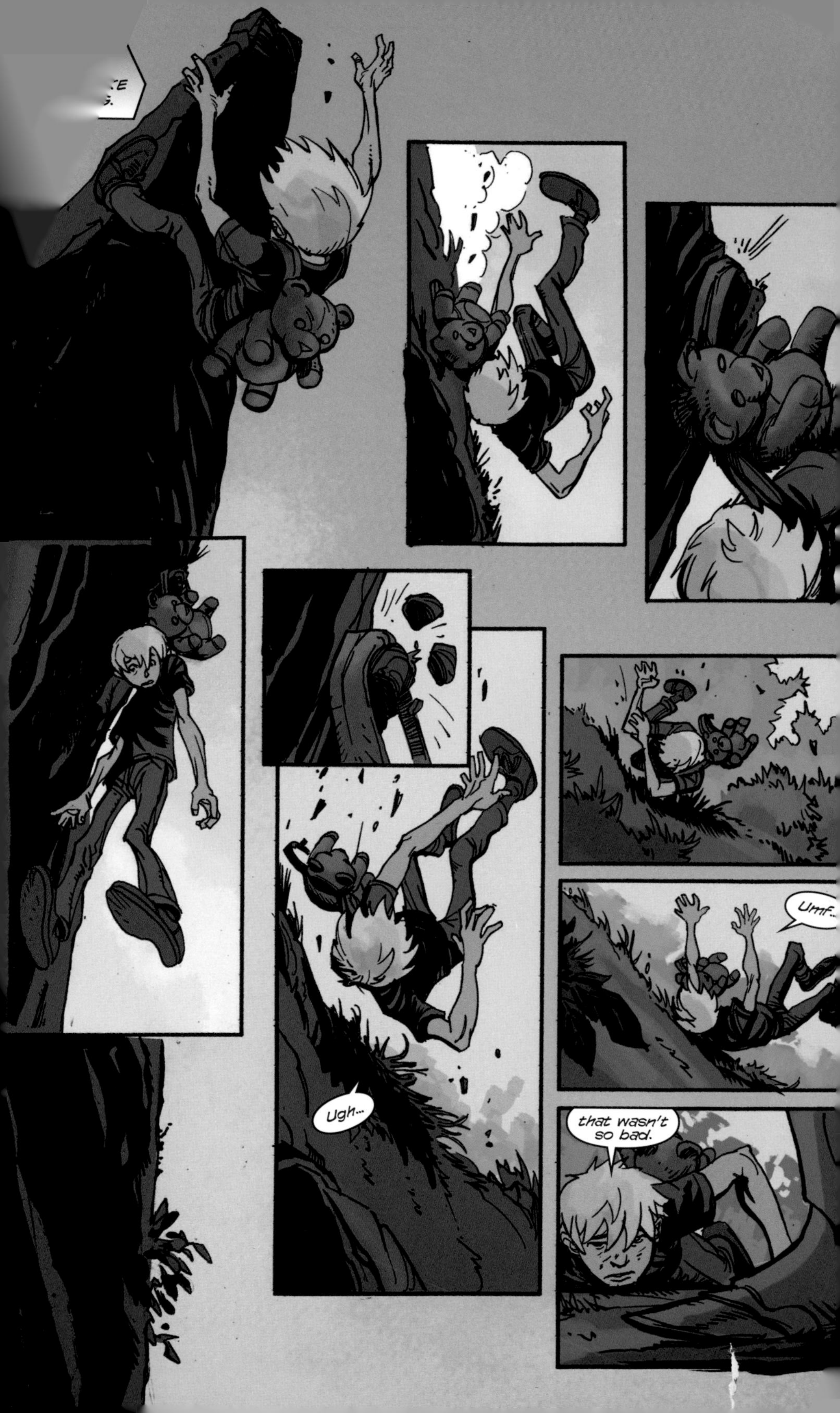
Ugh...
Umf...
that wasn't so bad.

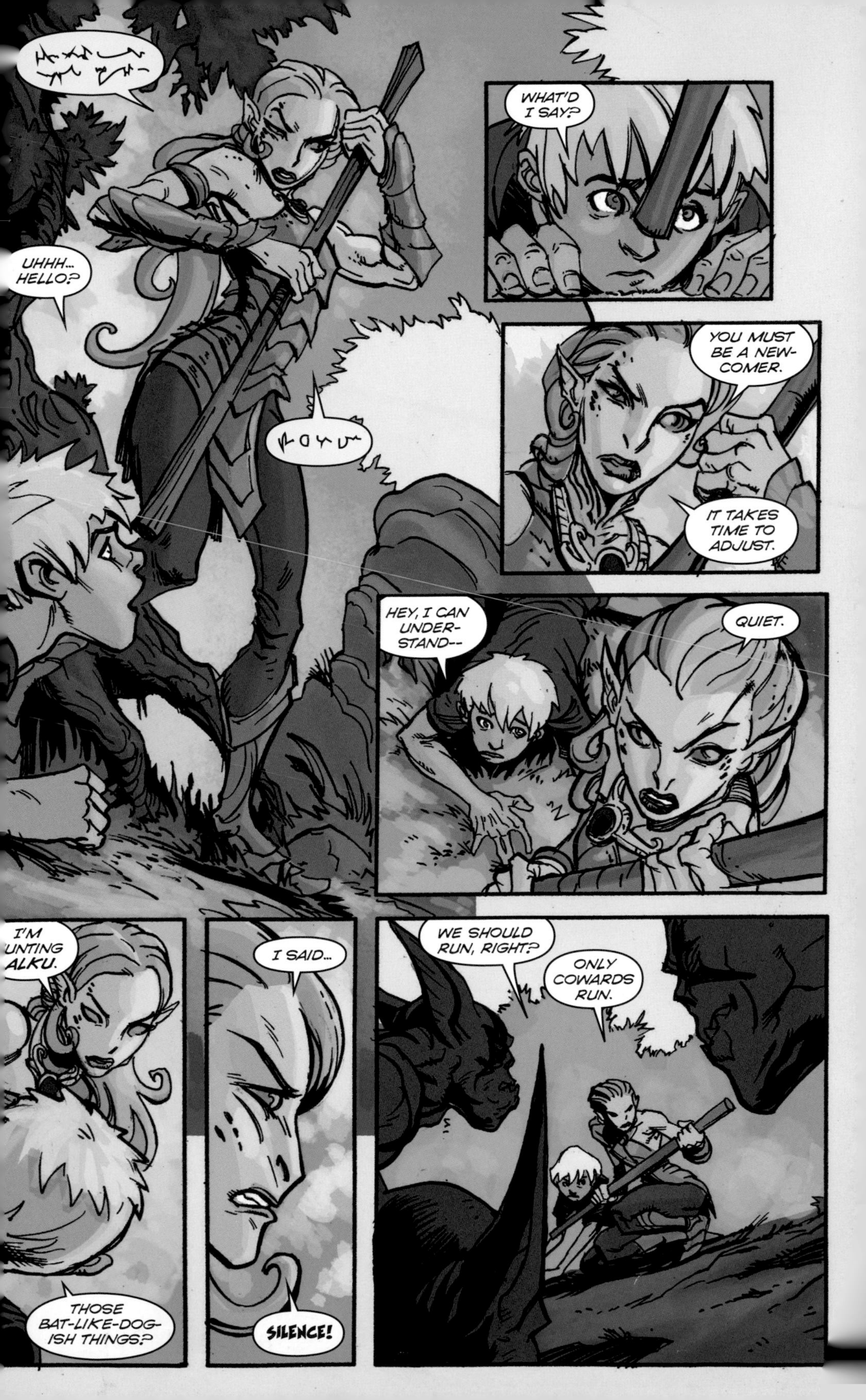
UHHH... HELLO?
WHAT'D I SAY?
YOU MUST BE A NEW-COMER.
IT TAKES TIME TO ADJUST.
HEY, I CAN UNDER-STAND--
QUIET.
I'M
UNTING
ALKU.
THOSE BAT-LIKE-DOG-ISH THINGS?
I SAID...
SILENCE!
WE SHOULD RUN, RIGHT?
ONLY COWARDS RUN.

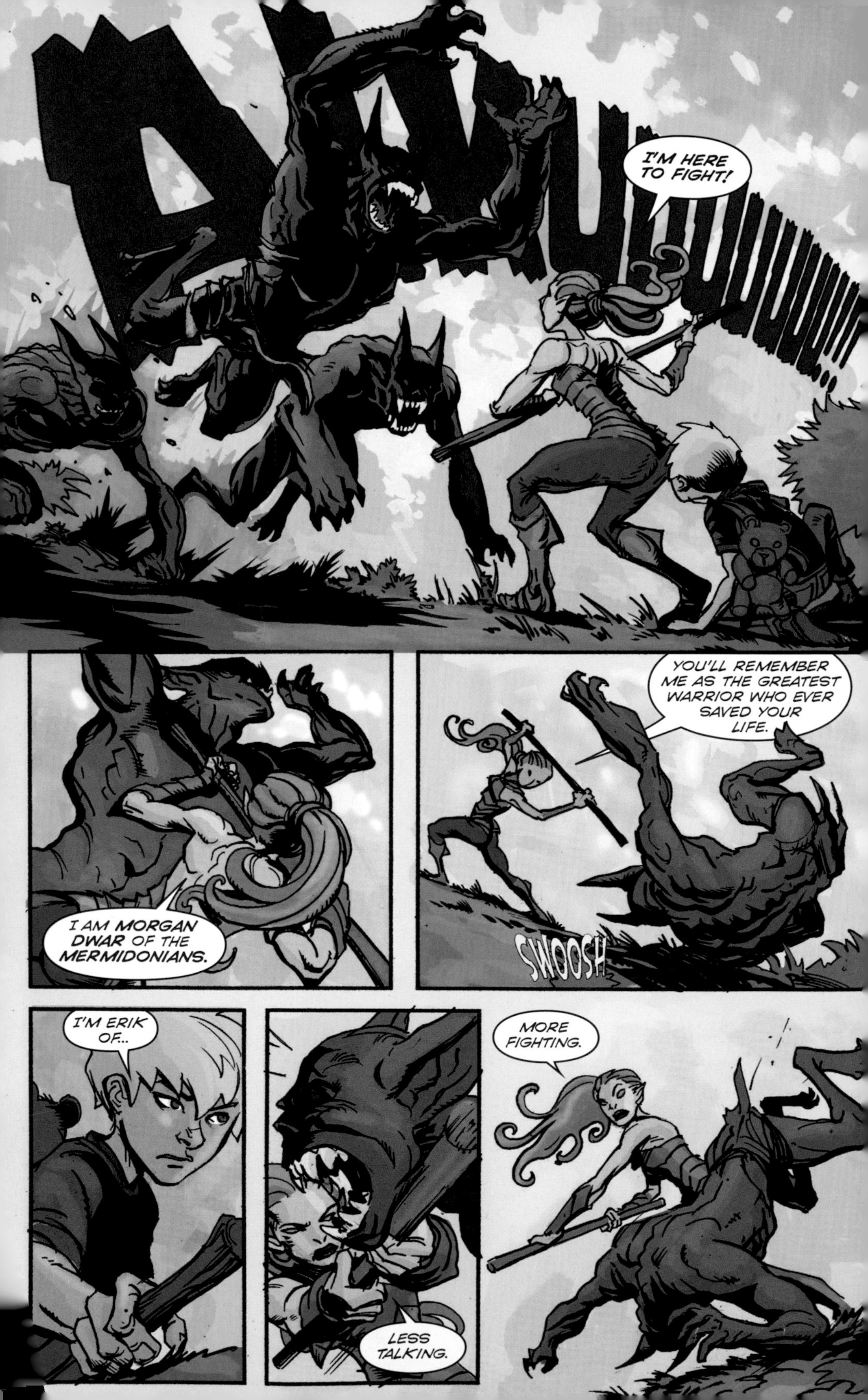
I'M HERE TO FIGHT!
I AM MORGAN DWAR OF THE MERMIDONIANS.
YOU'LL REMEMBER ME AS THE GREATEST WARRIOR WHO EVER SAVED YOUR LIFE.
SWOOSH
I'M ERIK OF...
LESS TALKING.
MORE FIGHTING.

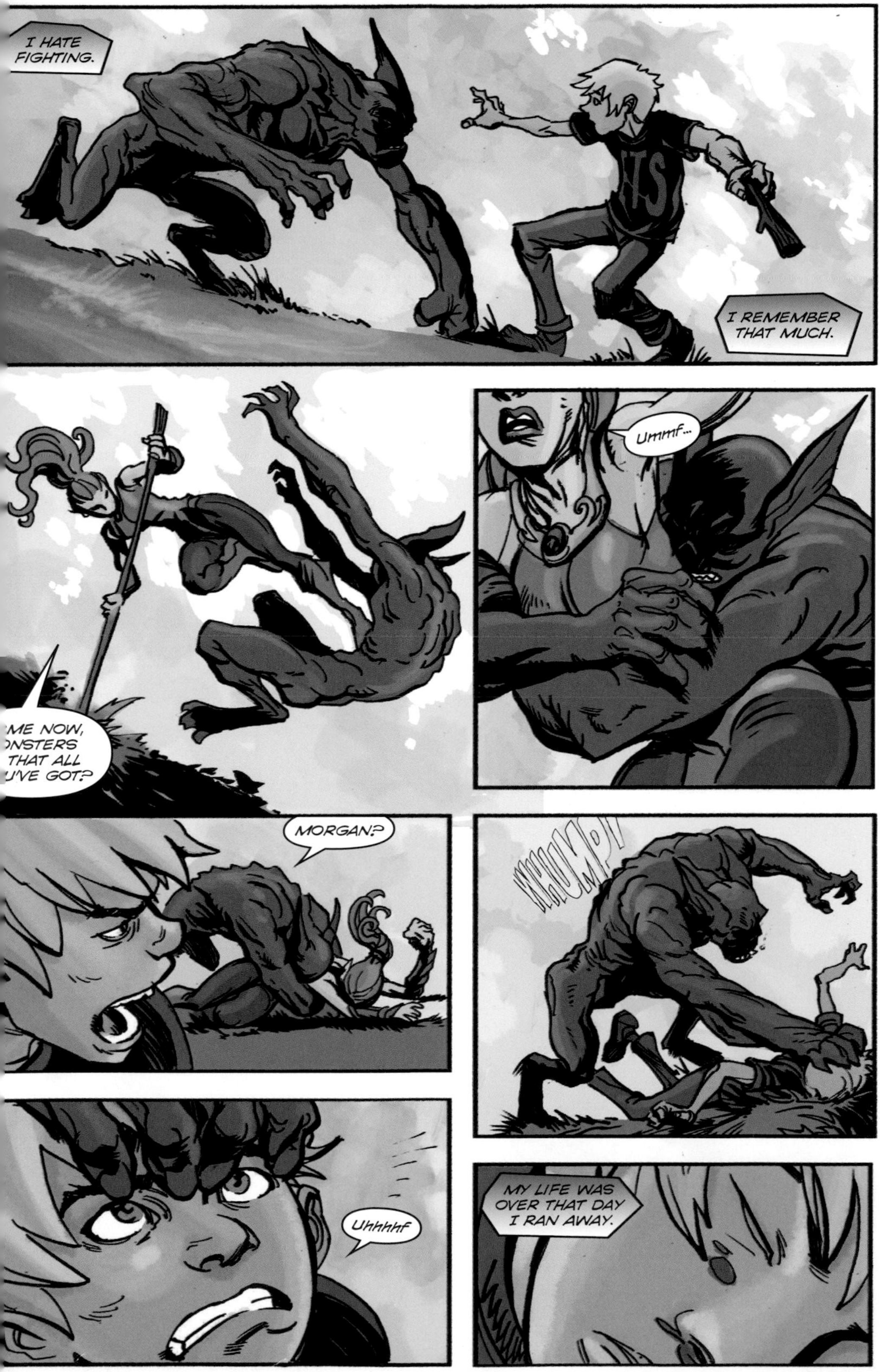

I HATE FIGHTING.
I REMEMBER THAT MUCH.
ME NOW, ONSTERS THAT ALL U'VE GOT?
Ummf...
MORGAN?
WHUMP!
Uhhhhf
MY LIFE WAS OVER THAT DAY I RAN AWAY.

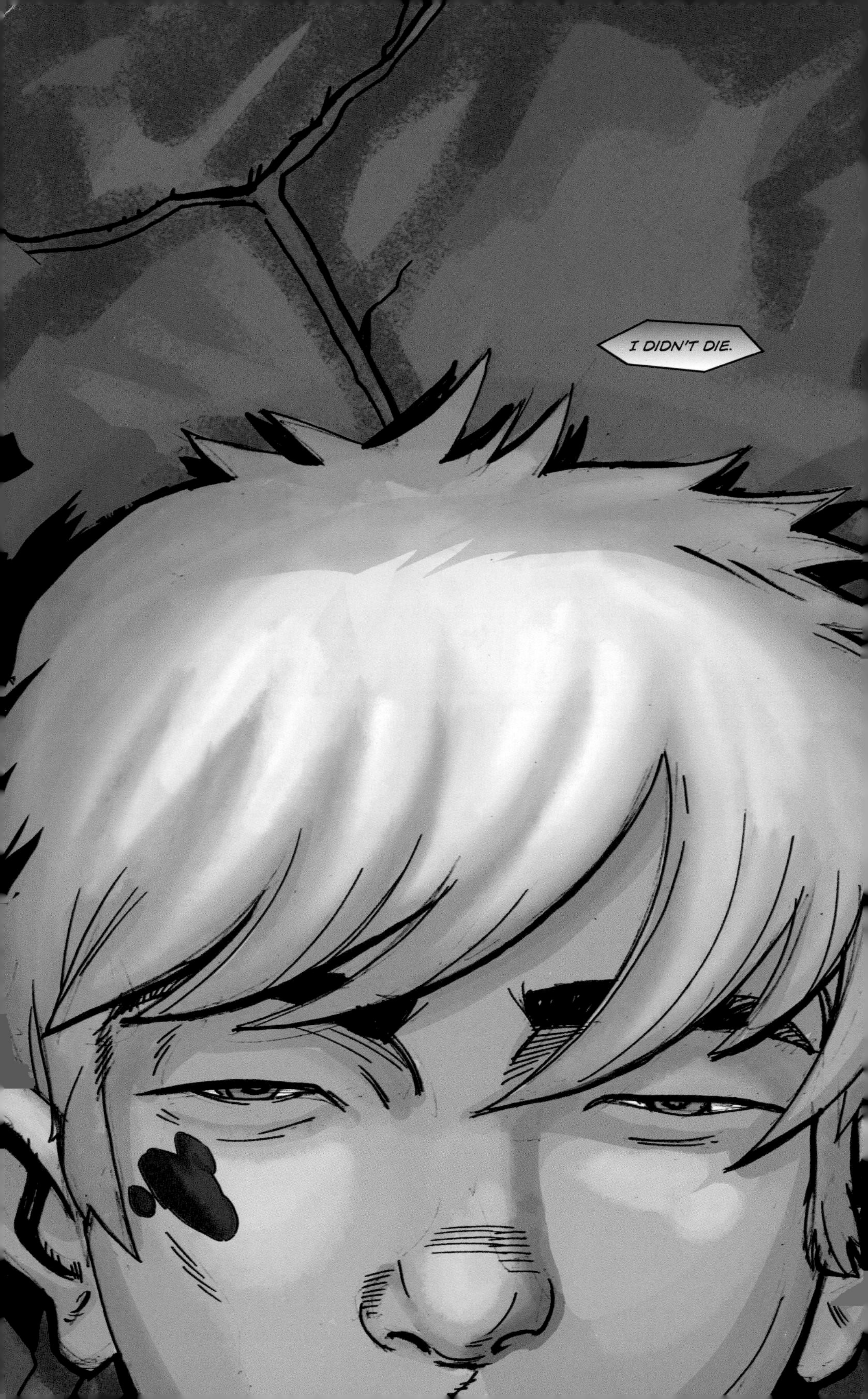
I DIDN'T DIE.

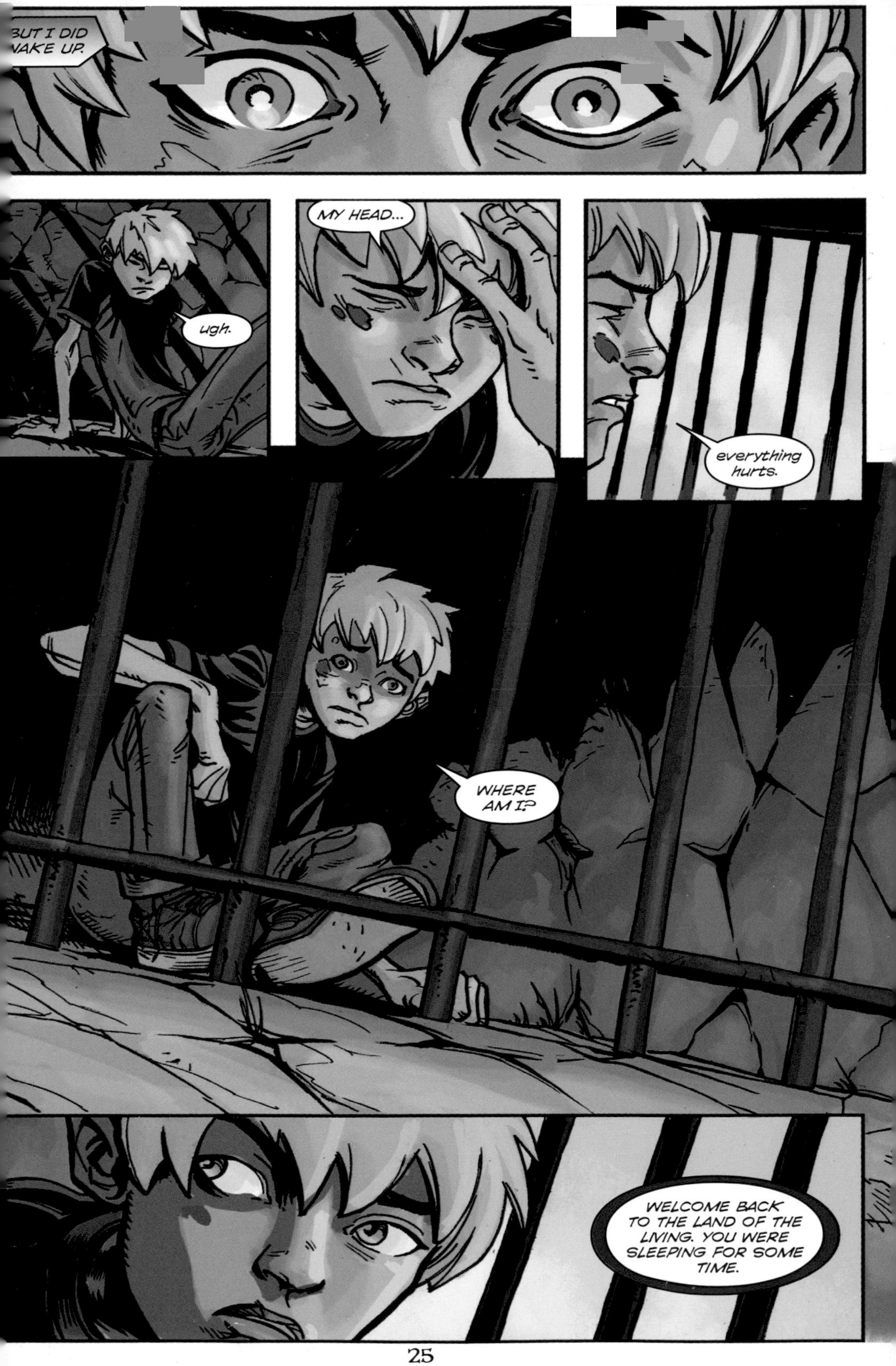
BUT I DID WAKE UP.
ugh.
MY HEAD...
everything hurts.
WHERE AM I?
WELCOME BACK TO THE LAND OF THE LIVING. YOU WERE SLEEPING FOR SOME TIME.

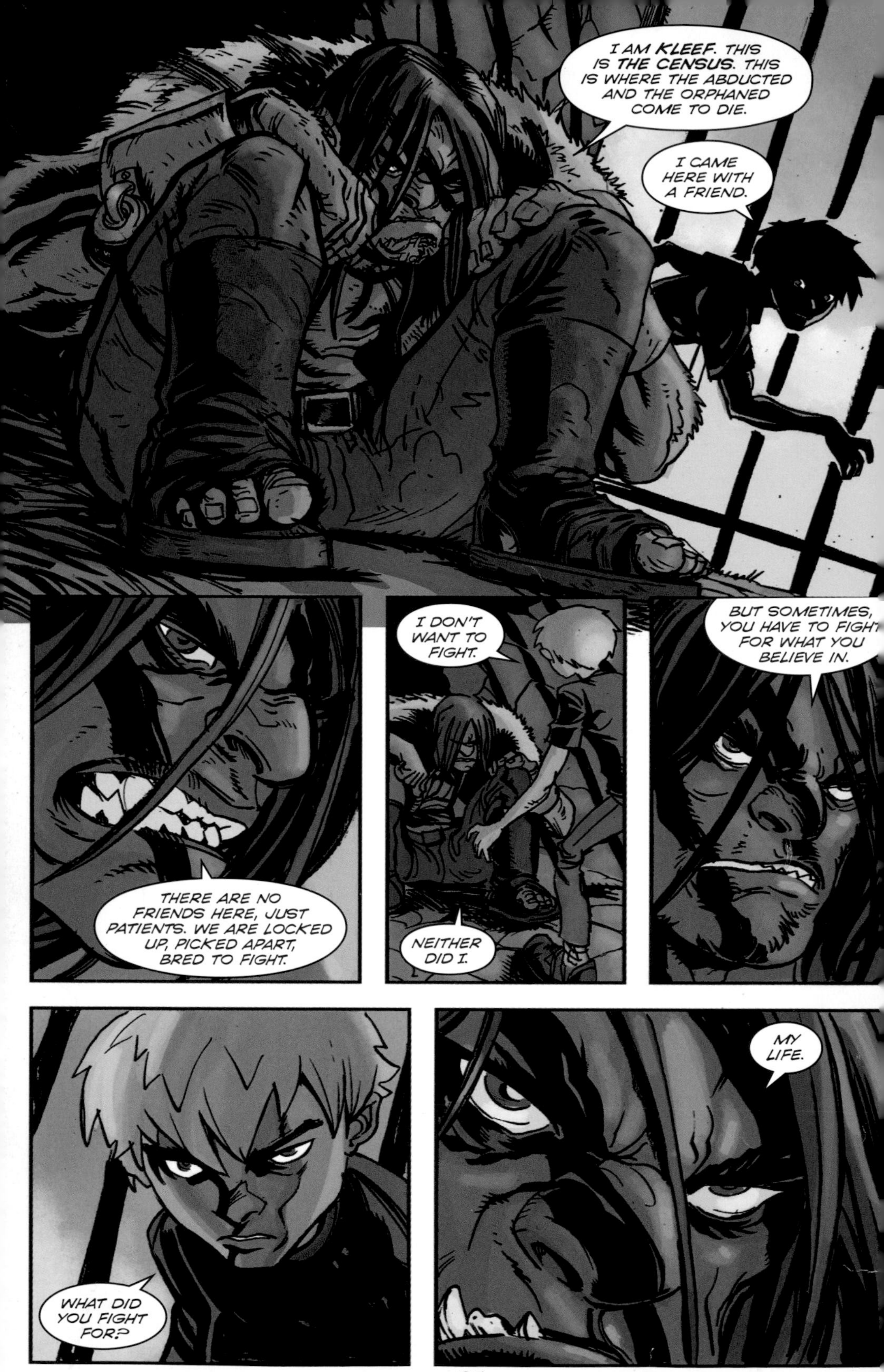
I AM KLEEF. THIS IS THE CENSUS. THIS IS WHERE THE ABDUCTED AND THE ORPHANED COME TO DIE.
I CAME HERE WITH A FRIEND.
THERE ARE NO FRIENDS HERE, JUST PATIENTS. WE ARE LOCKED UP, PICKED APART, BRED TO FIGHT.
I DON'T WANT TO FIGHT.
NEITHER DID I.
BUT SOMETIMES, YOU HAVE TO FIGHT FOR WHAT YOU BELIEVE IN.
WHAT DID YOU FIGHT FOR?
MY LIFE.

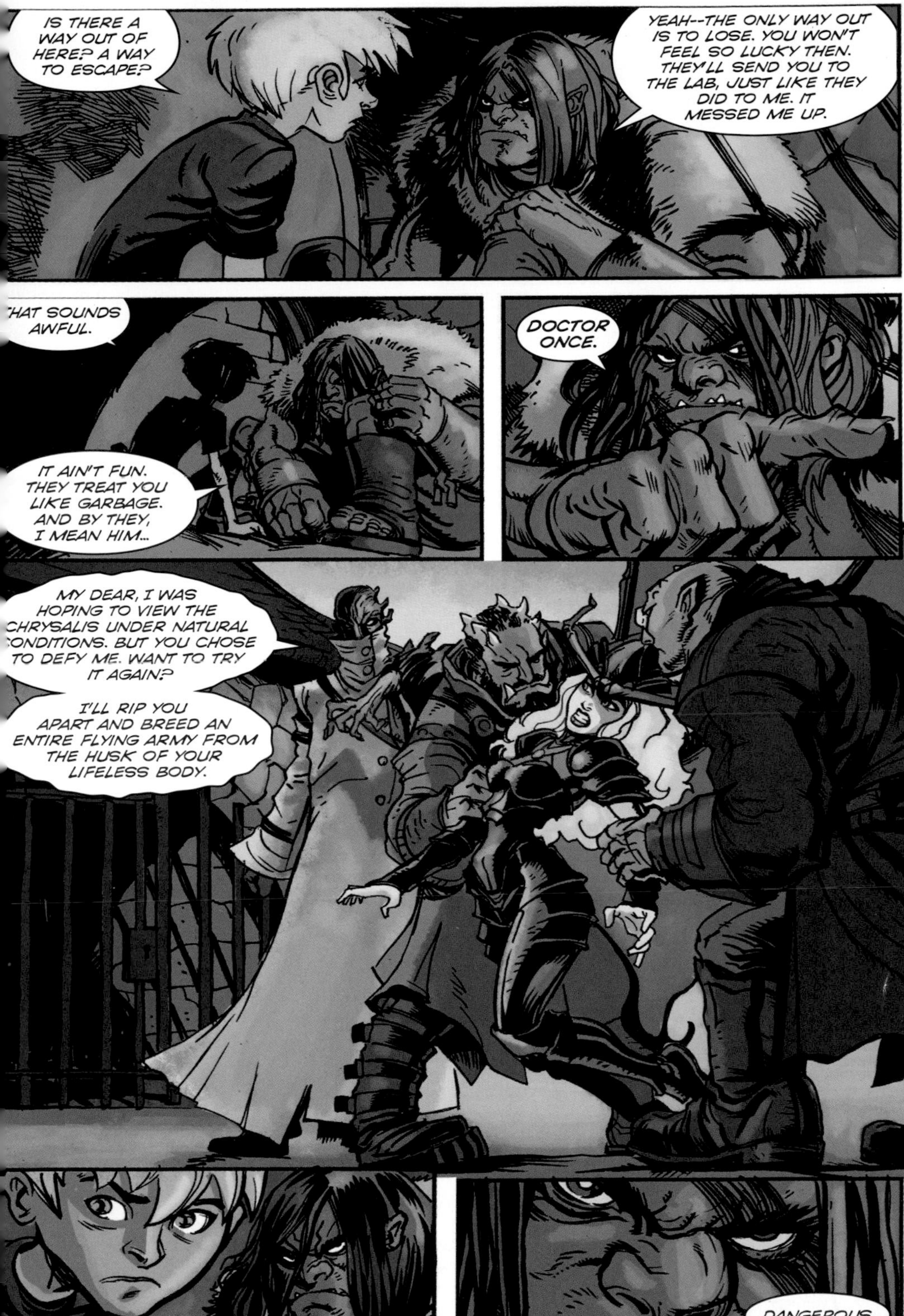
IS THERE A WAY OUT OF HERE? A WAY TO ESCAPE?
YEAH--THE ONLY WAY OUT IS TO LOSE. YOU WON'T FEEL SO LUCKY THEN. THEY'LL SEND YOU TO THE LAB, JUST LIKE THEY DID TO ME. IT MESSED ME UP.
THAT SOUNDS AWFUL.
IT AIN'T FUN. THEY TREAT YOU LIKE GARBAGE. AND BY THEY, I MEAN HIM...
DOCTOR ONCE.
MY DEAR, I WAS HOPING TO VIEW THE CHRYSALIS UNDER NATURAL CONDITIONS. BUT YOU CHOSE TO DEFY ME. WANT TO TRY IT AGAIN?
I'LL RIP YOU APART AND BREED AN ENTIRE FLYING ARMY FROM THE HUSK OF YOUR LIFELESS BODY.
AND THE GIRL? WHO IS SHE?
DANGEROUS.

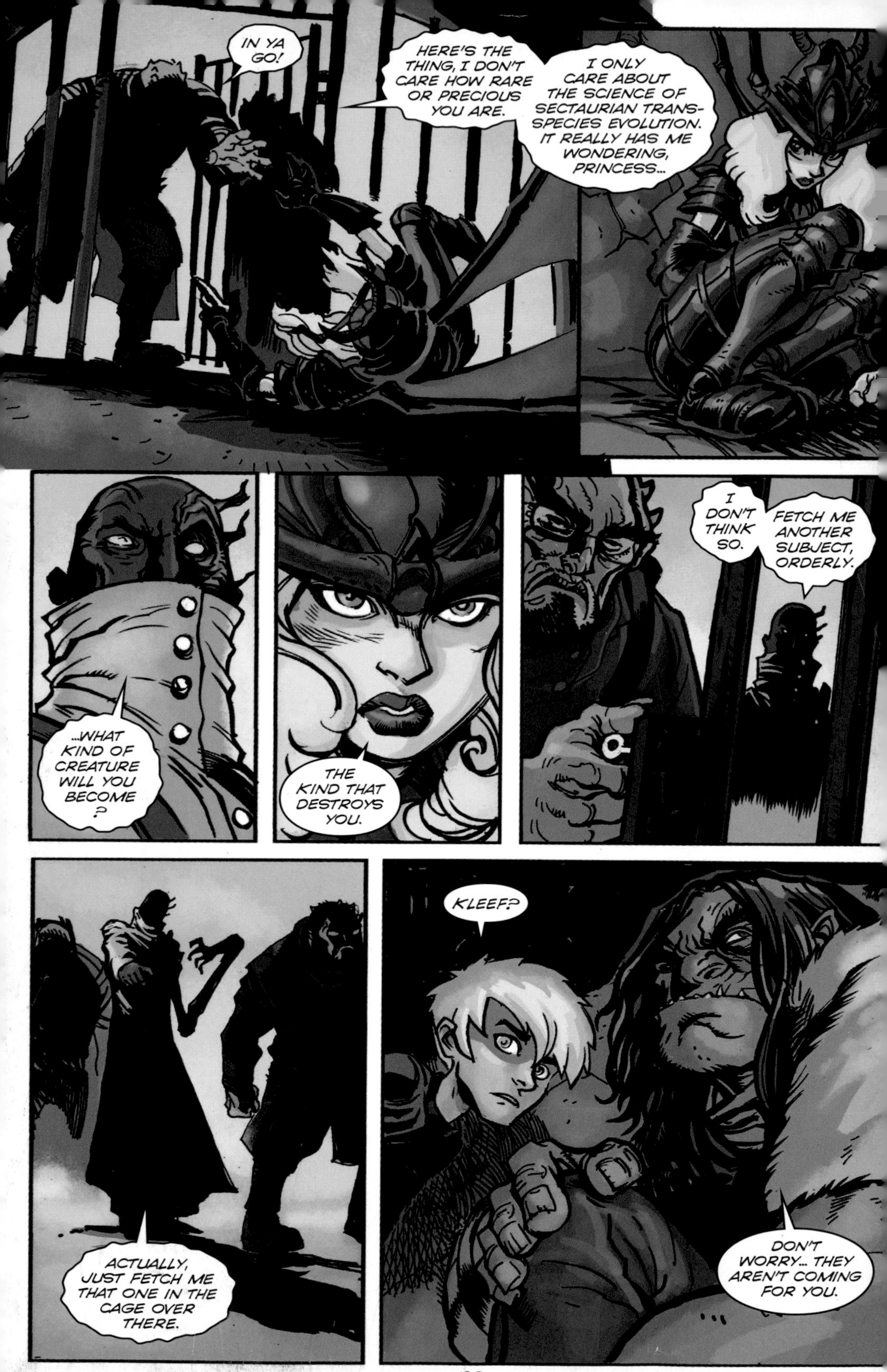
IN YA GO!
HERE'S THE THING, I DON'T CARE HOW RARE OR PRECIOUS YOU ARE.
I ONLY CARE ABOUT THE SCIENCE OF SECTAURIAN TRANS-SPECIES EVOLUTION. IT REALLY HAS ME WONDERING, PRINCESS...
...WHAT KIND OF CREATURE WILL YOU BECOME ?
THE KIND THAT DESTROYS YOU.
I DON'T THINK SO.
FETCH ME ANOTHER SUBJECT, ORDERLY.
ACTUALLY, JUST FETCH ME THAT ONE IN THE CAGE OVER THERE.
KLEEF?
DON'T WORRY... THEY AREN'T COMING FOR YOU.

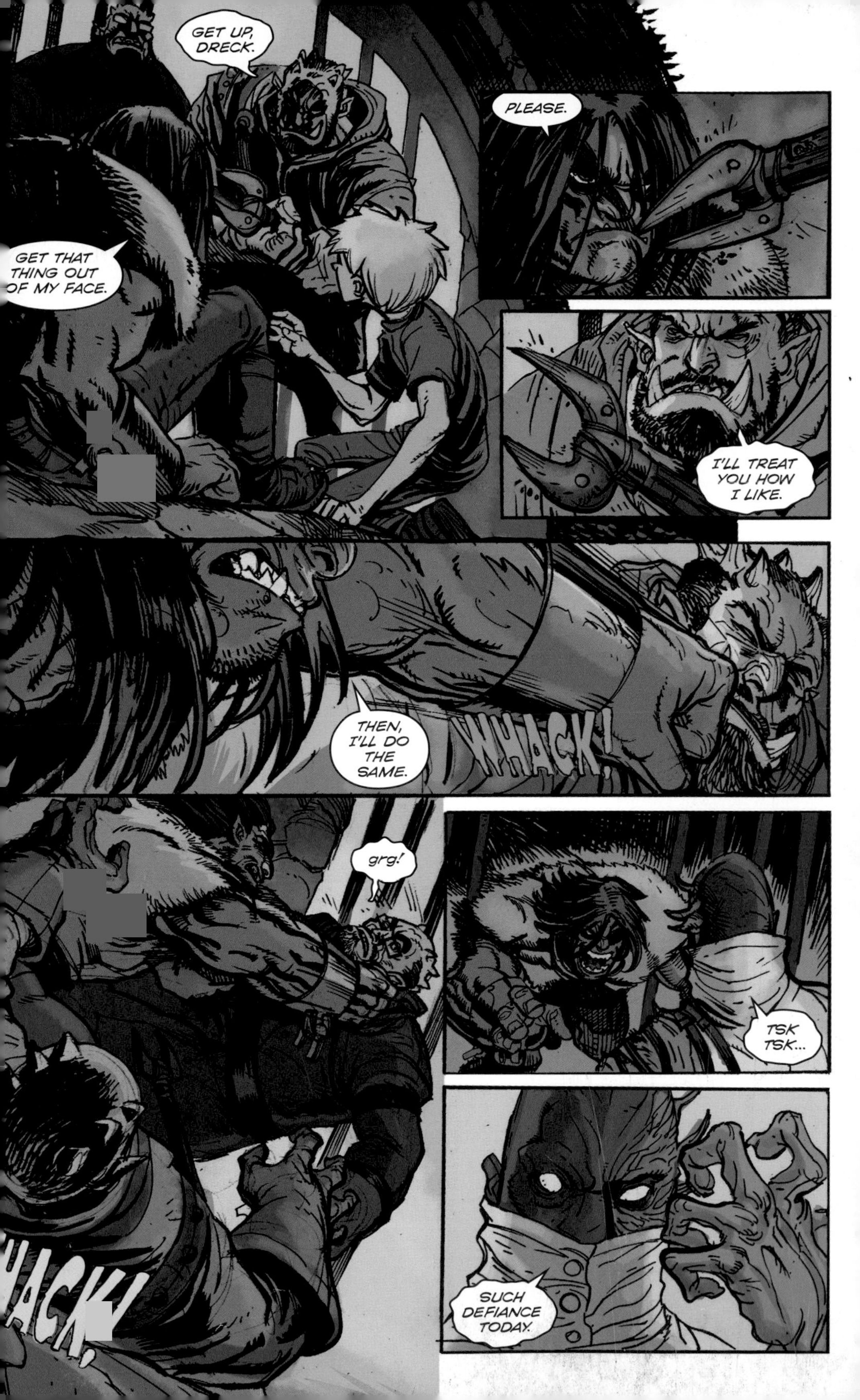
GET UP, DRECK.
GET THAT THING OUT OF MY FACE.
PLEASE.
I'LL TREAT YOU HOW I LIKE.
THEN, I'LL DO THE SAME.
WHACK!
grg!
HACK!
TSK TSK...
SUCH DEFIANCE TODAY.

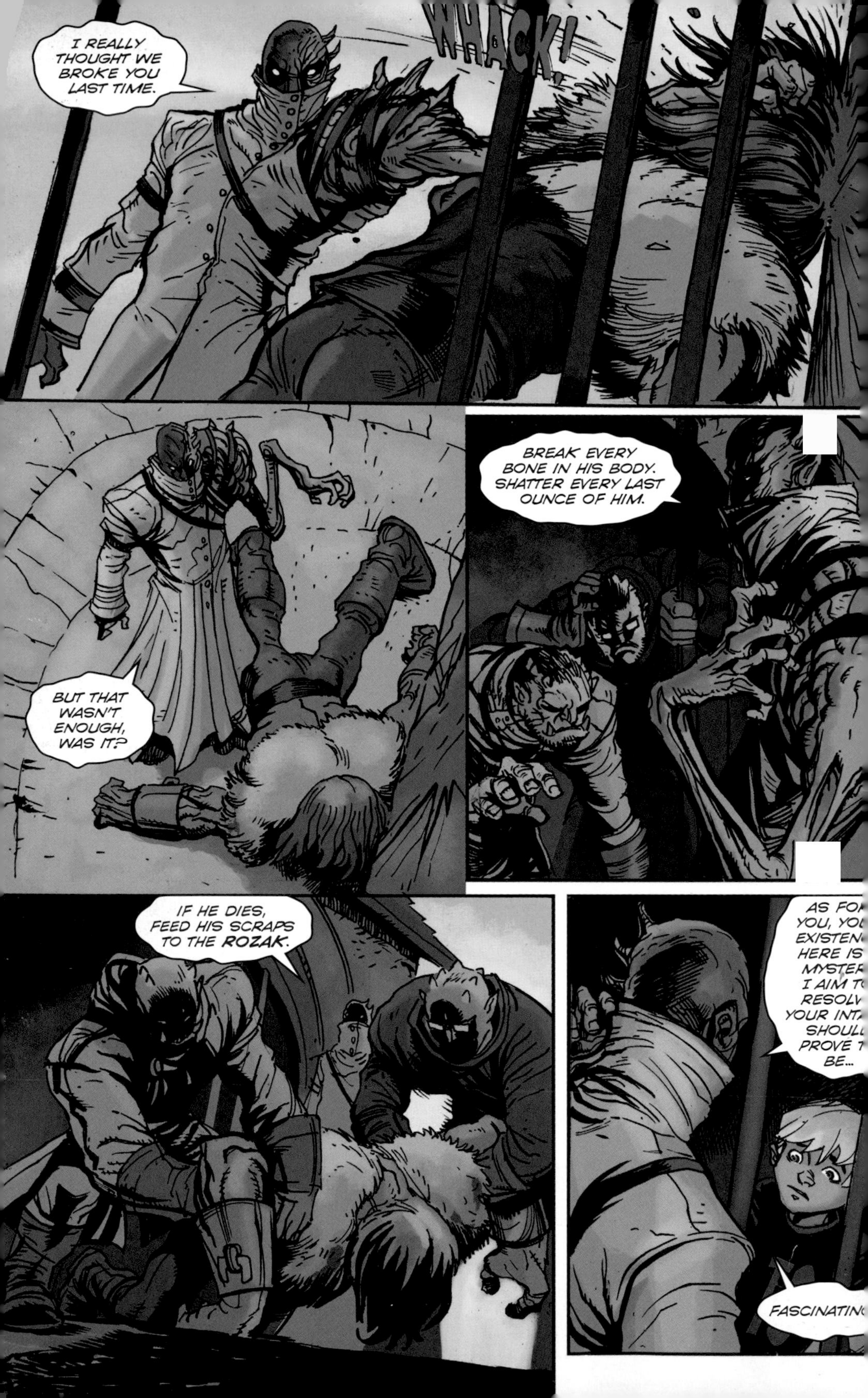

WHACK!
I REALLY THOUGHT WE BROKE YOU LAST TIME.
BUT THAT WASN'T ENOUGH, WAS IT?
BREAK EVERY BONE IN HIS BODY. SHATTER EVERY LAST OUNCE OF HIM.
IF HE DIES, FEED HIS SCRAPS TO THE ROZAK.
FASCINATIN

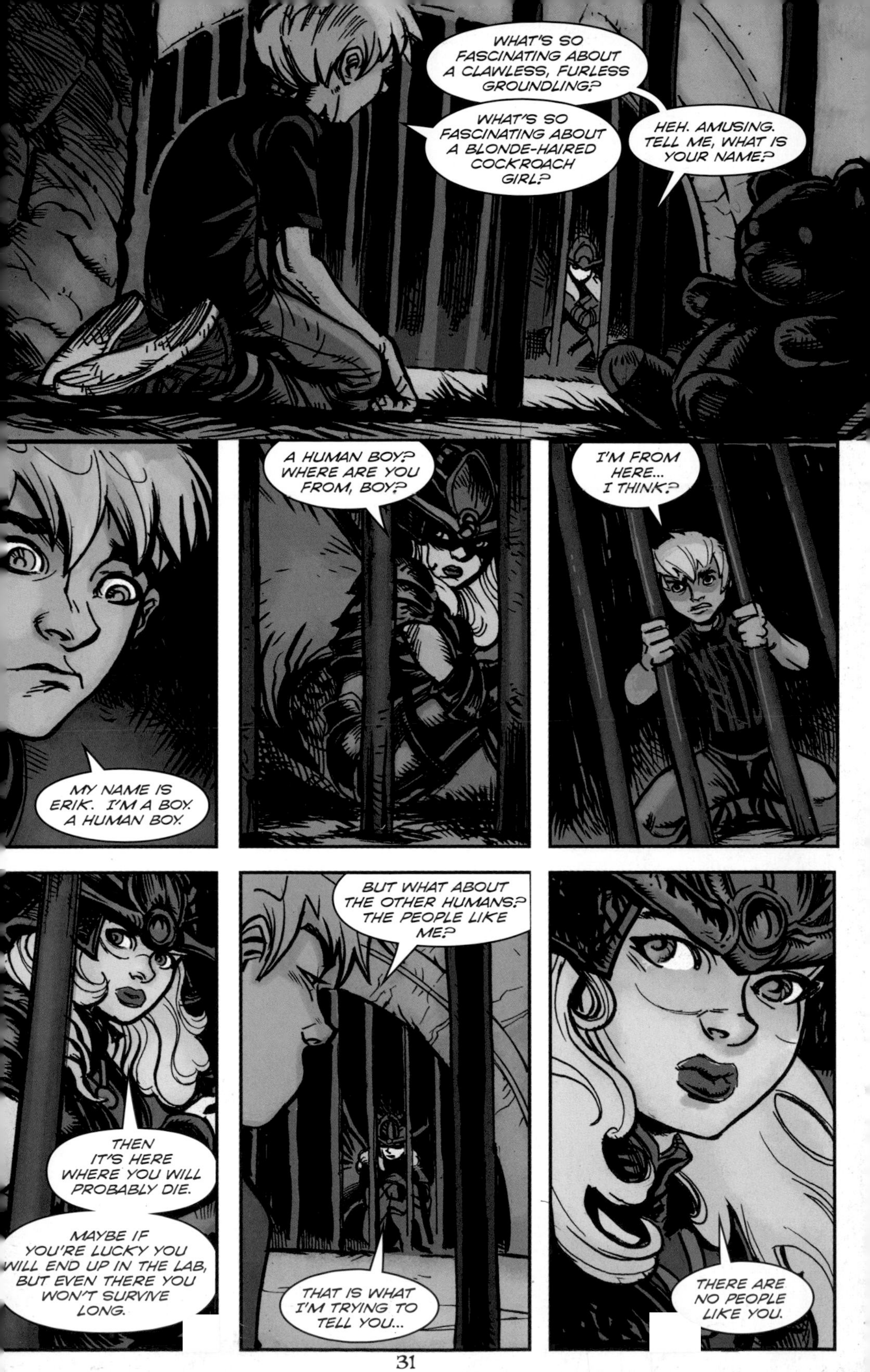
WHAT'S SO FASCINATING ABOUT A CLAWLESS, FURLESS GROUNDLING?
WHAT'S SO FASCINATING ABOUT A BLONDE-HAIRED COCKROACH GIRL?
HEH. AMUSING. TELL ME, WHAT IS YOUR NAME?
MY NAME IS ERIK. I'M A BOY. A HUMAN BOY.
A HUMAN BOY? WHERE ARE YOU FROM, BOY?
I'M FROM HERE... I THINK?
THEN IT'S HERE WHERE YOU WILL PROBABLY DIE.
MAYBE IF YOU'RE LUCKY YOU WILL END UP IN THE LAB, BUT EVEN THERE YOU WON'T SURVIVE LONG.
BUT WHAT ABOUT THE OTHER HUMANS? THE PEOPLE LIKE ME?
THAT IS WHAT I'M TRYING TO TELL YOU...
THERE ARE NO PEOPLE LIKE YOU.

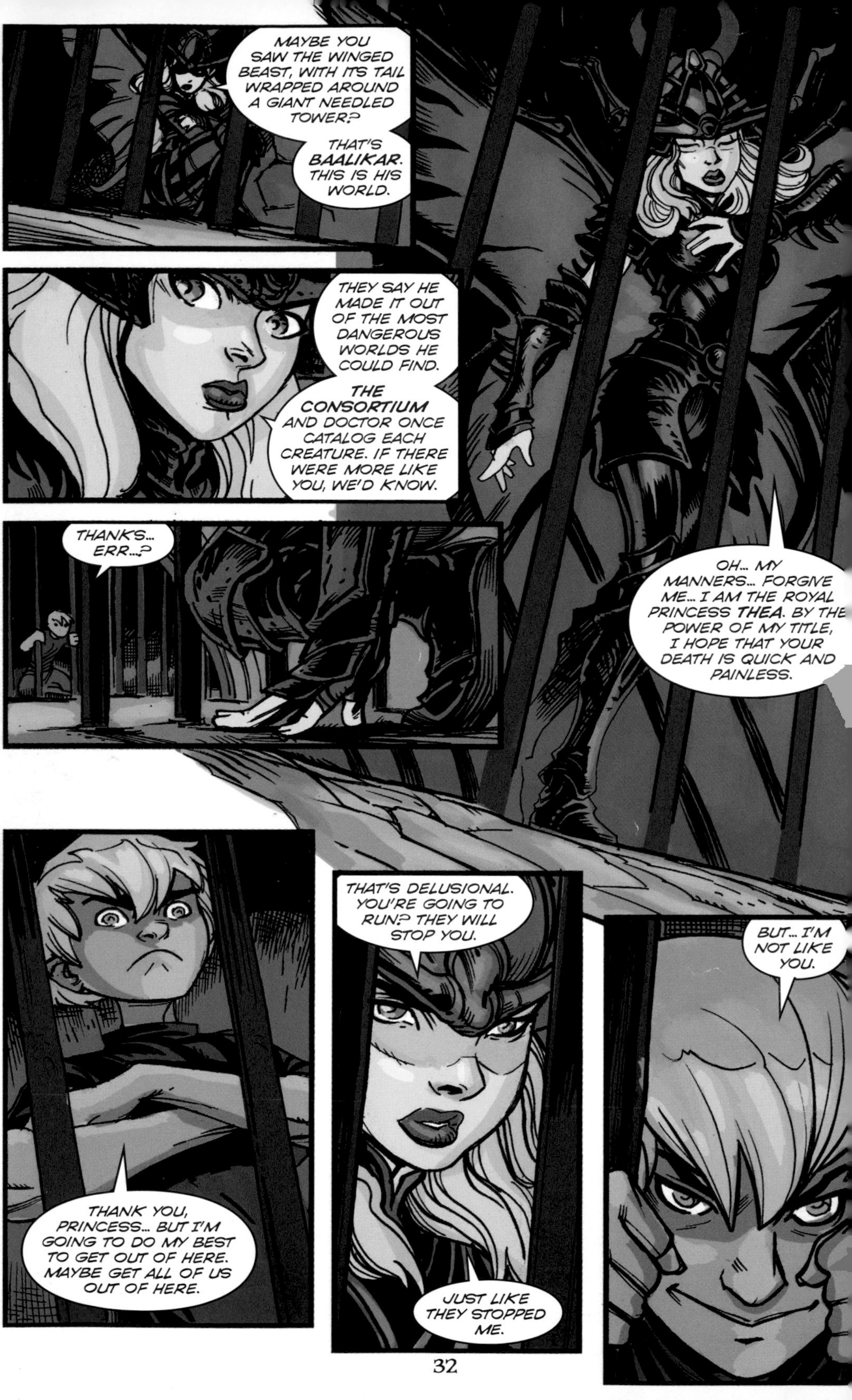
MAYBE YOU SAW THE WINGED BEAST, WITH ITS TAIL WRAPPED AROUND A GIANT NEEDLED TOWER?
THAT'S **BAALIKAR**. THIS IS HIS WORLD.
THEY SAY HE MADE IT OUT OF THE MOST DANGEROUS WORLDS HE COULD FIND.
THE CONSORTIUM AND DOCTOR ONCE CATALOG EACH CREATURE. IF THERE WERE MORE LIKE YOU, WE'D KNOW.
THANKS... ERR...?
OH... MY MANNERS... FORGIVE ME... I AM THE ROYAL PRINCESS **THEA**. BY THE POWER OF MY TITLE, I HOPE THAT YOUR DEATH IS QUICK AND PAINLESS.
THANK YOU, PRINCESS... BUT I'M GOING TO DO MY BEST TO GET OUT OF HERE. MAYBE GET ALL OF US OUT OF HERE.
THAT'S DELUSIONAL. YOU'RE GOING TO RUN? THEY WILL STOP YOU.
JUST LIKE THEY STOPPED ME.
BUT... I'M NOT LIKE YOU.

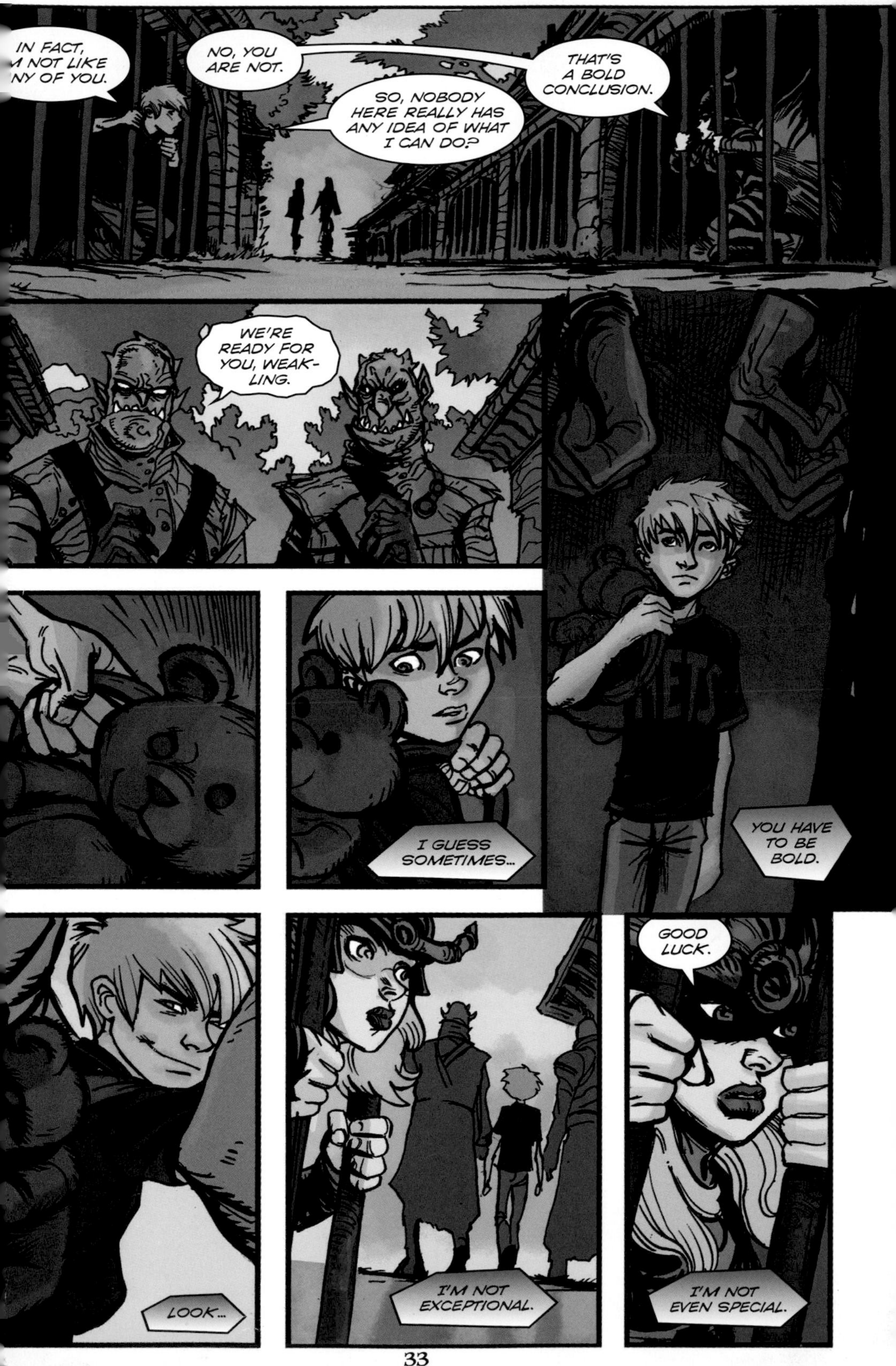
IN FACT,
M NOT LIKE
NY OF YOU.
NO, YOU
ARE NOT.
SO, NOBODY
HERE REALLY HAS
ANY IDEA OF WHAT
I CAN DO?
THAT'S
A BOLD
CONCLUSION.
WE'RE
READY FOR
YOU, WEAK-
LING.
YOU HAVE
TO BE
BOLD.
I GUESS
SOMETIMES...
LOOK...
I'M NOT
EXCEPTIONAL.
GOOD
LUCK.
I'M NOT
EVEN SPECIAL.

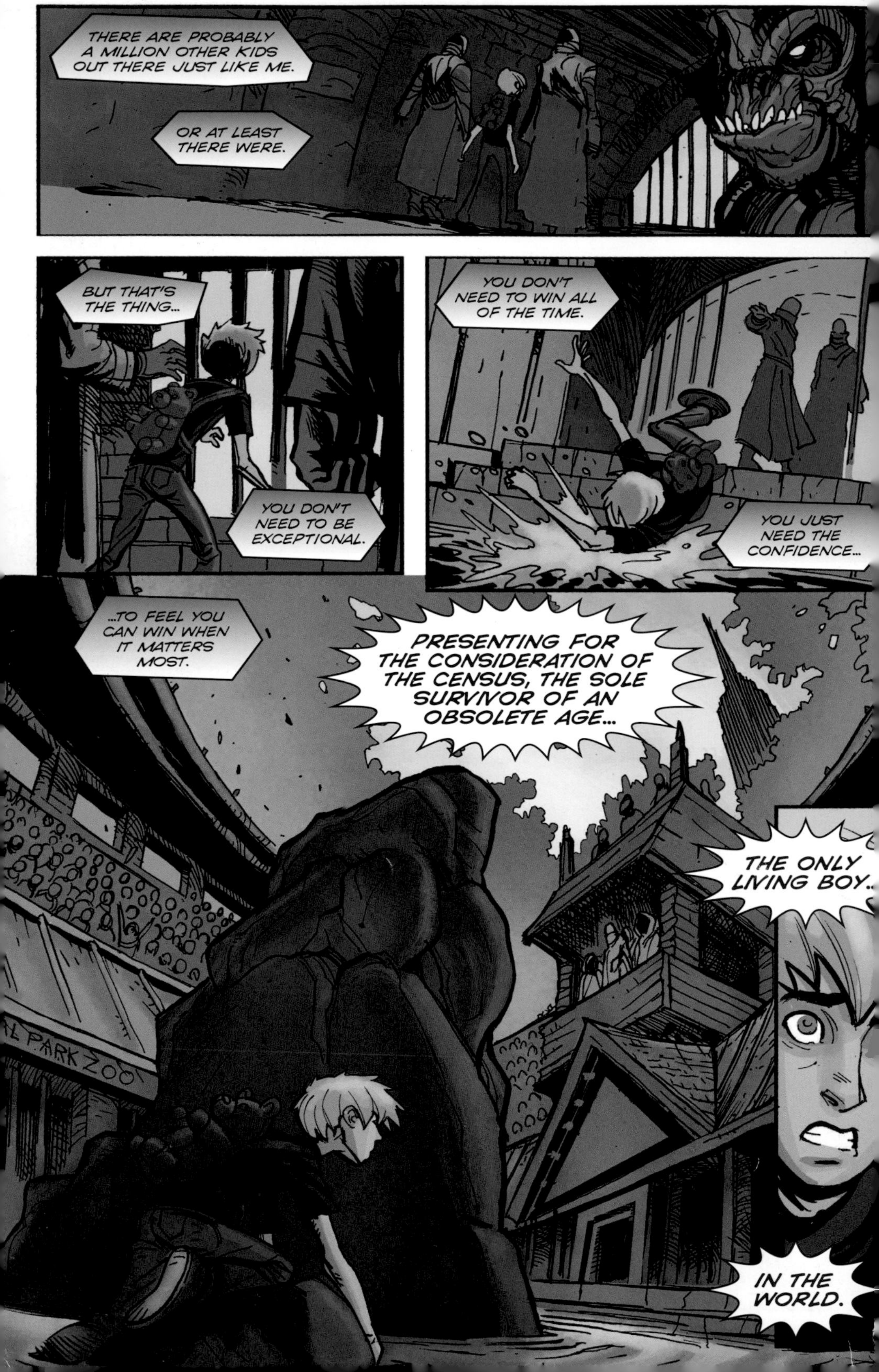
THERE ARE PROBABLY A MILLION OTHER KIDS OUT THERE JUST LIKE ME.
OR AT LEAST THERE WERE.
BUT THAT'S THE THING...
YOU DON'T NEED TO BE EXCEPTIONAL.
YOU DON'T NEED TO WIN ALL OF THE TIME.
YOU JUST NEED THE CONFIDENCE...
...TO FEEL YOU CAN WIN WHEN IT MATTERS MOST.
PRESENTING FOR THE CONSIDERATION OF THE CENSUS, THE SOLE SURVIVOR OF AN OBSOLETE AGE...
THE ONLY LIVING BOY...
IN THE WORLD.
L PARK ZOO

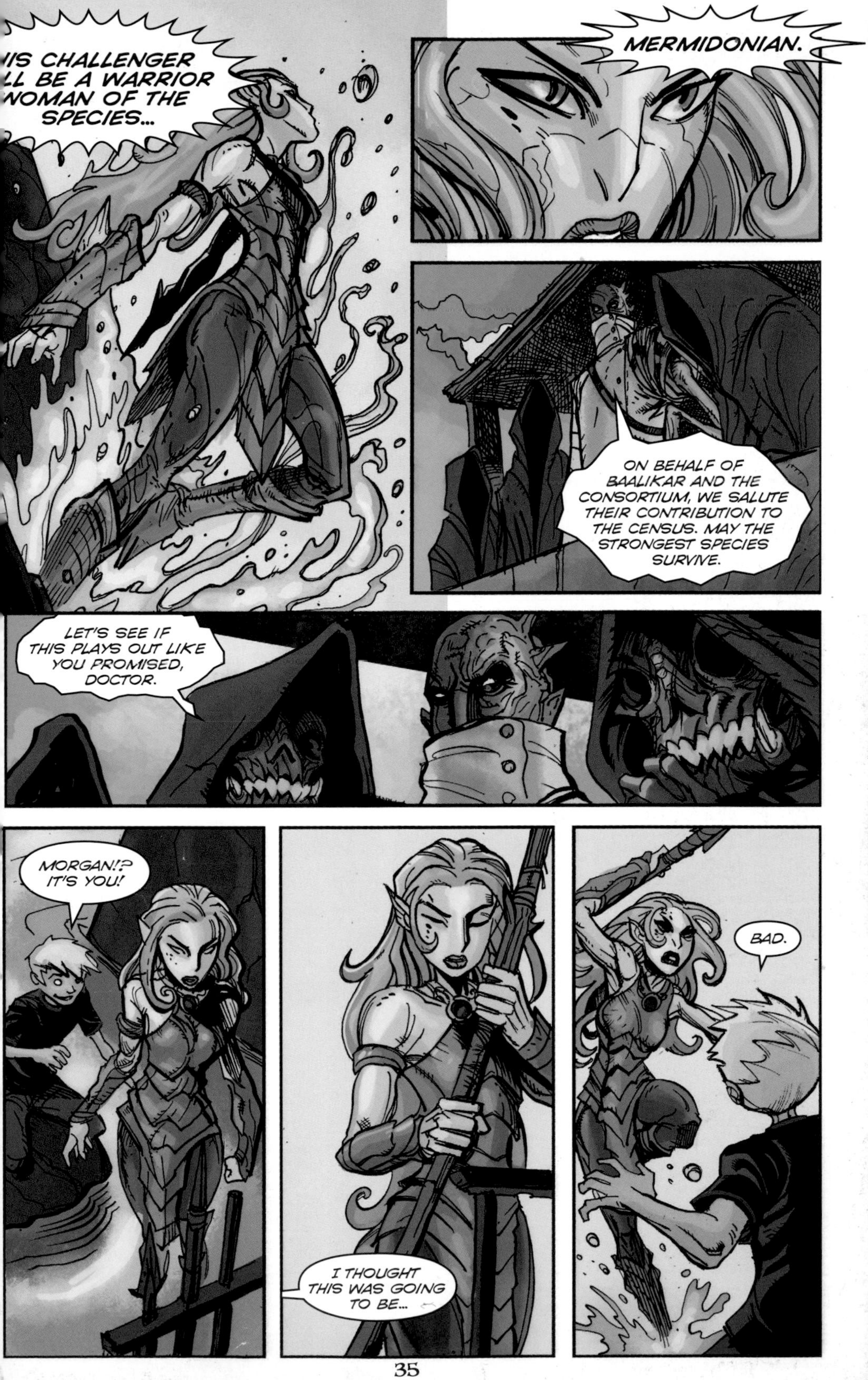
IS CHALLENGER
LL BE A WARRIOR
WOMAN OF THE
SPECIES...
MERMIDONIAN.
ON BEHALF OF BAALIKAR AND THE CONSORTIUM, WE SALUTE THEIR CONTRIBUTION TO THE CENSUS. MAY THE STRONGEST SPECIES SURVIVE.
LET'S SEE IF THIS PLAYS OUT LIKE YOU PROMISED, DOCTOR.
MORGAN!? IT'S YOU!
I THOUGHT THIS WAS GOING TO BE...
BAD.

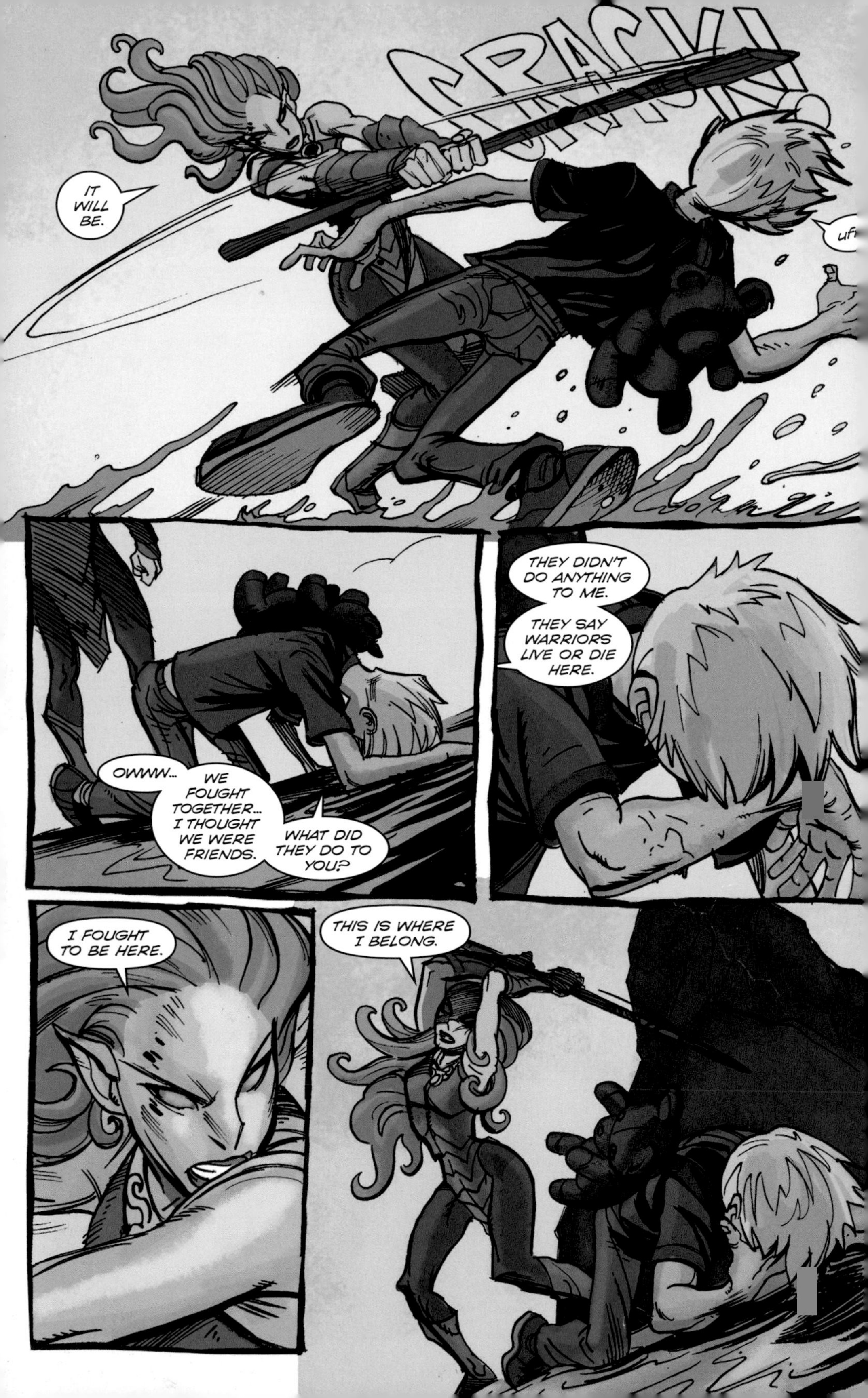
CRACK!
IT WILL BE.
uff
OWWW...
WE FOUGHT TOGETHER... I THOUGHT WE WERE FRIENDS.
WHAT DID THEY DO TO YOU?
THEY DIDN'T DO ANYTHING TO ME.
THEY SAY WARRIORS LIVE OR DIE HERE.
I FOUGHT TO BE HERE.
THIS IS WHERE I BELONG.

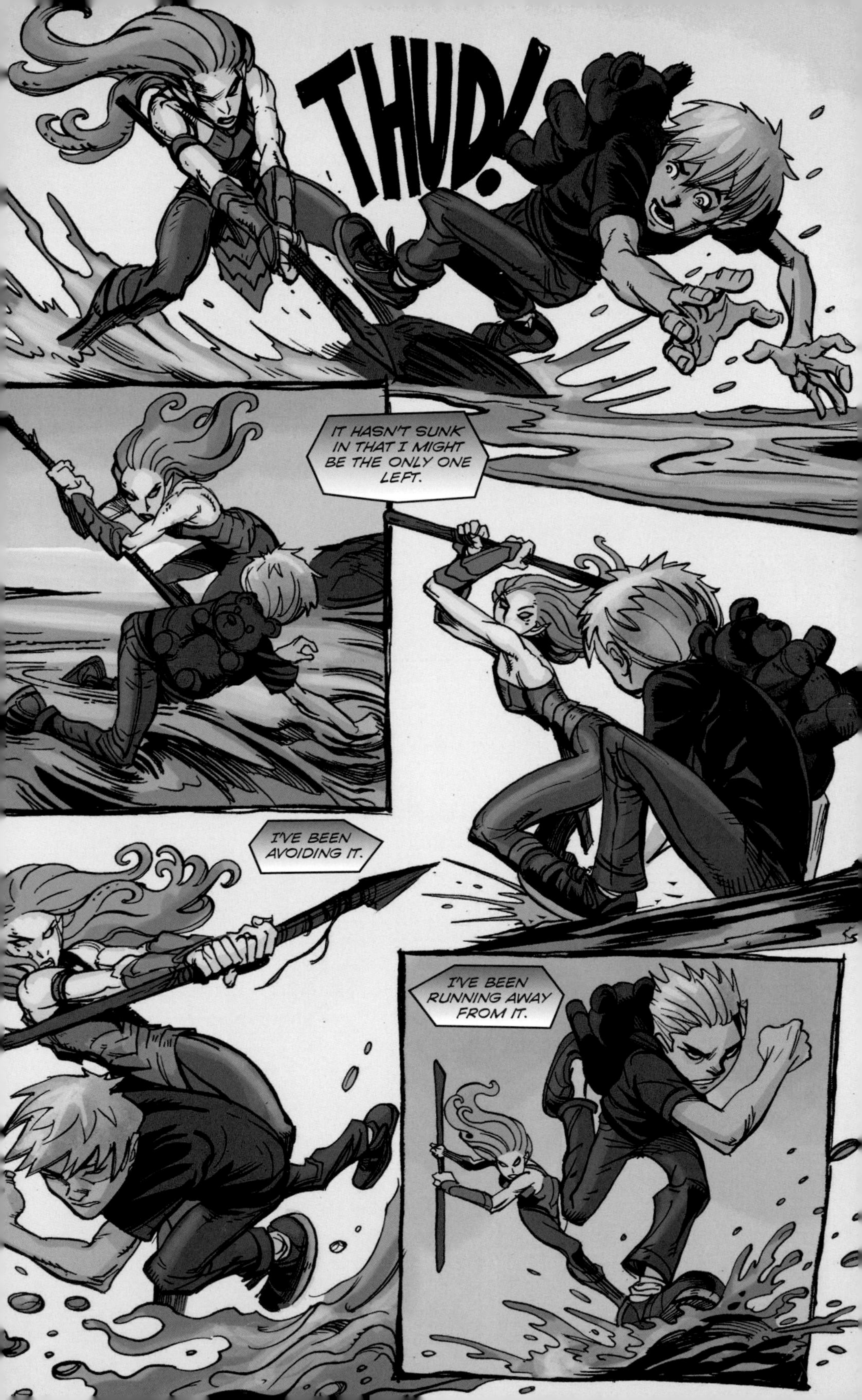
THUD!
IT HASN'T SUNK IN THAT I MIGHT BE THE ONLY ONE LEFT.
I'VE BEEN AVOIDING IT.
I'VE BEEN RUNNING AWAY FROM IT.

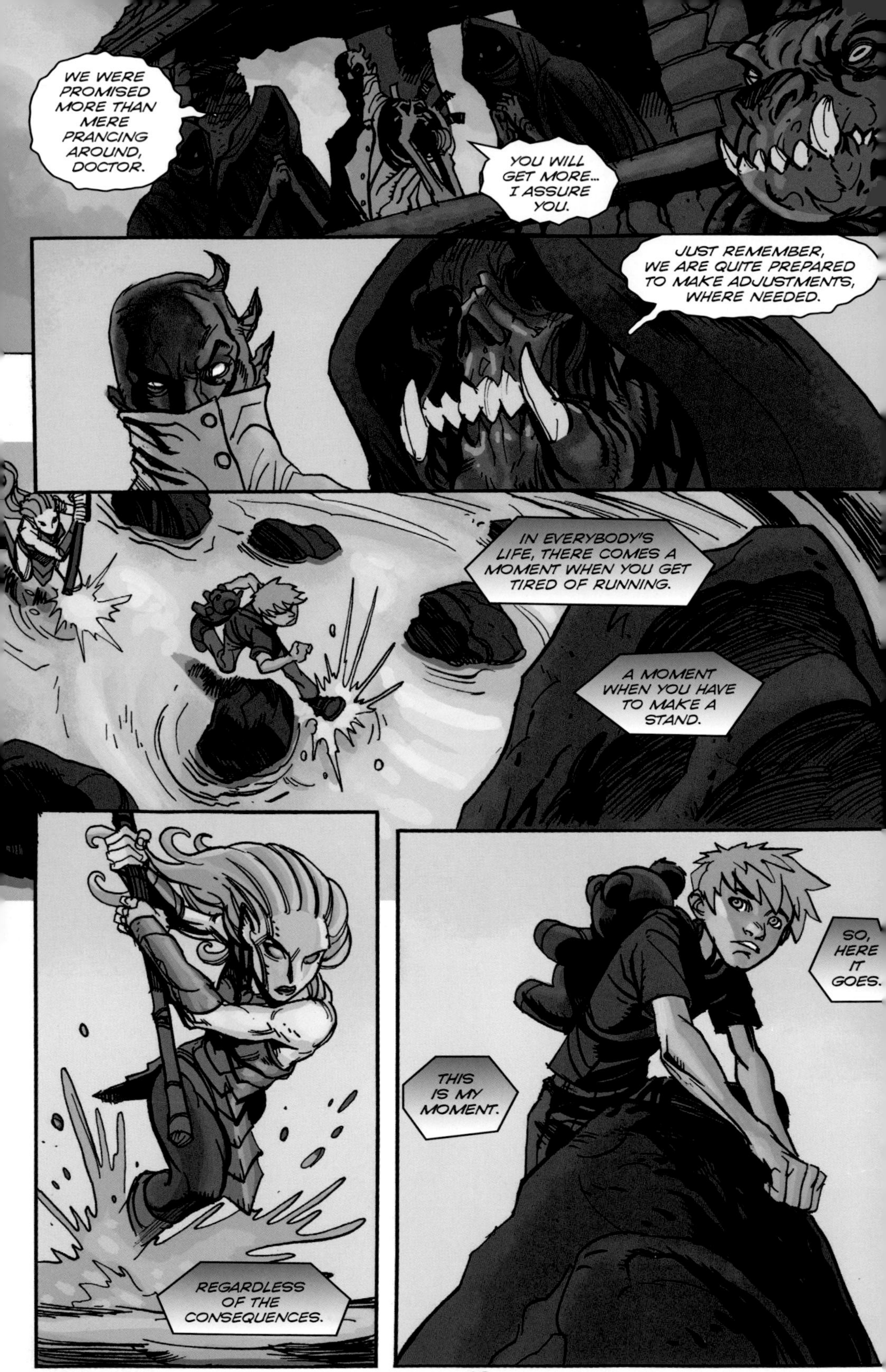
WE WERE PROMISED MORE THAN MERE PRANCING AROUND, DOCTOR.
YOU WILL GET MORE... I ASSURE YOU.
JUST REMEMBER, WE ARE QUITE PREPARED TO MAKE ADJUSTMENTS, WHERE NEEDED.
IN EVERYBODY'S LIFE, THERE COMES A MOMENT WHEN YOU GET TIRED OF RUNNING.
A MOMENT WHEN YOU HAVE TO MAKE A STAND.
REGARDLESS OF THE CONSEQUENCES.
SO, HERE IT GOES.
THIS IS MY MOMENT.

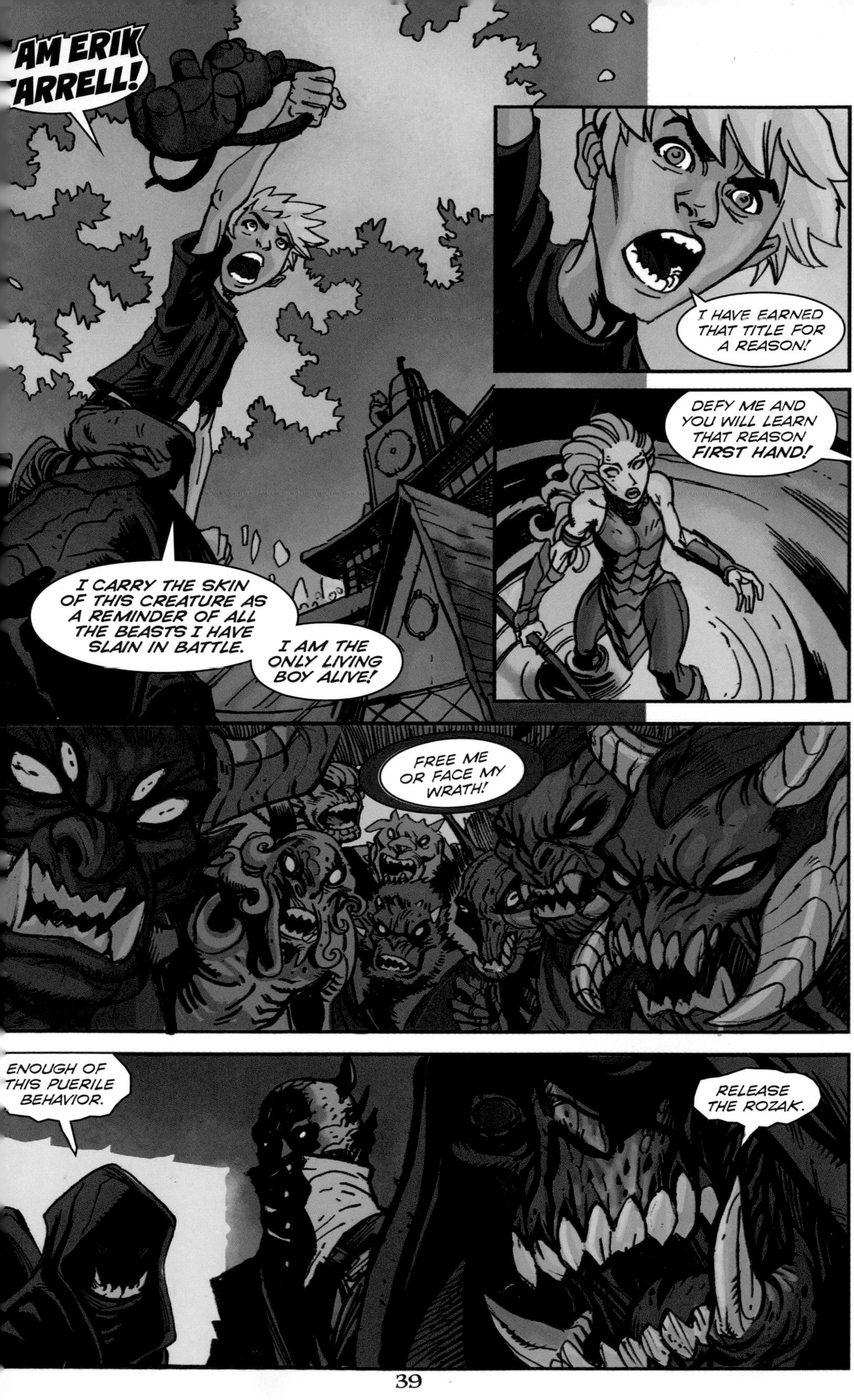
AM ERIK
ARRELL!
I HAVE EARNED THAT TITLE FOR A REASON!
I CARRY THE SKIN OF THIS CREATURE AS A REMINDER OF ALL THE BEASTS I HAVE SLAIN IN BATTLE.
I AM THE ONLY LIVING BOY ALIVE!
DEFY ME AND YOU WILL LEARN THAT REASON FIRST HAND!
FREE ME OR FACE MY WRATH!
ENOUGH OF THIS PUERILE BEHAVIOR.
RELEASE THE ROZAK.

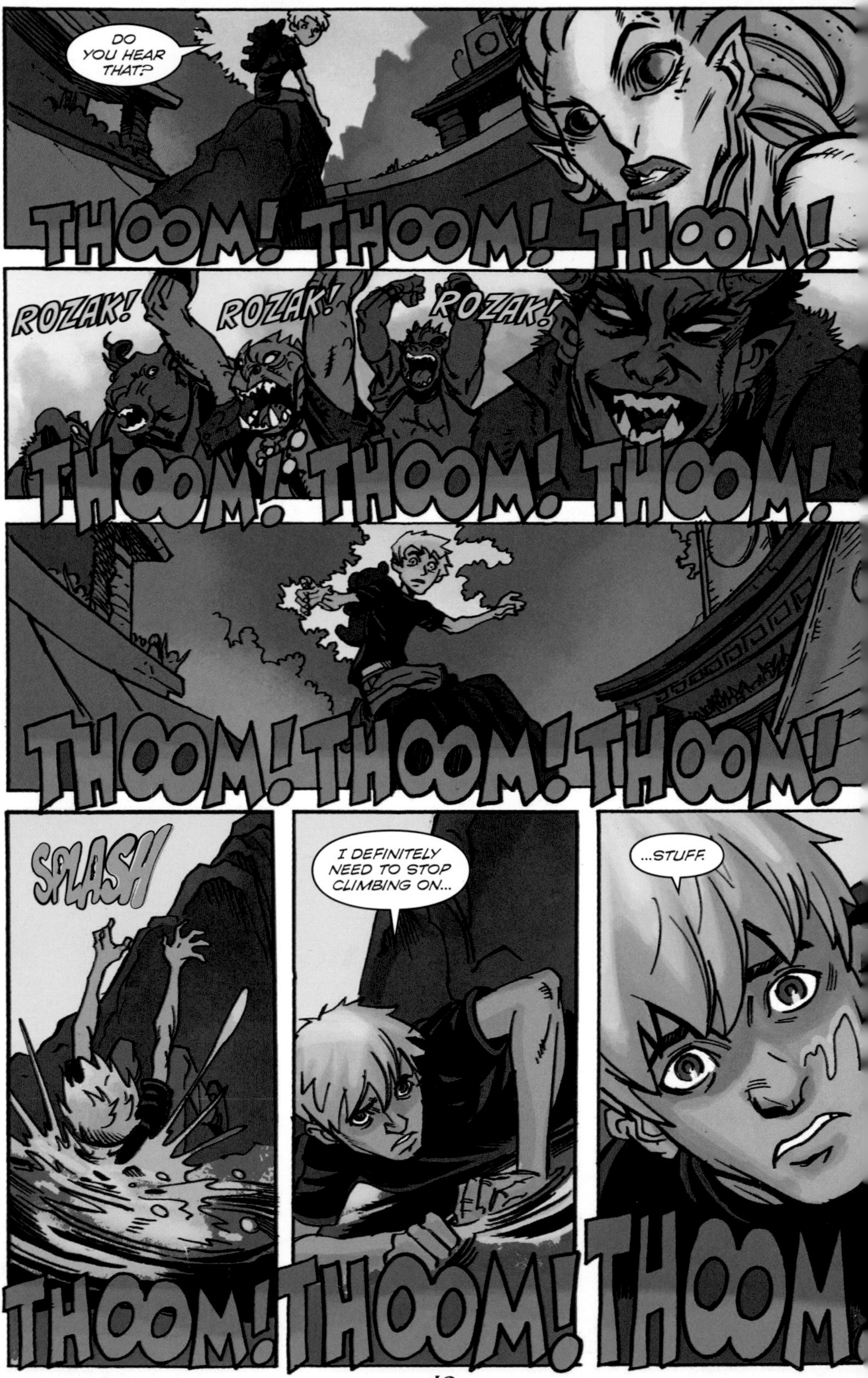
DO YOU HEAR THAT?
THOOM! THOOM! THOOM!
ROZAK! ROZAK! ROZAK!
THOOM! THOOM! THOOM!
THOOM! THOOM! THOOM!
SPLASH
I DEFINITELY NEED TO STOP CLIMBING ON...
...STUFF.
THOOM! THOOM! THOOM

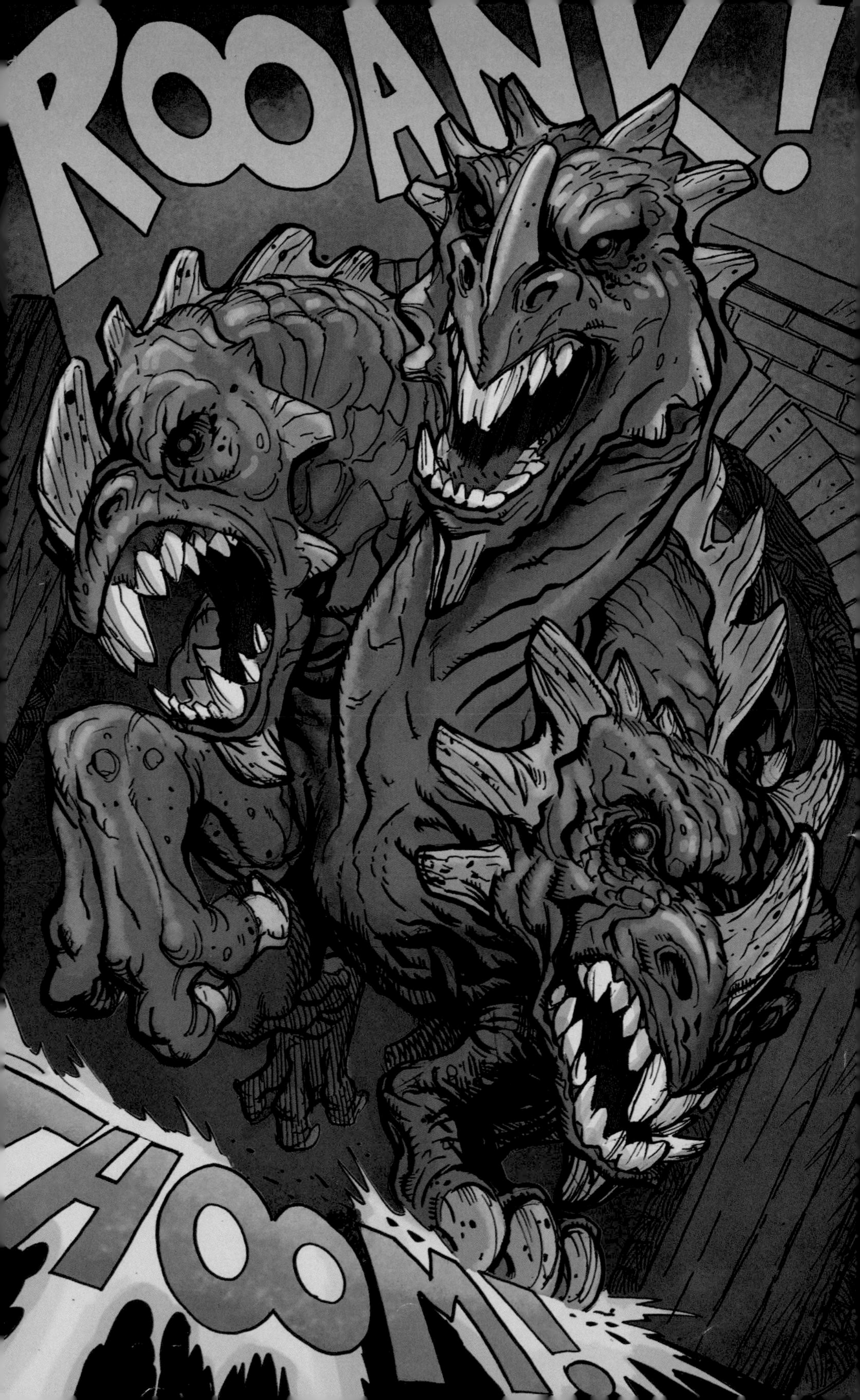
ROOANK!
HOOM!

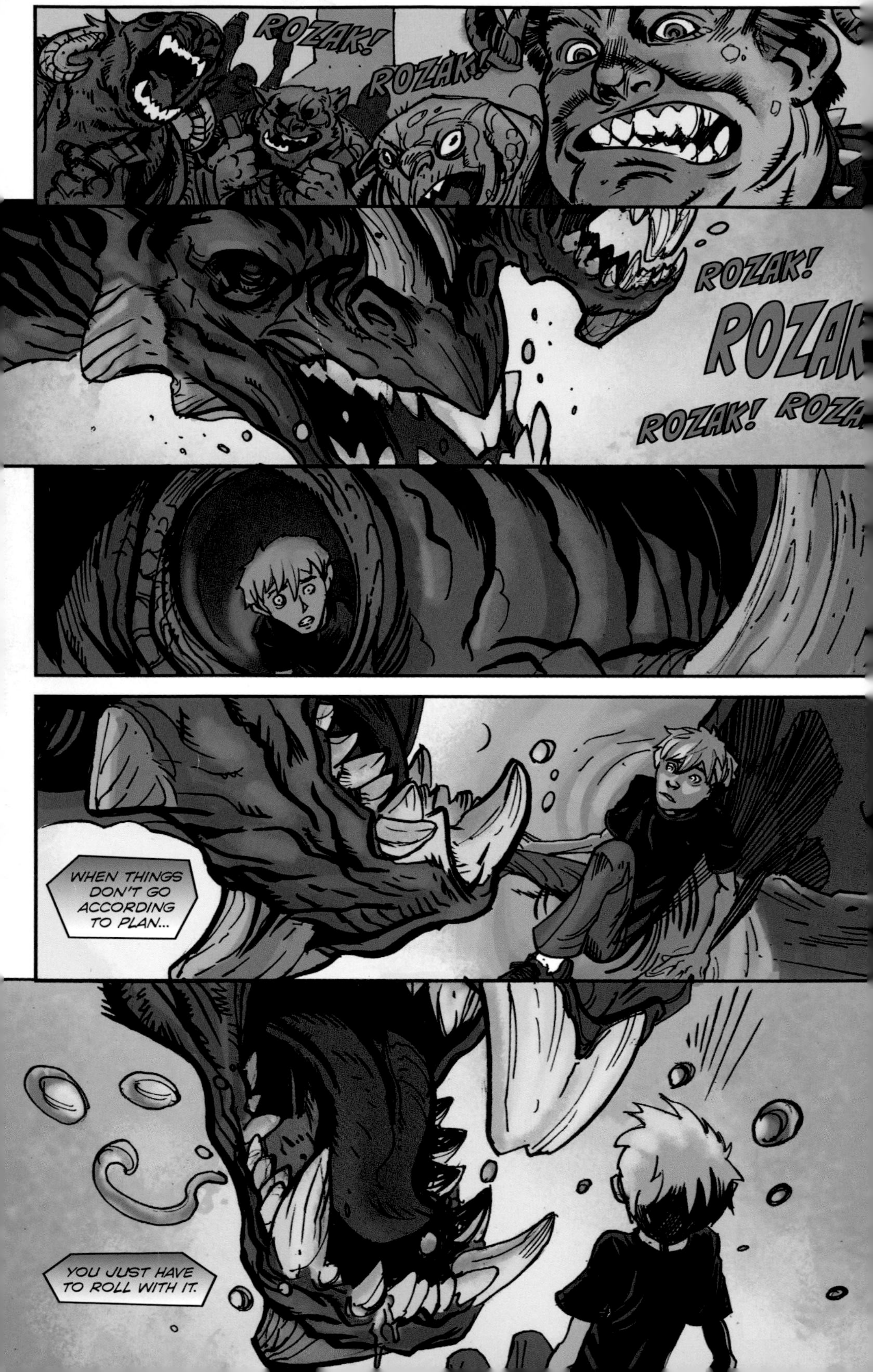
ROZAK!
ROZAK!
ROZAK!
ROZAK
ROZAK! ROZA
WHEN THINGS DON'T GO ACCORDING TO PLAN...
YOU JUST HAVE TO ROLL WITH IT.

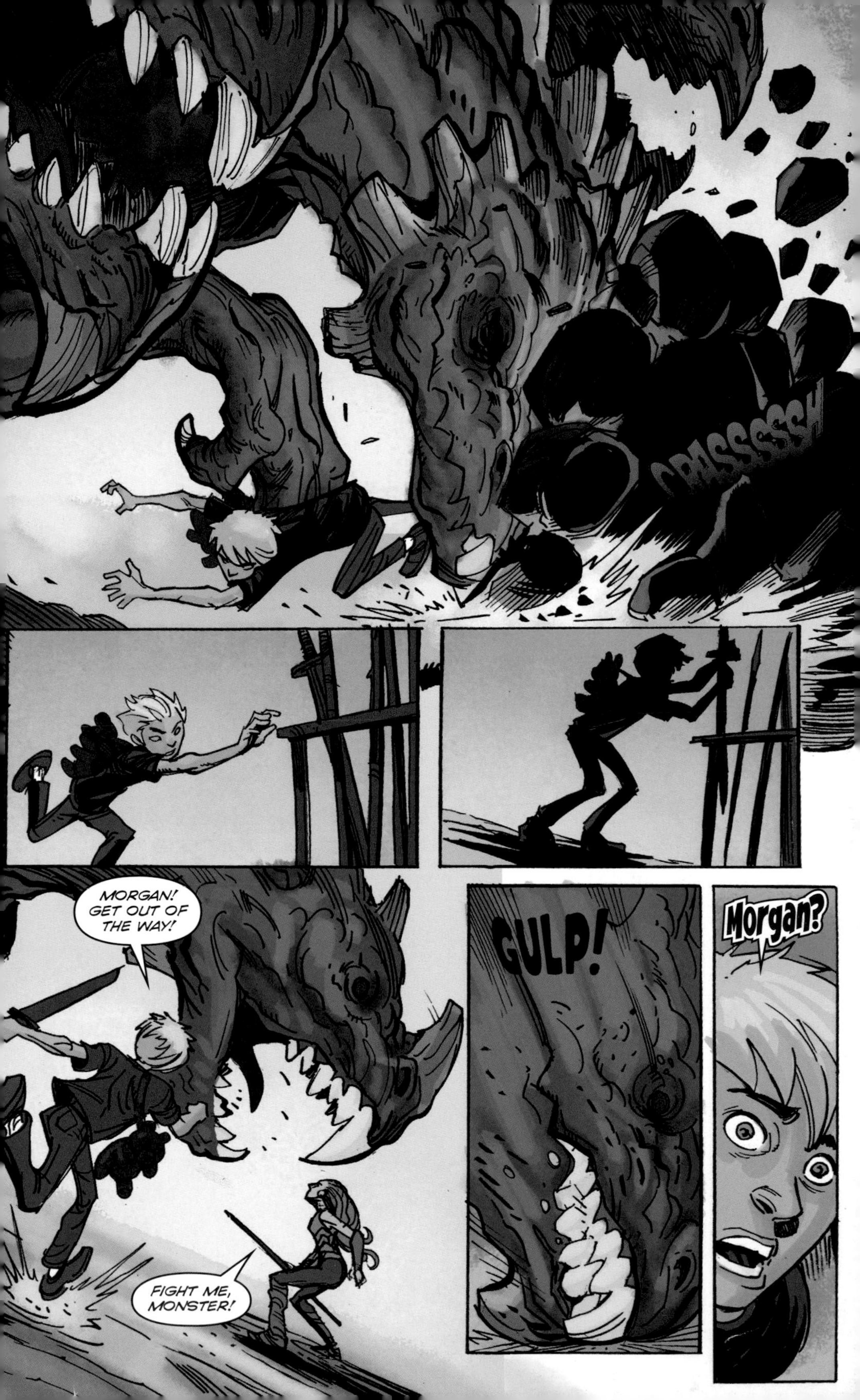
CRASSSSSH
MORGAN! GET OUT OF THE WAY!
FIGHT ME, MONSTER!
GULP!
Morgan?

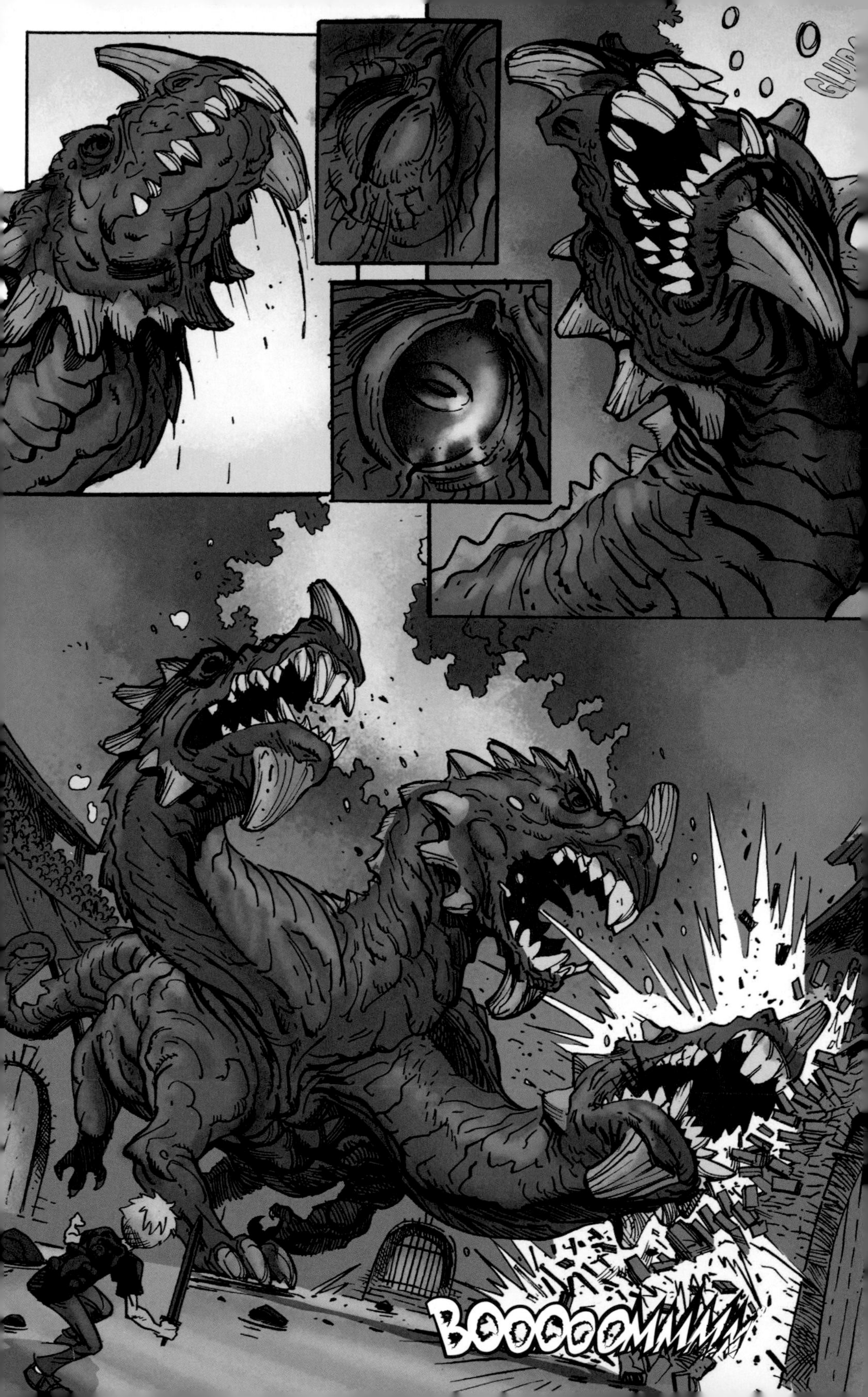
GLUB
BOOOOOMMMM

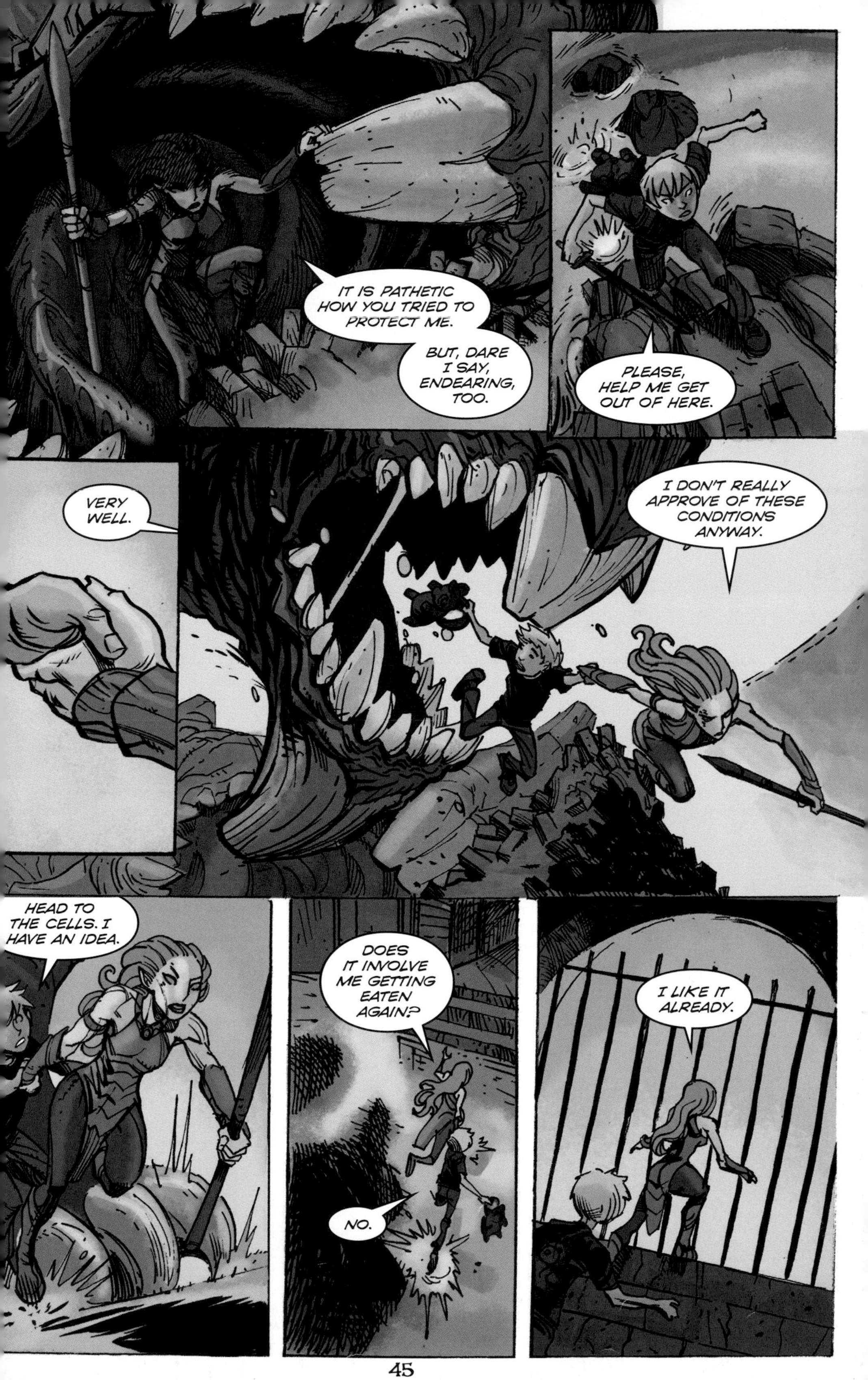
IT IS PATHETIC HOW YOU TRIED TO PROTECT ME.
BUT, DARE I SAY, ENDEARING, TOO.
PLEASE, HELP ME GET OUT OF HERE.
VERY WELL.
I DON'T REALLY APPROVE OF THESE CONDITIONS ANYWAY.
HEAD TO THE CELLS. I HAVE AN IDEA.
DOES IT INVOLVE ME GETTING EATEN AGAIN?
NO.
I LIKE IT ALREADY.

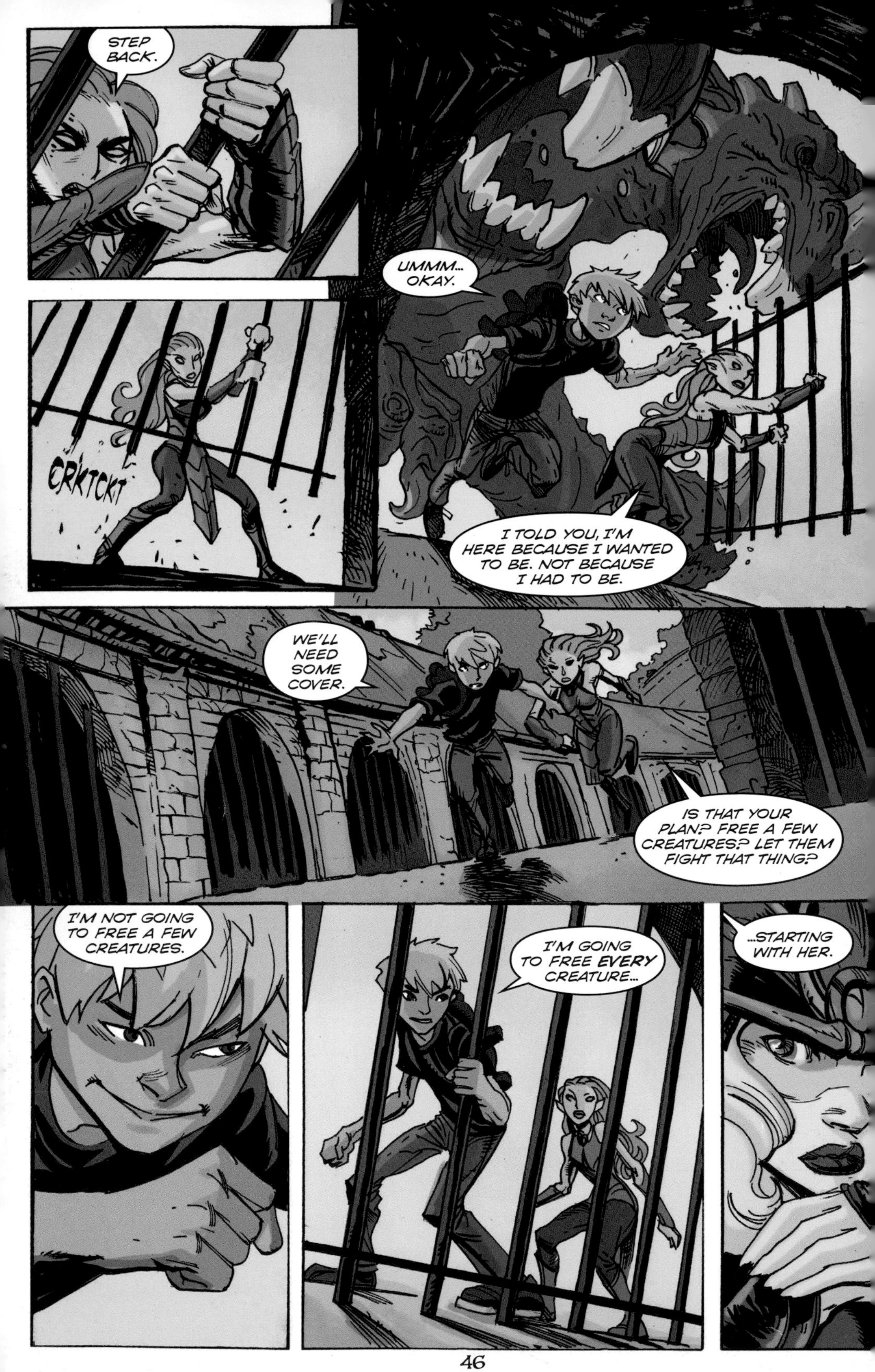
STEP BACK.
UMMM... OKAY.
CRKTCKT
I TOLD YOU, I'M HERE BECAUSE I WANTED TO BE. NOT BECAUSE I HAD TO BE.
WE'LL NEED SOME COVER.
IS THAT YOUR PLAN? FREE A FEW CREATURES? LET THEM FIGHT THAT THING?
I'M NOT GOING TO FREE A FEW CREATURES.
I'M GOING TO FREE **EVERY** CREATURE...
...STARTING WITH HER.

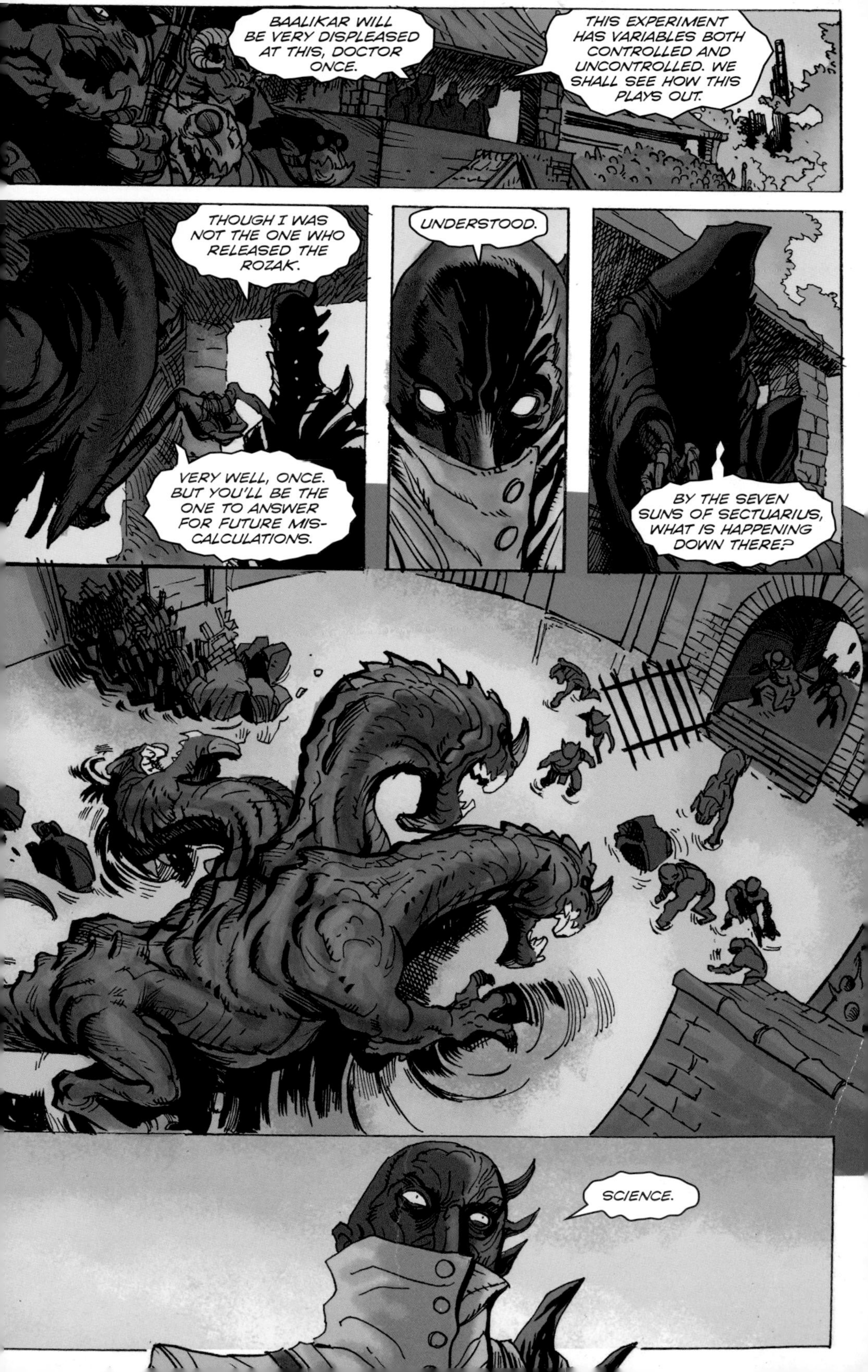
BAALIKAR WILL BE VERY DISPLEASED AT THIS, DOCTOR ONCE.
THIS EXPERIMENT HAS VARIABLES BOTH CONTROLLED AND UNCONTROLLED. WE SHALL SEE HOW THIS PLAYS OUT.
THOUGH I WAS NOT THE ONE WHO RELEASED THE ROZAK.
VERY WELL, ONCE. BUT YOU'LL BE THE ONE TO ANSWER FOR FUTURE MIS-CALCULATIONS.
UNDERSTOOD.
BY THE SEVEN SUNS OF SECTUARIUS, WHAT IS HAPPENING DOWN THERE?
SCIENCE.

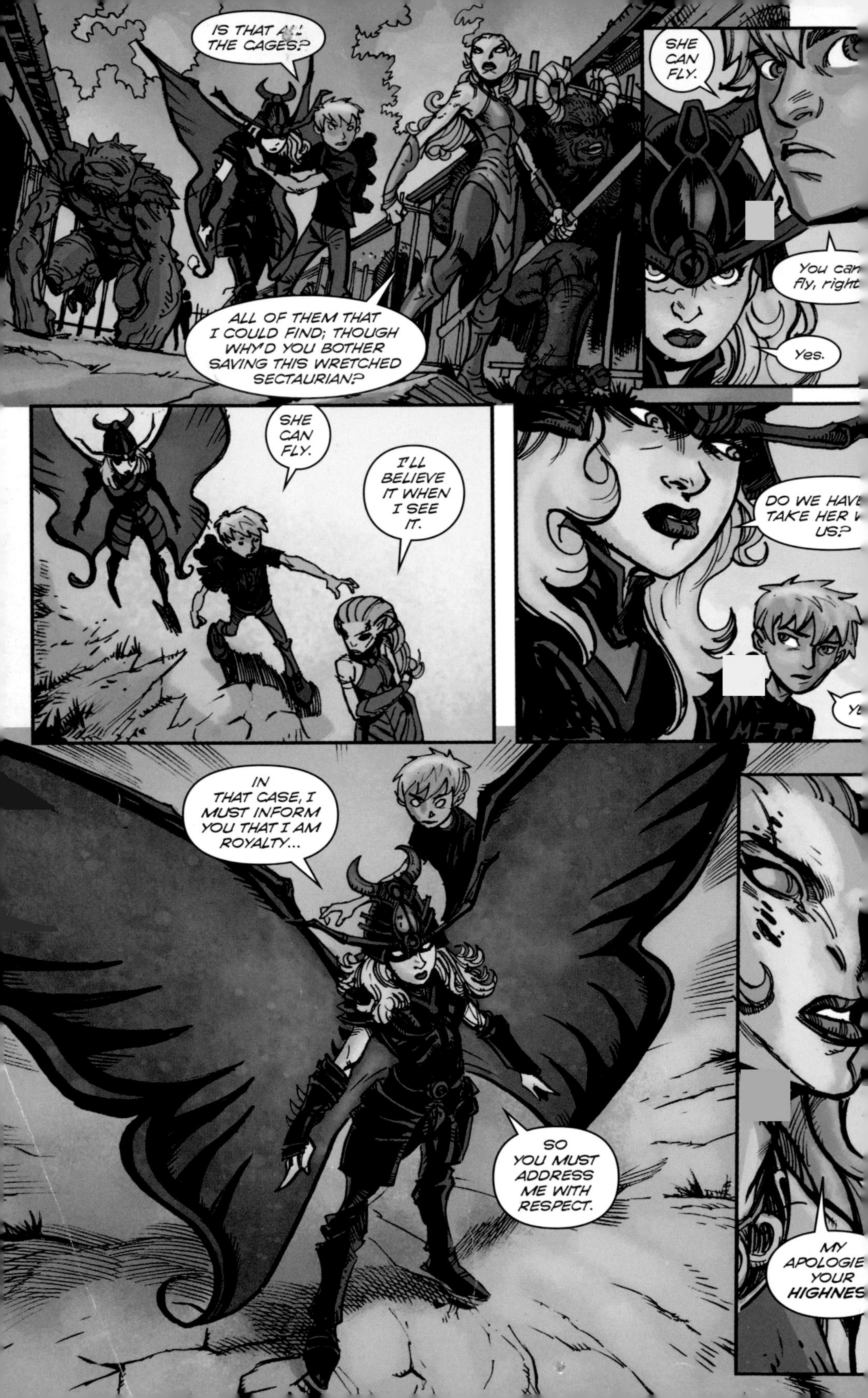
IS THAT ALL THE CAGES?
ALL OF THEM THAT I COULD FIND; THOUGH WHY'D YOU BOTHER SAVING THIS WRETCHED SECTAURIAN?
SHE CAN FLY.
You can fly, right
Yes.
SHE CAN FLY.
I'LL BELIEVE IT WHEN I SEE IT.
DO WE HAVE TAKE HER W US?
IN THAT CASE, I MUST INFORM YOU THAT I AM ROYALTY...
SO YOU MUST ADDRESS ME WITH RESPECT.
MY APOLOGIE YOUR HIGHNES

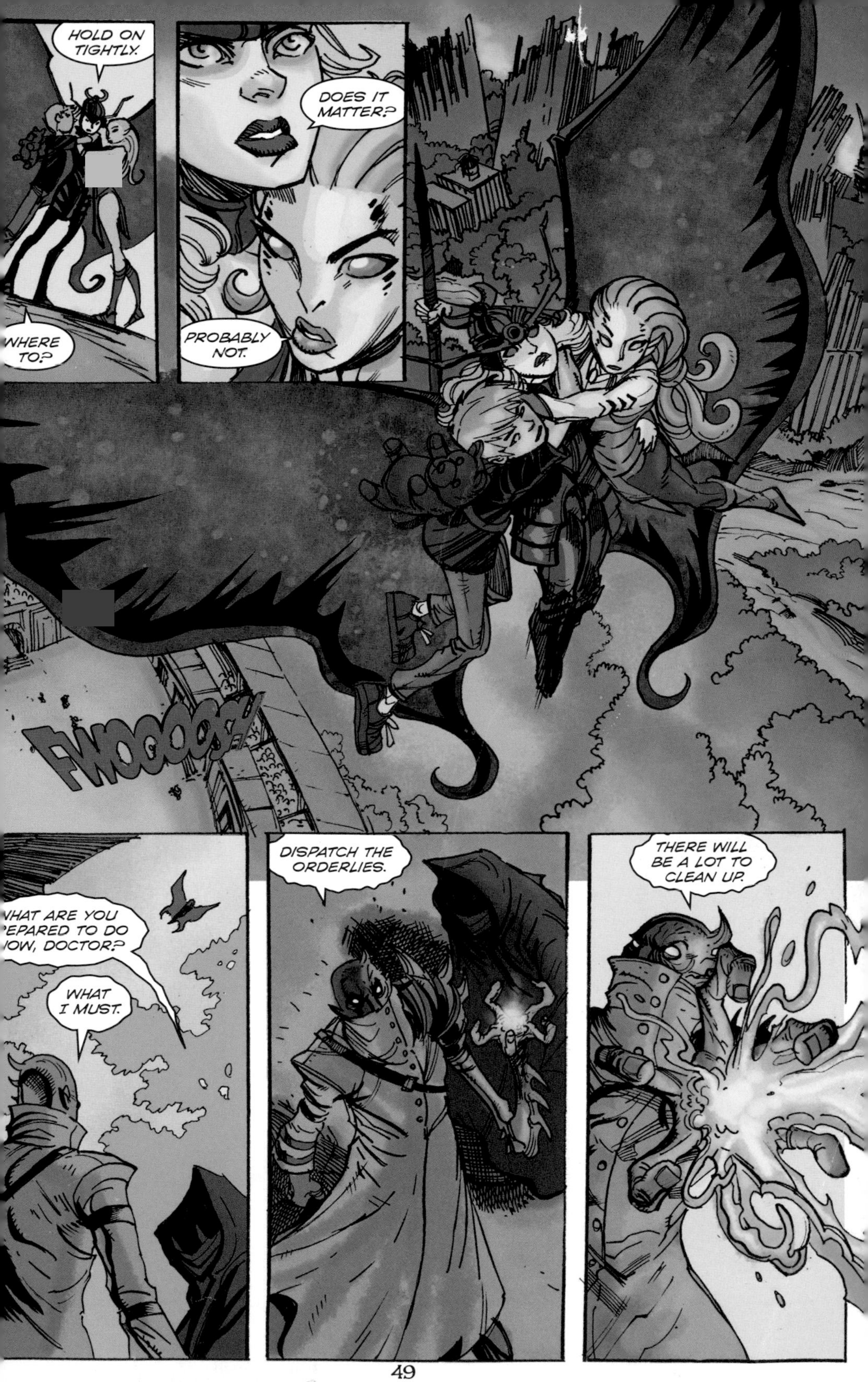
HOLD ON TIGHTLY.
HERE TO?
DOES IT MATTER?
PROBABLY NOT.
FWOOOS
HAT ARE YOU EPARED TO DO OW, DOCTOR?
WHAT I MUST.
DISPATCH THE ORDERLIES.
THERE WILL BE A LOT TO CLEAN UP.

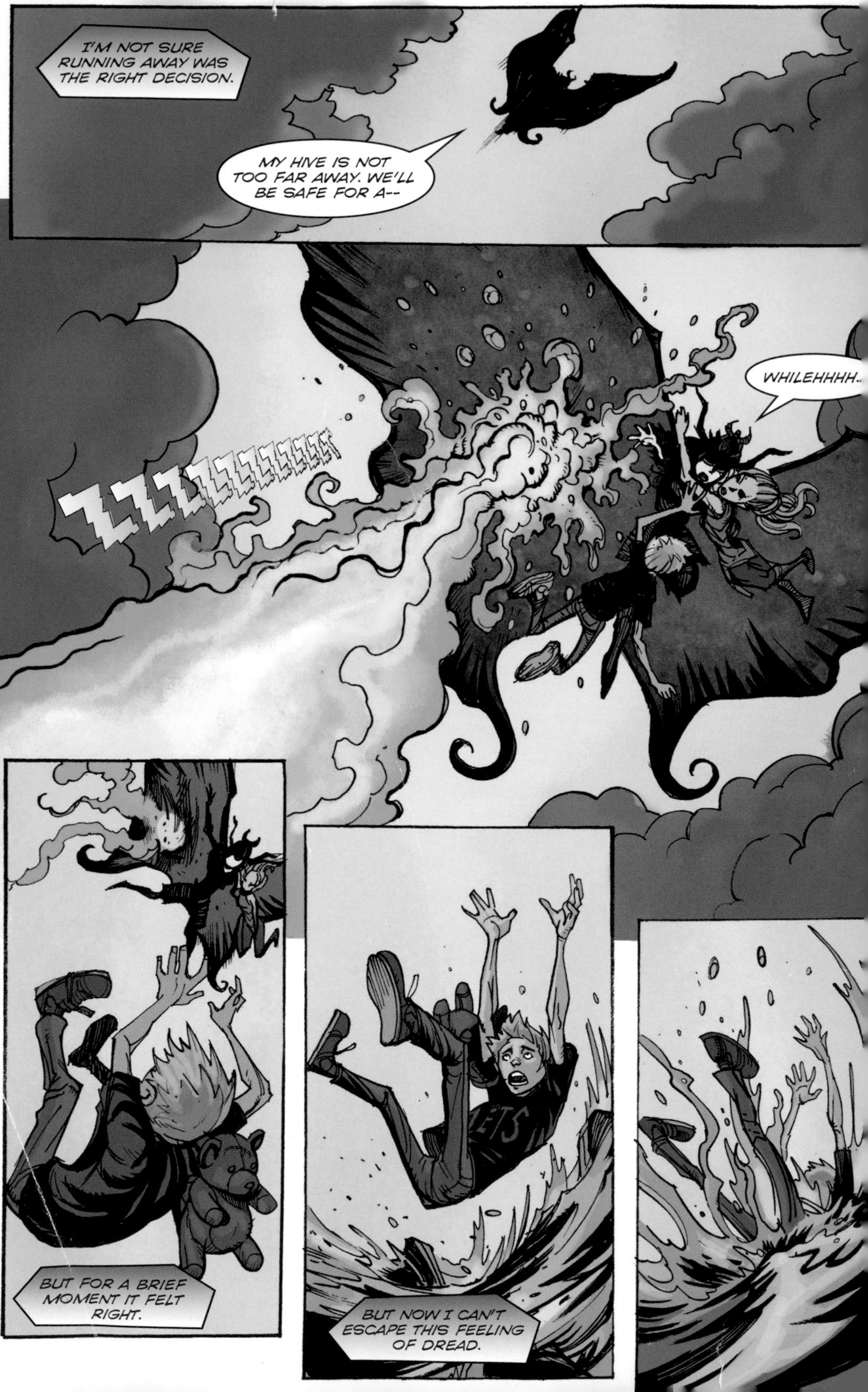
I'M NOT SURE RUNNING AWAY WAS THE RIGHT DECISION.
MY HIVE IS NOT TOO FAR AWAY. WE'LL BE SAFE FOR A--
WHILEHHHH...
BUT FOR A BRIEF MOMENT IT FELT RIGHT.
BUT NOW I CAN'T ESCAPE THIS FEELING OF DREAD.

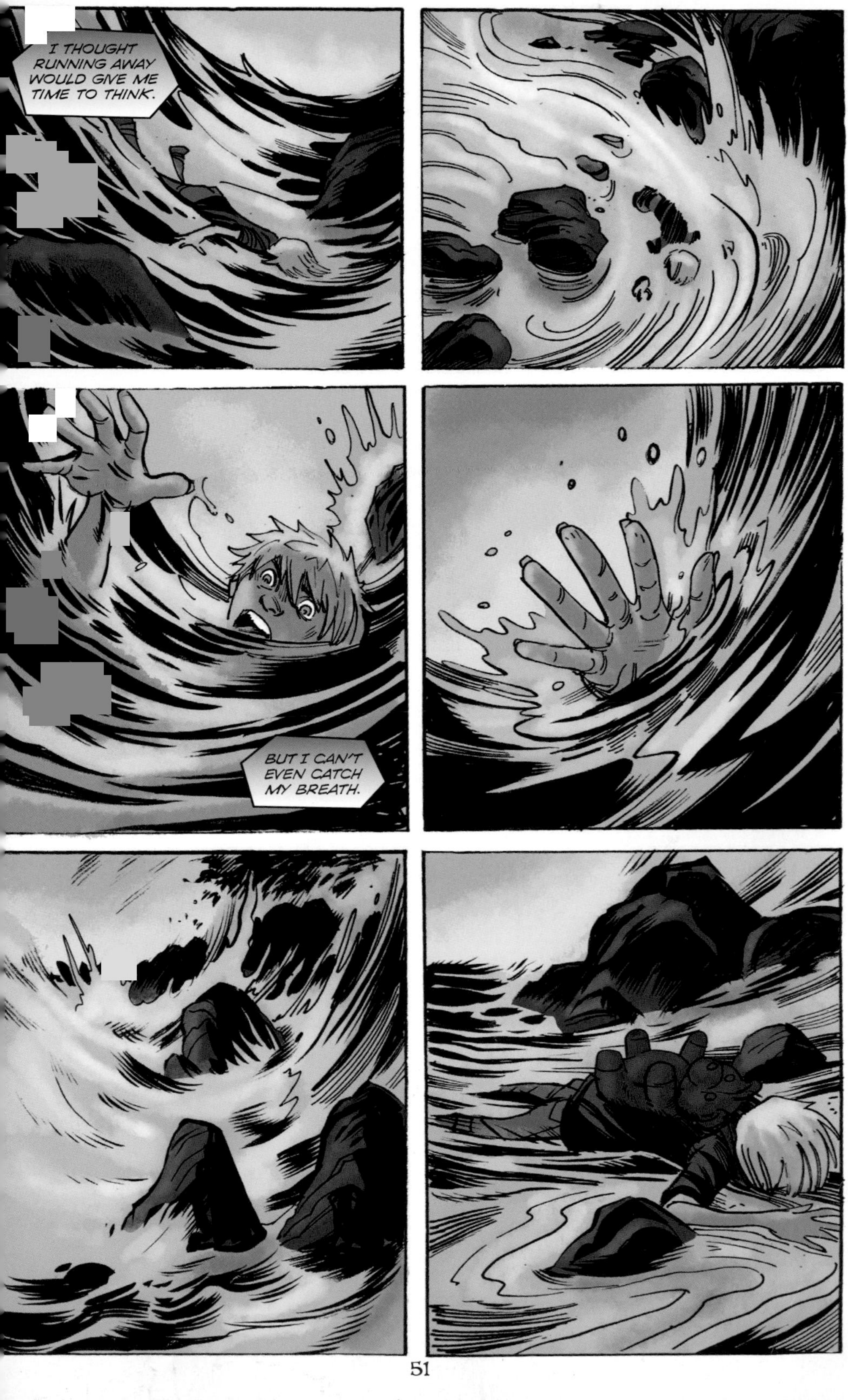

I THOUGHT RUNNING AWAY WOULD GIVE ME TIME TO THINK.
BUT I CAN'T EVEN CATCH MY BREATH.

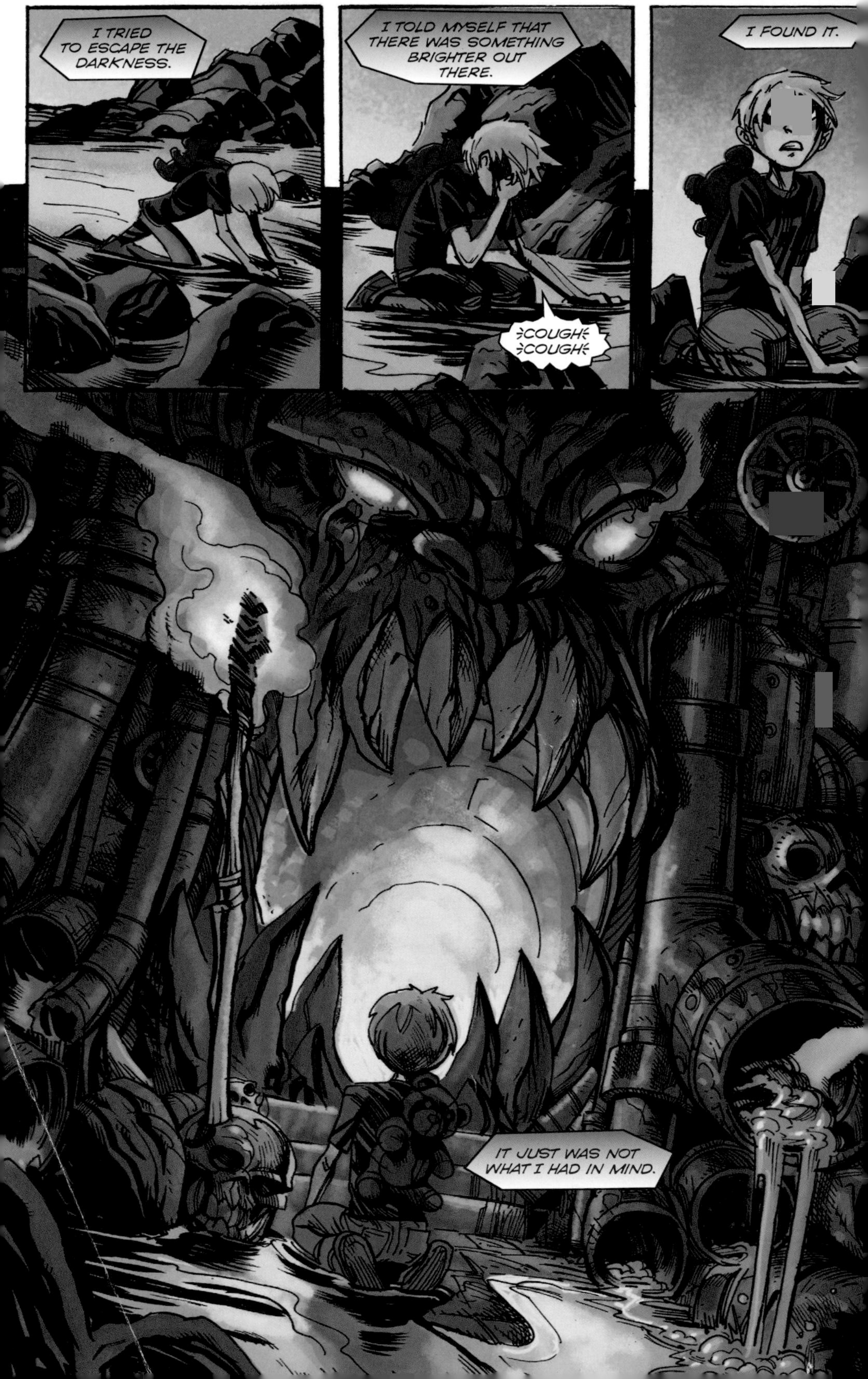
I TRIED TO ESCAPE THE DARKNESS.
I TOLD MYSELF THAT THERE WAS SOMETHING BRIGHTER OUT THERE.
COUGH COUGH
I FOUND IT.
IT JUST WAS NOT WHAT I HAD IN MIND.

CHAPTER TWO

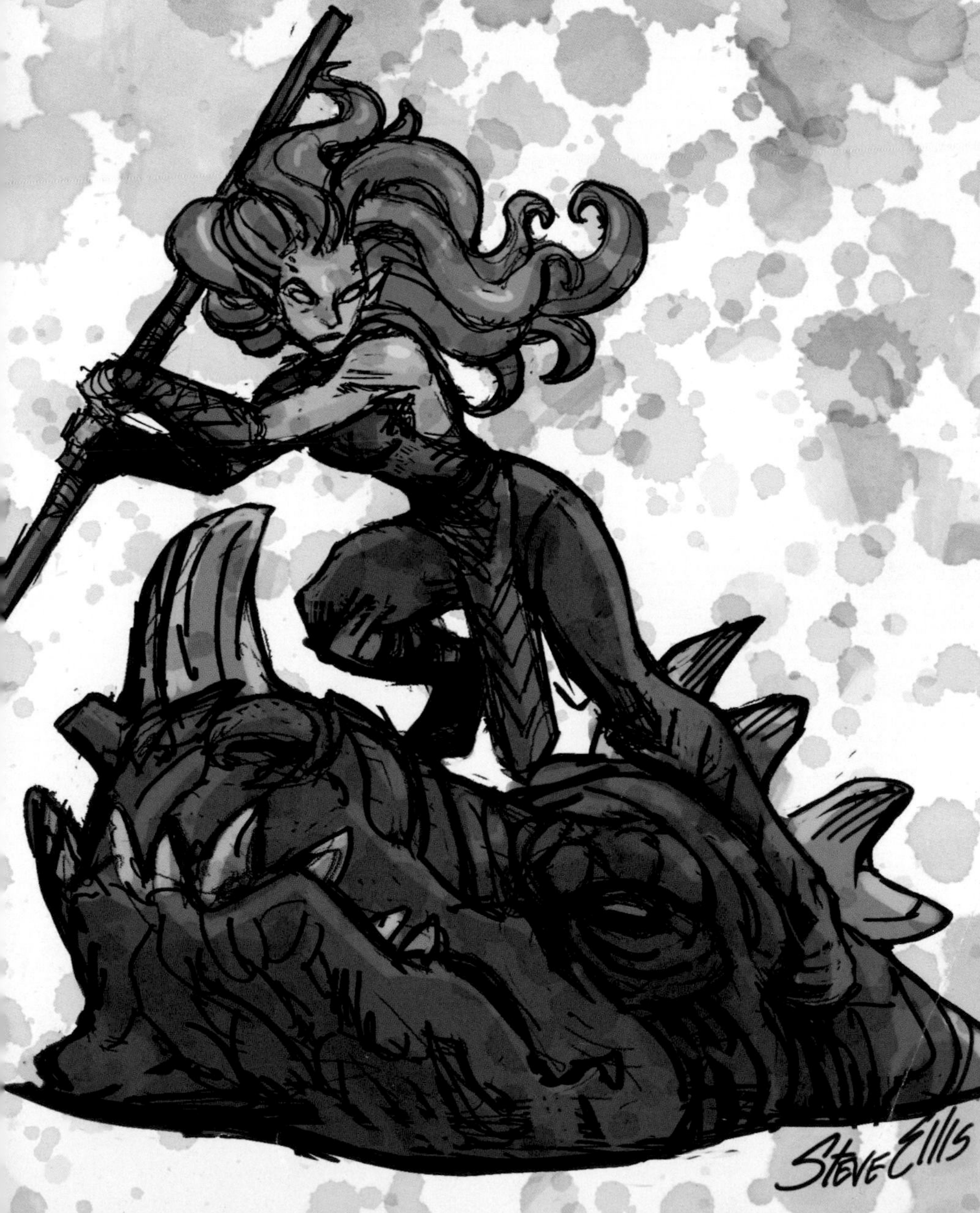
Steve Ellis

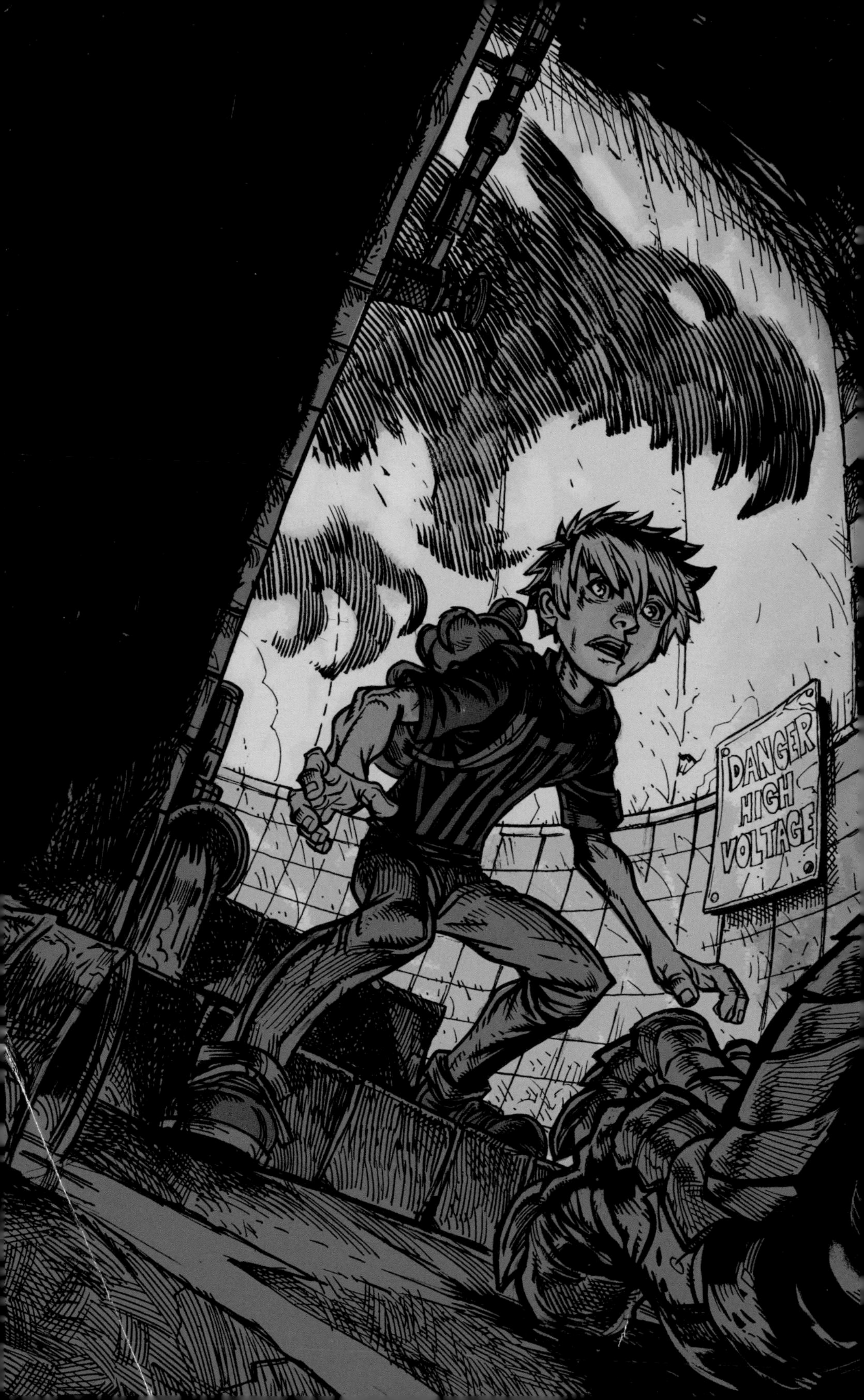
DANGER
HIGH
VOLTAGE

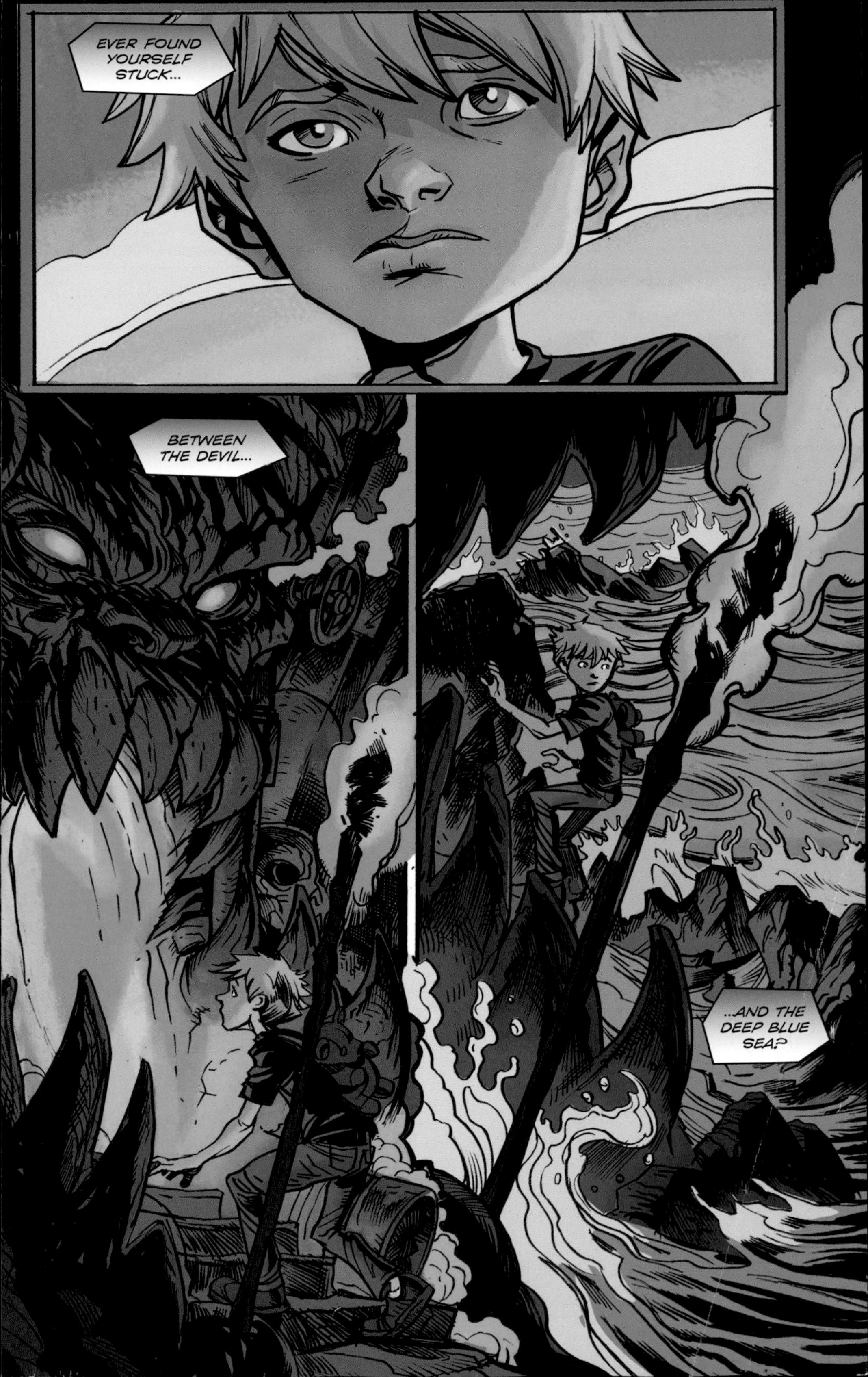
EVER FOUND YOURSELF STUCK...
BETWEEN THE DEVIL...
...AND THE DEEP BLUE SEA?

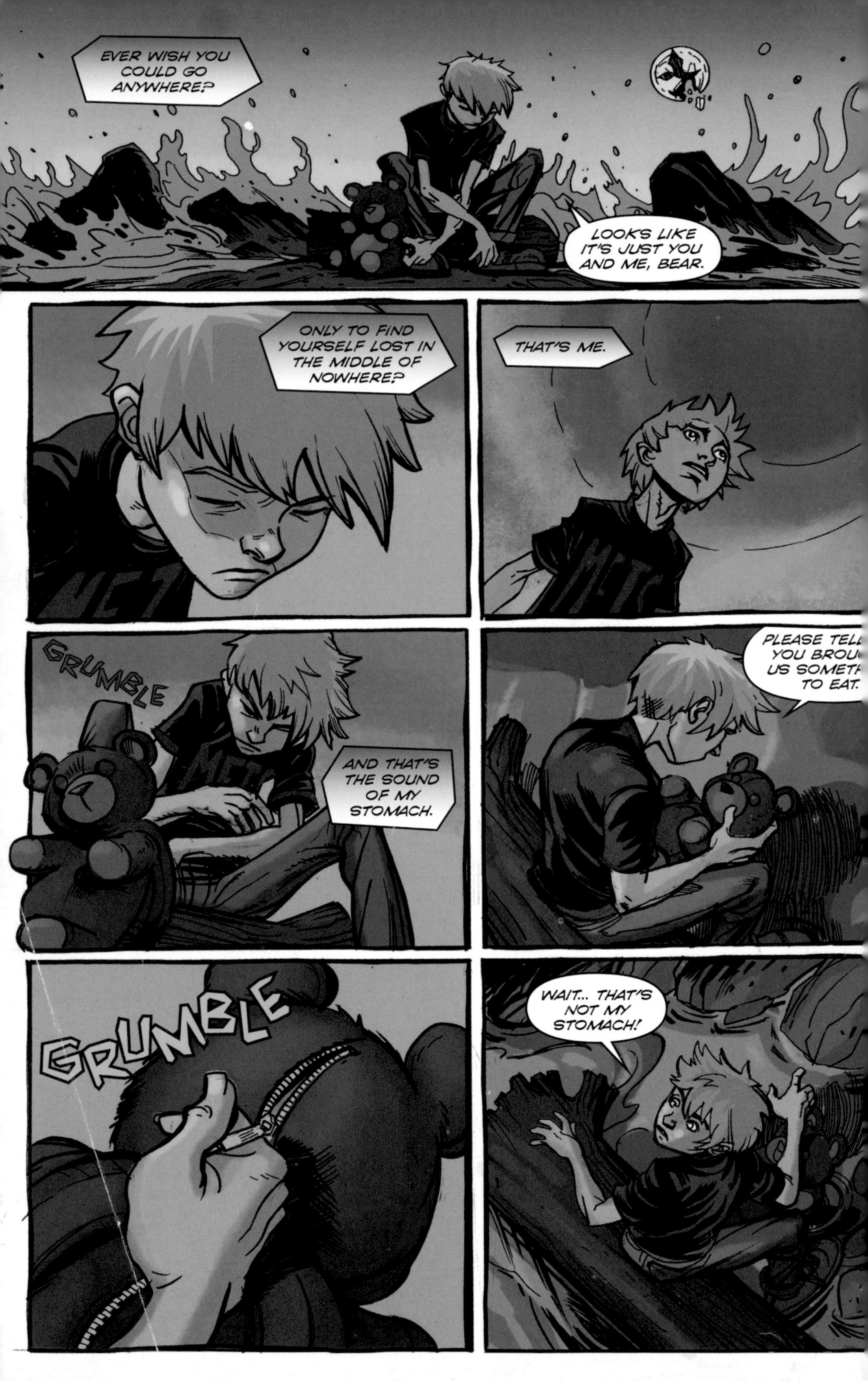

EVER WISH YOU COULD GO ANYWHERE?
LOOKS LIKE IT'S JUST YOU AND ME, BEAR.
ONLY TO FIND YOURSELF LOST IN THE MIDDLE OF NOWHERE?
THAT'S ME.
GRUMBLE
AND THAT'S THE SOUND OF MY STOMACH.
PLEASE TELL YOU BROU US SOMETH TO EAT.
GRUMBLE
WAIT... THAT'S NOT MY STOMACH!

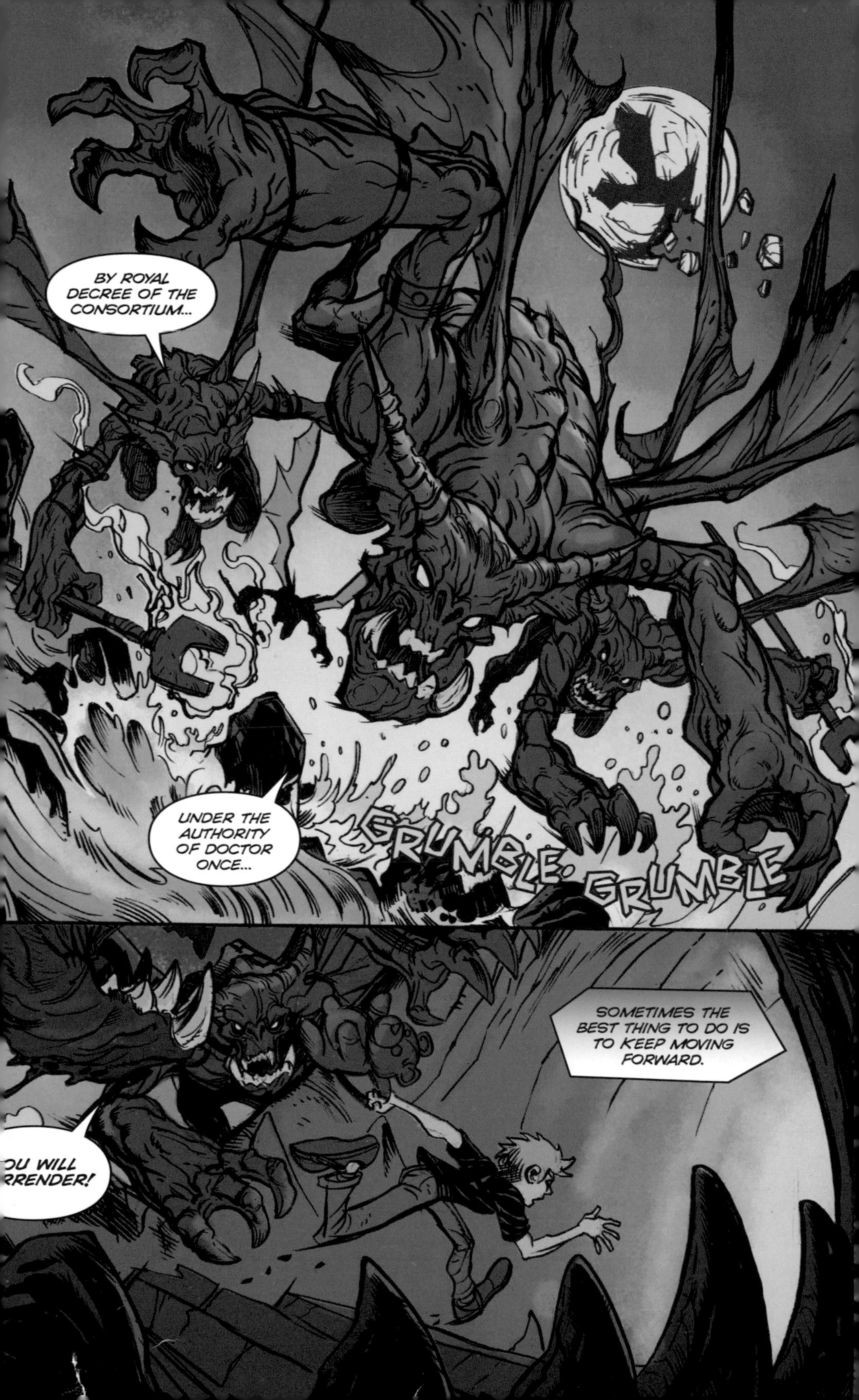
BY ROYAL DECREE OF THE CONSORTIUM...
UNDER THE AUTHORITY OF DOCTOR ONCE...
GRUMBLE GRUMBLE
SOMETIMES THE BEST THING TO DO IS TO KEEP MOVING FORWARD.
OU WILL RRENDER!

WE DON'T HAVE TO TAKE YOU ALIVE.

WAITING AROUND FOR SOMETHING TO HAPPEN...

ONLY MAKES THINGS WORSE.

CRIFA

RIIII P

LIFE IS FULL OF LITTLE SURPRISES.

OKAY, THAT WAS A FREEBIE.

WE NEV KNOW W WILL HAP NEX?

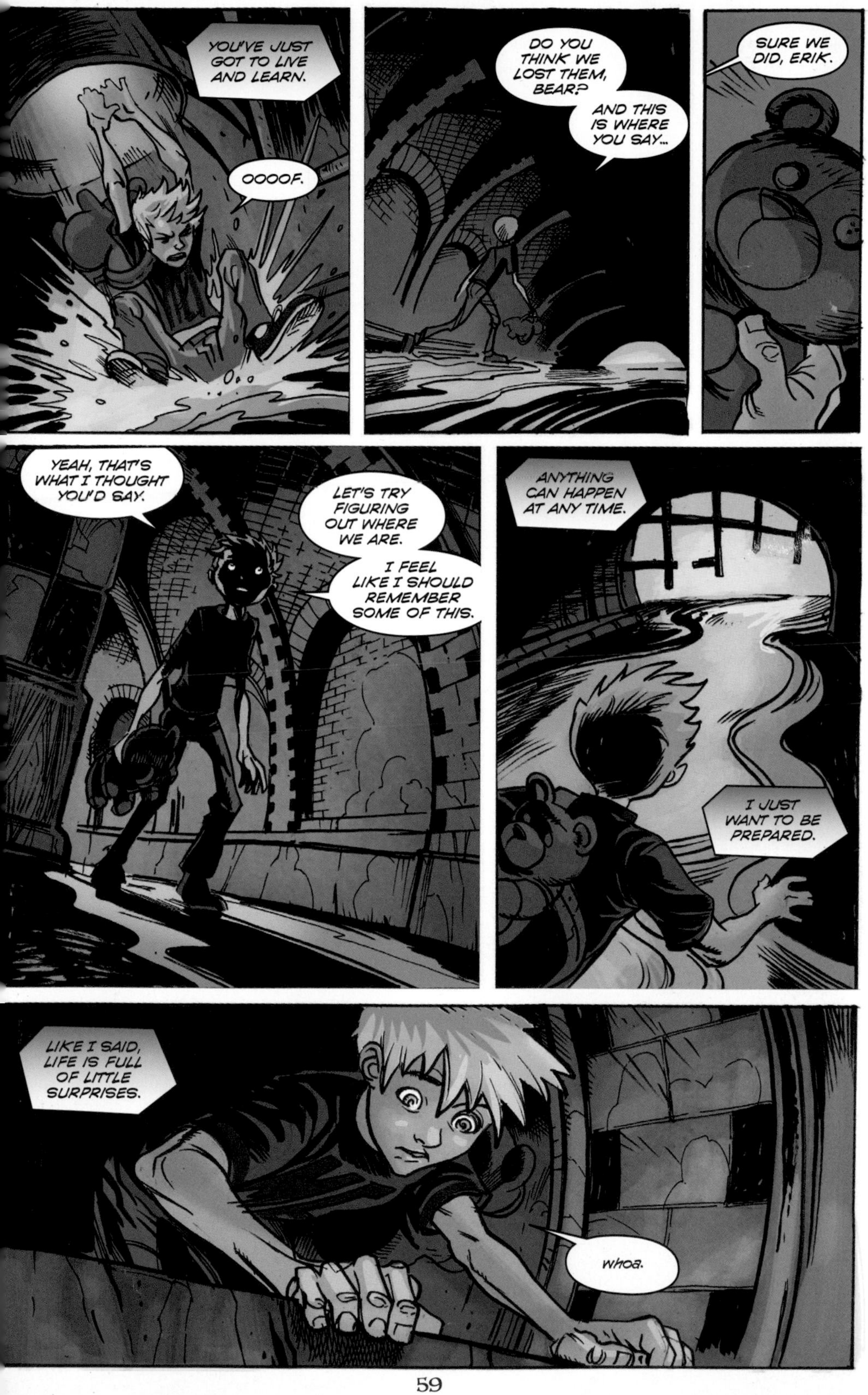
YOU'VE JUST GOT TO LIVE AND LEARN.
OOOOF.
DO YOU THINK WE LOST THEM, BEAR?
AND THIS IS WHERE YOU SAY...
SURE WE DID, ERIK.
YEAH, THAT'S WHAT I THOUGHT YOU'D SAY.
LET'S TRY FIGURING OUT WHERE WE ARE.
I FEEL LIKE I SHOULD REMEMBER SOME OF THIS.
ANYTHING CAN HAPPEN AT ANY TIME.
I JUST WANT TO BE PREPARED.
LIKE I SAID, LIFE IS FULL OF LITTLE SURPRISES.
whoa.

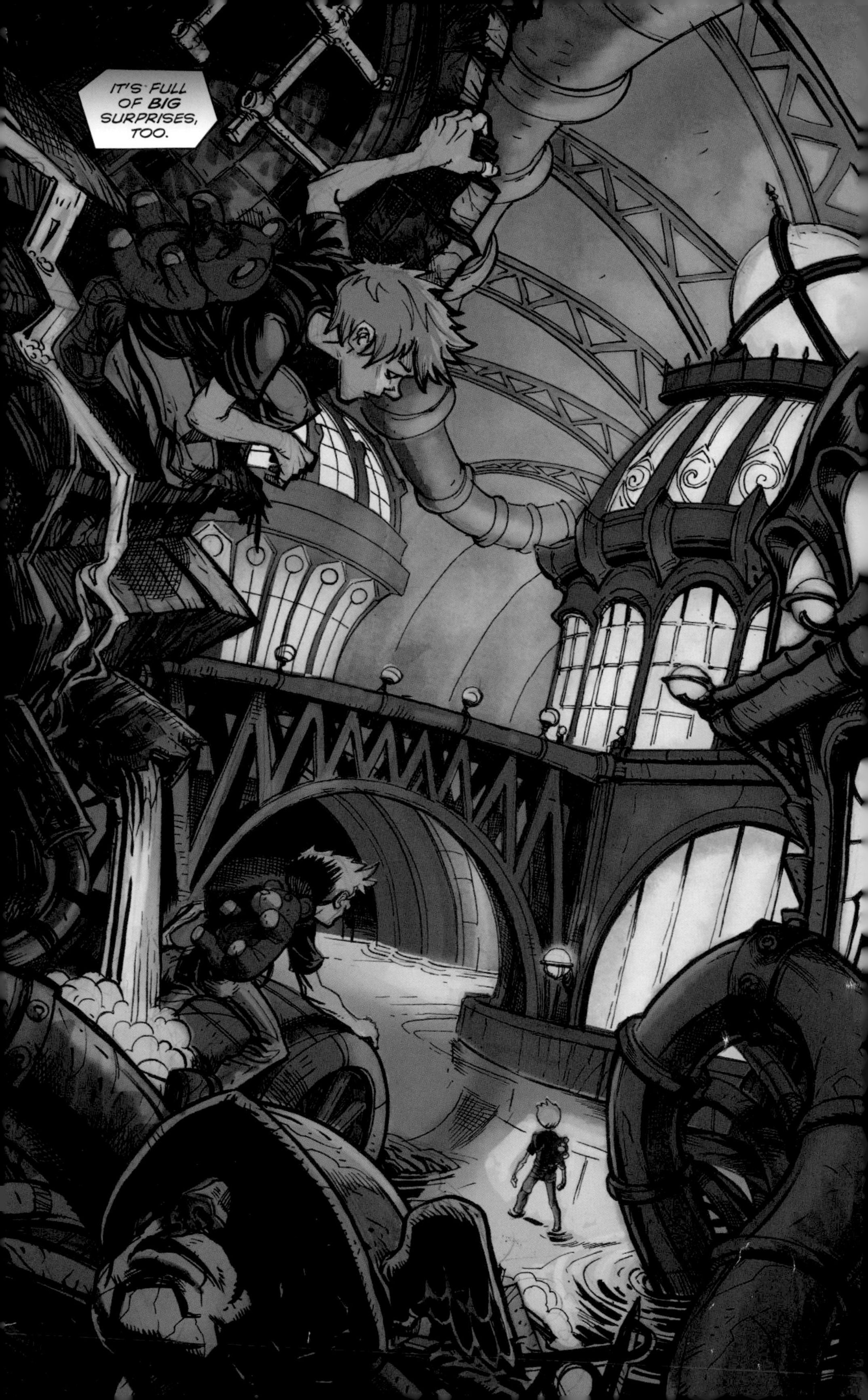
IT'S FULL OF BIG SURPRISES, TOO.

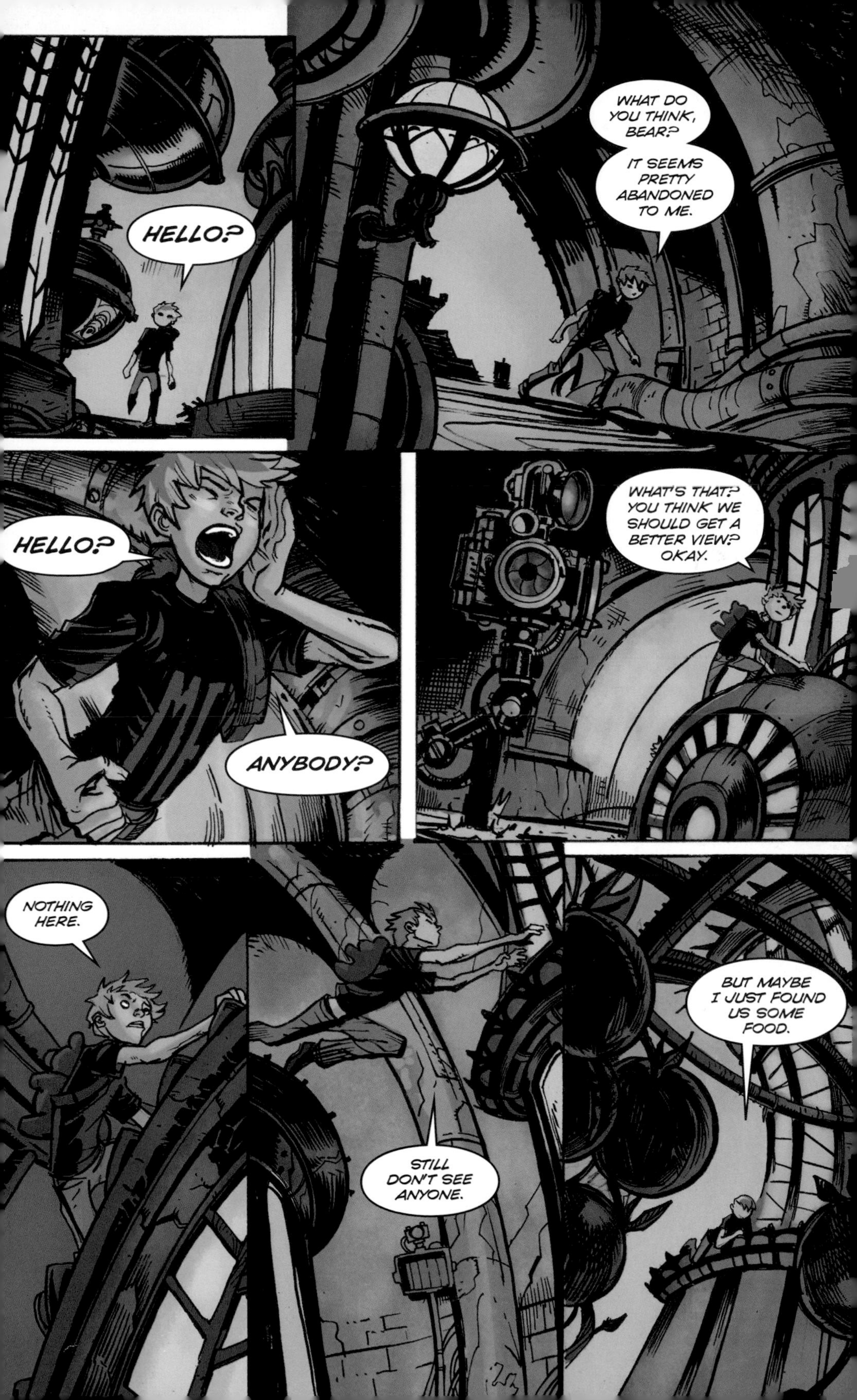
HELLO?
WHAT DO YOU THINK, BEAR?
IT SEEMS PRETTY ABANDONED TO ME.
HELLO?
ANYBODY?
WHAT'S THAT? YOU THINK WE SHOULD GET A BETTER VIEW? OKAY.
NOTHING HERE.
STILL DON'T SEE ANYONE.
BUT MAYBE I JUST FOUND US SOME FOOD.

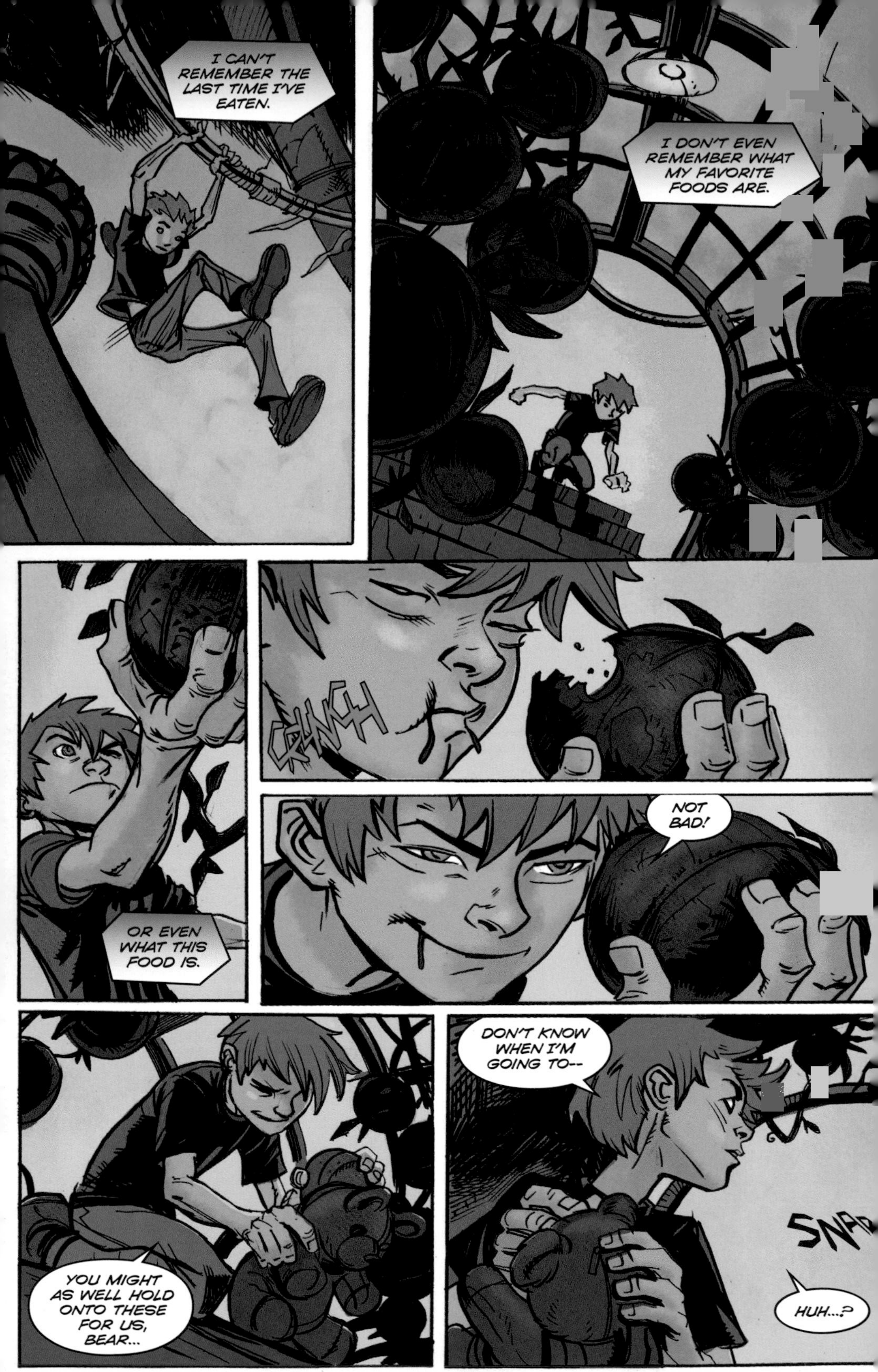
I CAN'T REMEMBER THE LAST TIME I'VE EATEN.
I DON'T EVEN REMEMBER WHAT MY FAVORITE FOODS ARE.
CRUNCH
OR EVEN WHAT THIS FOOD IS.
NOT BAD!
YOU MIGHT AS WELL HOLD ONTO THESE FOR US, BEAR...
DON'T KNOW WHEN I'M GOING TO--
SNAP
HUH...?

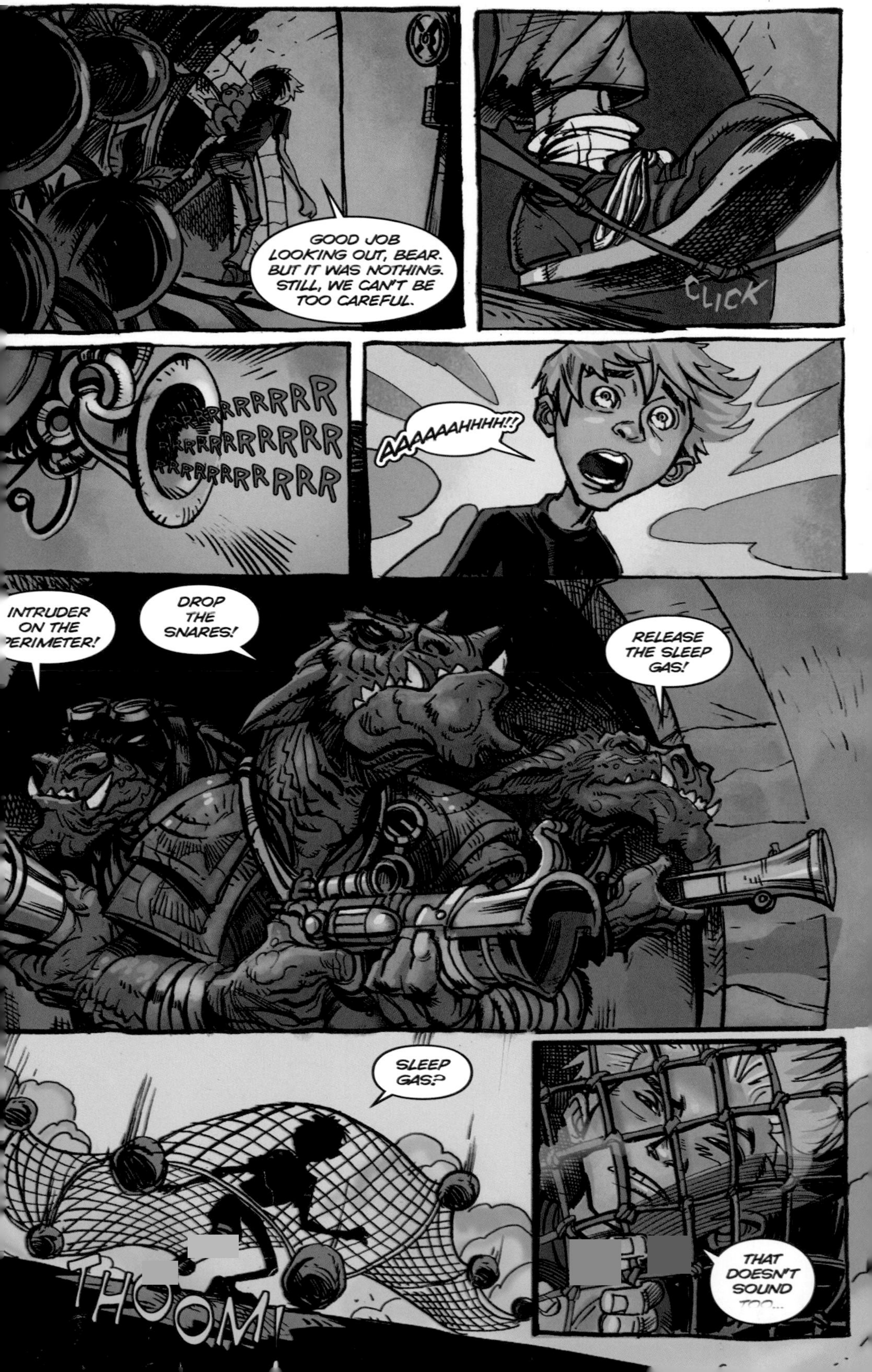
GOOD JOB LOOKING OUT, BEAR. BUT IT WAS NOTHING. STILL, WE CAN'T BE TOO CAREFUL.
CLICK
RRRRRRRRRRR RRRRRRRRRRRR RRRRRRRRRRRR
AAAAAAHHHH!!
INTRUDER ON THE PERIMETER!
DROP THE SNARES!
RELEASE THE SLEEP GAS!
SLEEP GAS?
THOOM!
THAT DOESN'T SOUND TOO...

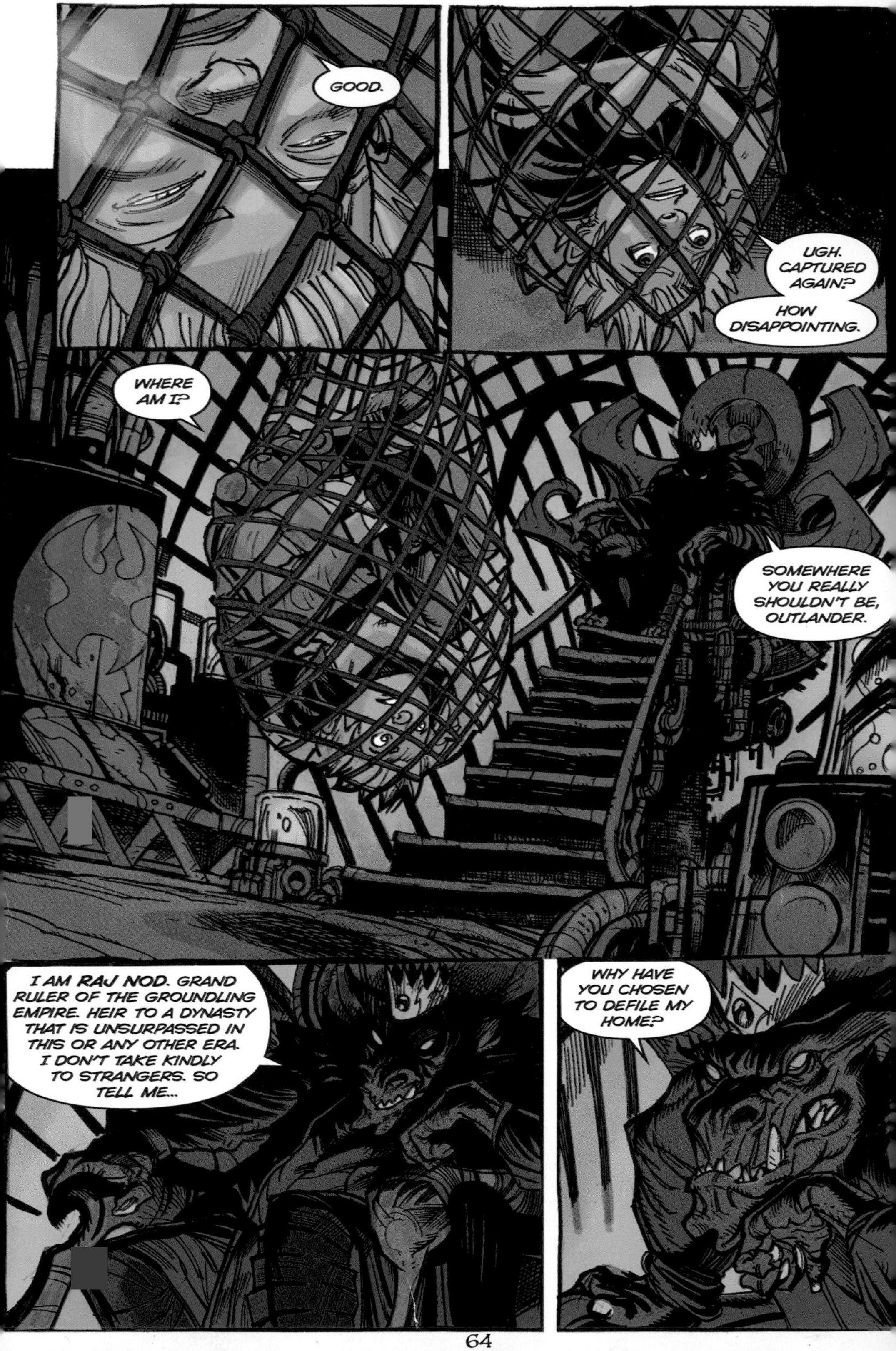

GOOD.
UGH. CAPTURED AGAIN?
HOW DISAPPOINTING.
WHERE AM I?
SOMEWHERE YOU REALLY SHOULDN'T BE, OUTLANDER.
I AM **RAJ NOD**. GRAND RULER OF THE GROUNDLING EMPIRE. HEIR TO A DYNASTY THAT IS UNSURPASSED IN THIS OR ANY OTHER ERA. I DON'T TAKE KINDLY TO STRANGERS. SO TELL ME...
WHY HAVE YOU CHOSEN TO DEFILE MY HOME?

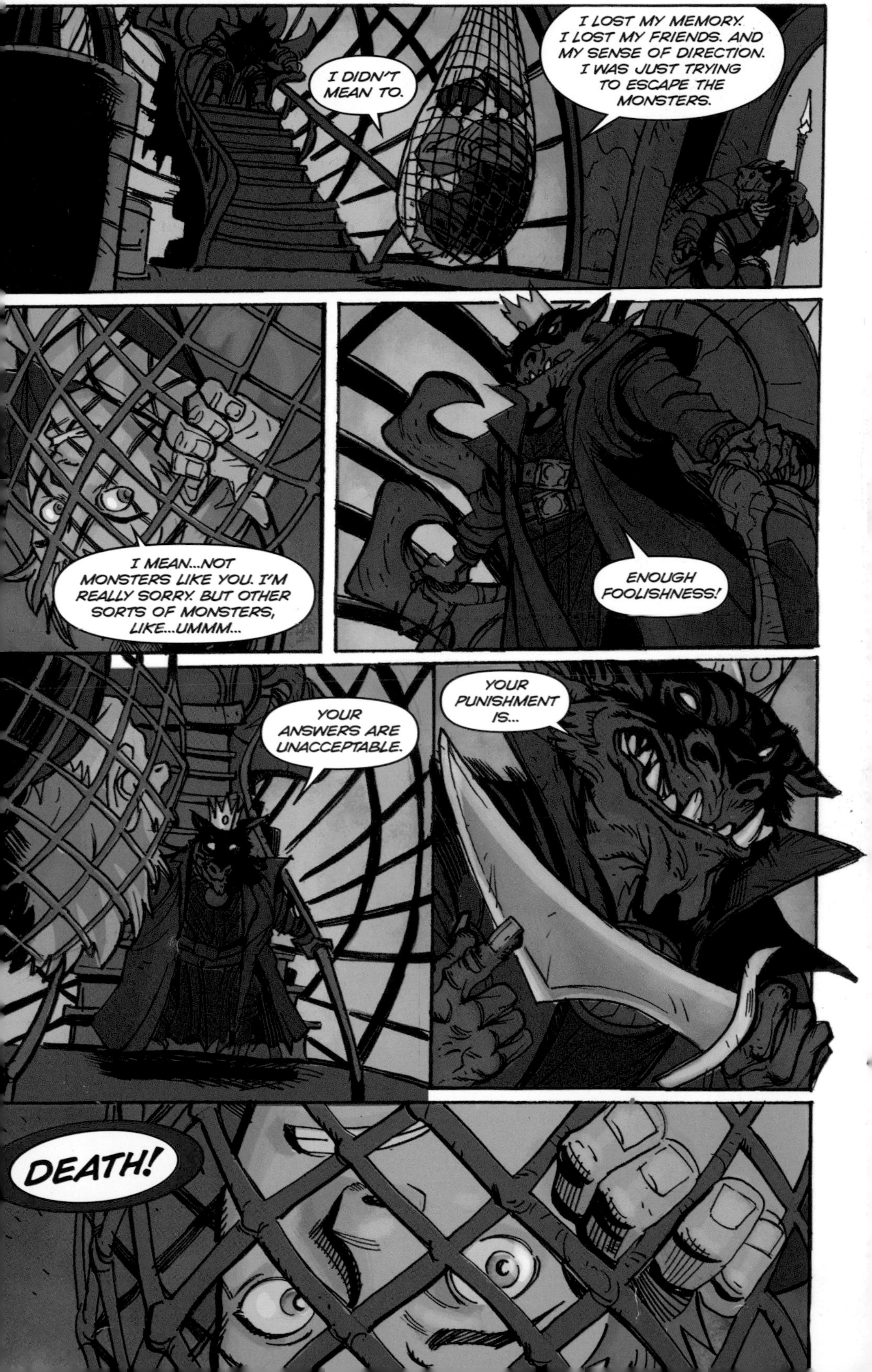
I DIDN'T MEAN TO.
I LOST MY MEMORY. I LOST MY FRIENDS. AND MY SENSE OF DIRECTION. I WAS JUST TRYING TO ESCAPE THE MONSTERS.
I MEAN...NOT MONSTERS LIKE YOU. I'M REALLY SORRY. BUT OTHER SORTS OF MONSTERS, LIKE...UMMM...
ENOUGH FOOLISHNESS!
YOUR ANSWERS ARE UNACCEPTABLE.
YOUR PUNISHMENT IS...
DEATH!

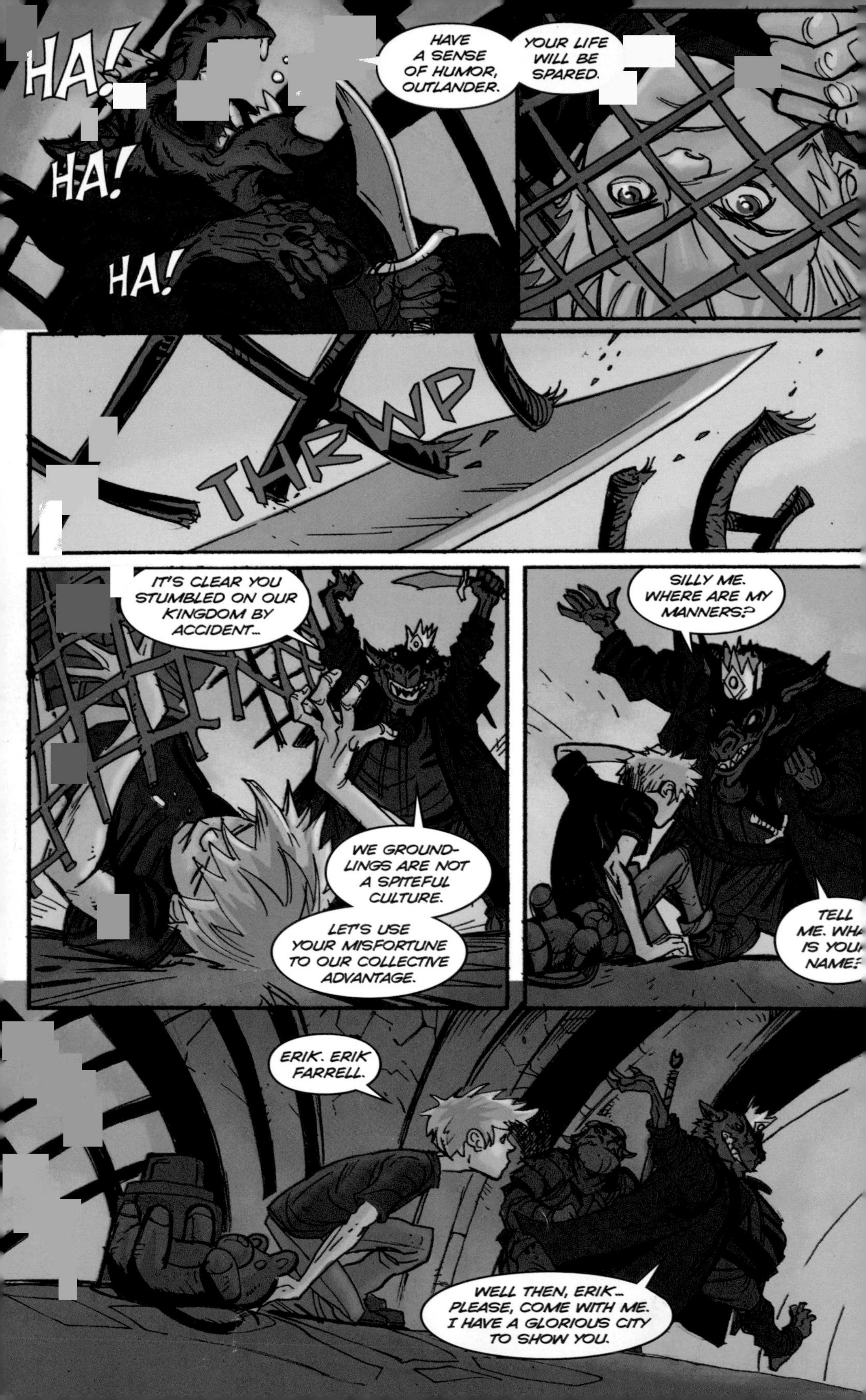
HA!
HA!
HA!
HAVE A SENSE OF HUMOR, OUTLANDER.
YOUR LIFE WILL BE SPARED.
THRWP
IT'S CLEAR YOU STUMBLED ON OUR KINGDOM BY ACCIDENT...
WE GROUNDLINGS ARE NOT A SPITEFUL CULTURE.
LET'S USE YOUR MISFORTUNE TO OUR COLLECTIVE ADVANTAGE.
SILLY ME. WHERE ARE MY MANNERS?
TELL ME. WHA IS YOU NAME?
ERIK. ERIK FARRELL.
WELL THEN, ERIK... PLEASE, COME WITH ME. I HAVE A GLORIOUS CITY TO SHOW YOU.

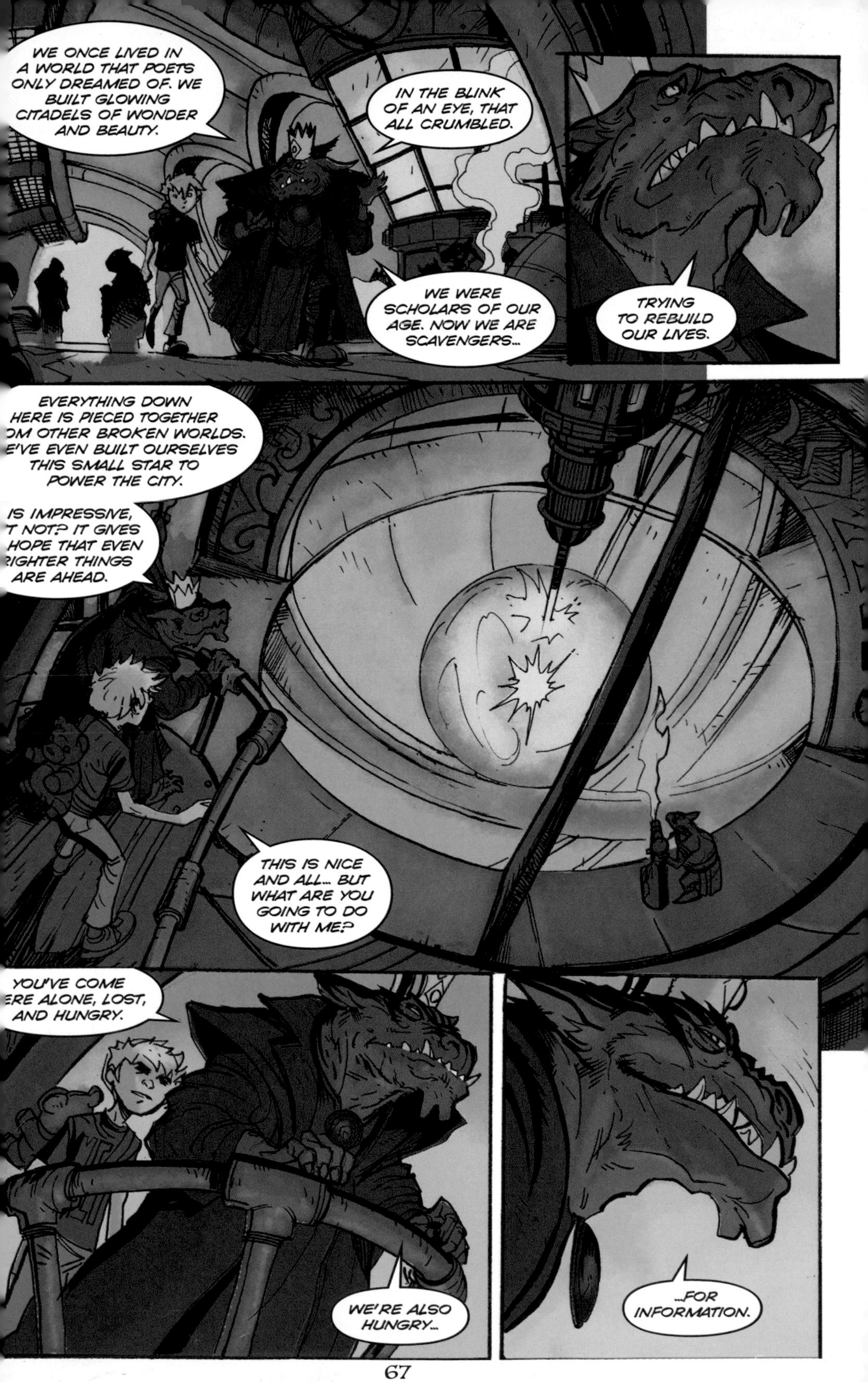
WE ONCE LIVED IN A WORLD THAT POETS ONLY DREAMED OF. WE BUILT GLOWING CITADELS OF WONDER AND BEAUTY.
IN THE BLINK OF AN EYE, THAT ALL CRUMBLED.
WE WERE SCHOLARS OF OUR AGE. NOW WE ARE SCAVENGERS...
TRYING TO REBUILD OUR LIVES.
EVERYTHING DOWN HERE IS PIECED TOGETHER OM OTHER BROKEN WORLDS. E'VE EVEN BUILT OURSELVES THIS SMALL STAR TO POWER THE CITY.
IS IMPRESSIVE, T NOT? IT GIVES HOPE THAT EVEN RIGHTER THINGS ARE AHEAD.
THIS IS NICE AND ALL... BUT WHAT ARE YOU GOING TO DO WITH ME?
YOU'VE COME ERE ALONE, LOST, AND HUNGRY.
WE'RE ALSO HUNGRY...
...FOR INFORMATION.

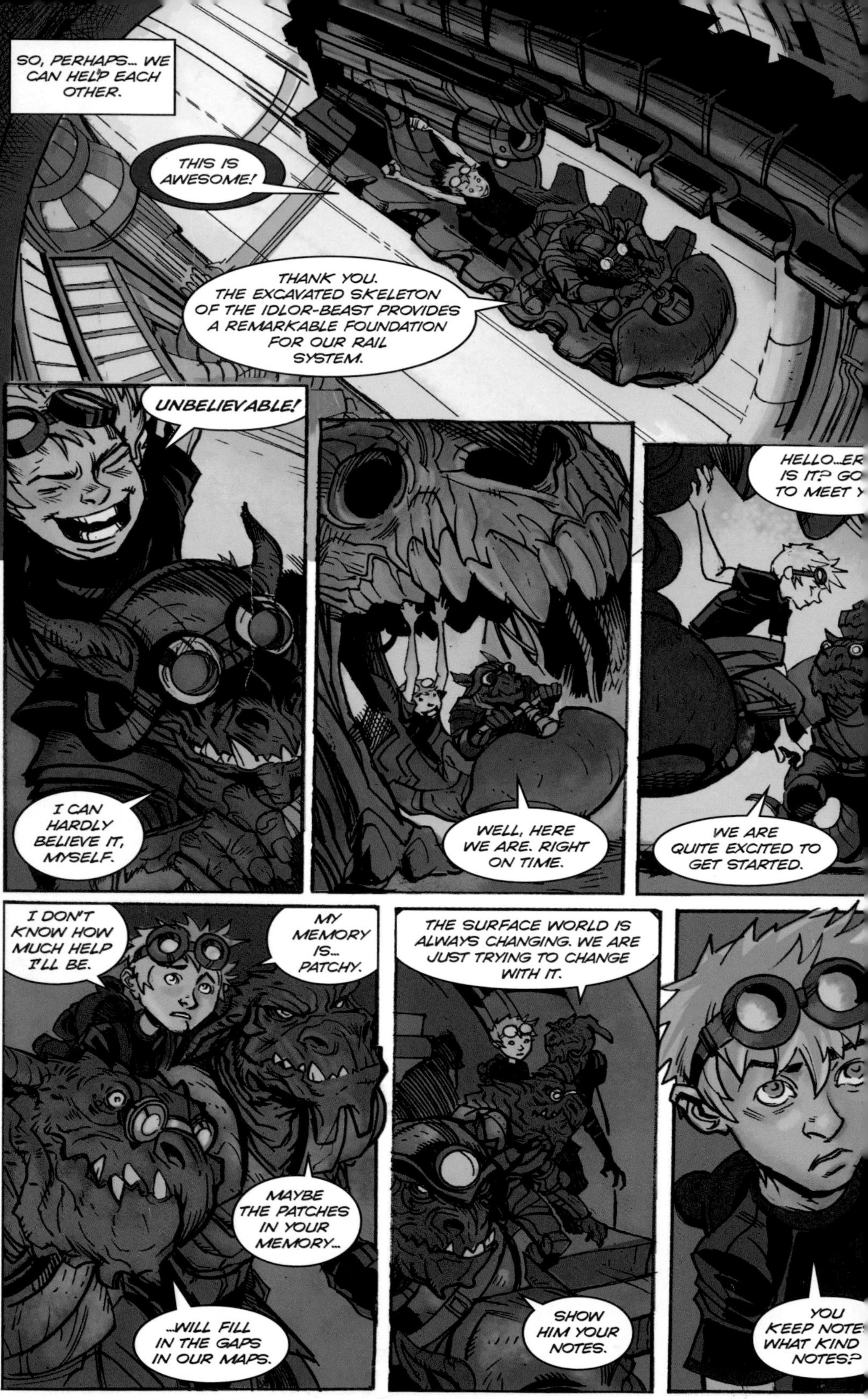
SO, PERHAPS... WE CAN HELP EACH OTHER.
THIS IS AWESOME!
THANK YOU. THE EXCAVATED SKELETON OF THE IDLOR-BEAST PROVIDES A REMARKABLE FOUNDATION FOR OUR RAIL SYSTEM.
UNBELIEVABLE!
I CAN HARDLY BELIEVE IT, MYSELF.
WELL, HERE WE ARE. RIGHT ON TIME.
WE ARE QUITE EXCITED TO GET STARTED.
I DON'T KNOW HOW MUCH HELP I'LL BE.
MY MEMORY IS... PATCHY.
MAYBE THE PATCHES IN YOUR MEMORY...
...WILL FILL IN THE GAPS IN OUR MAPS.
THE SURFACE WORLD IS ALWAYS CHANGING. WE ARE JUST TRYING TO CHANGE WITH IT.
SHOW HIM YOUR NOTES.

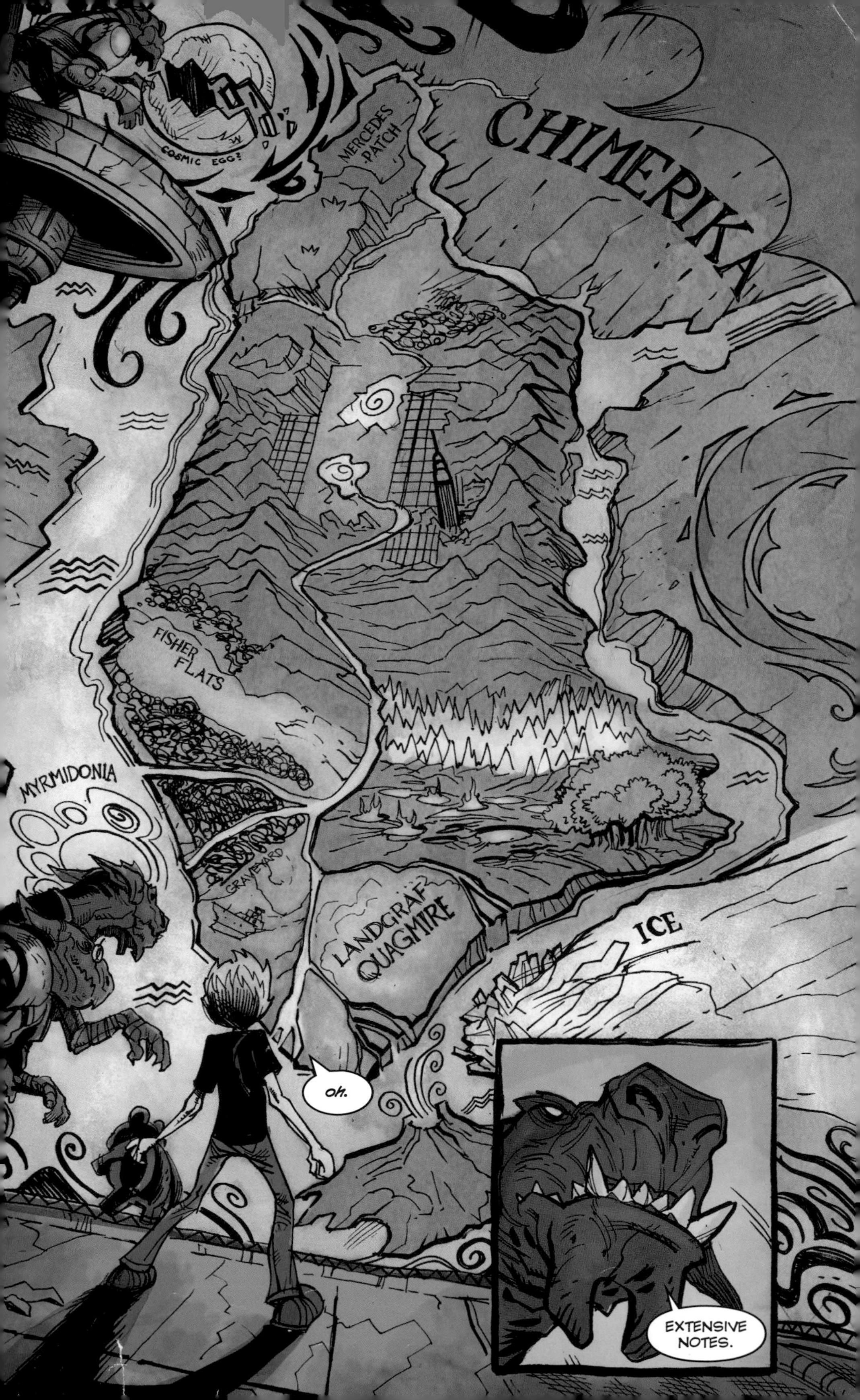

COSMIC EGG?
MERCEDES PATCH
CHIMERIKA
FISHER FLATS
MYRMIDONIA
GRAVEYARD
LANDGRAF QUAGMIRE
ICE
oh.
EXTENSIVE NOTES.

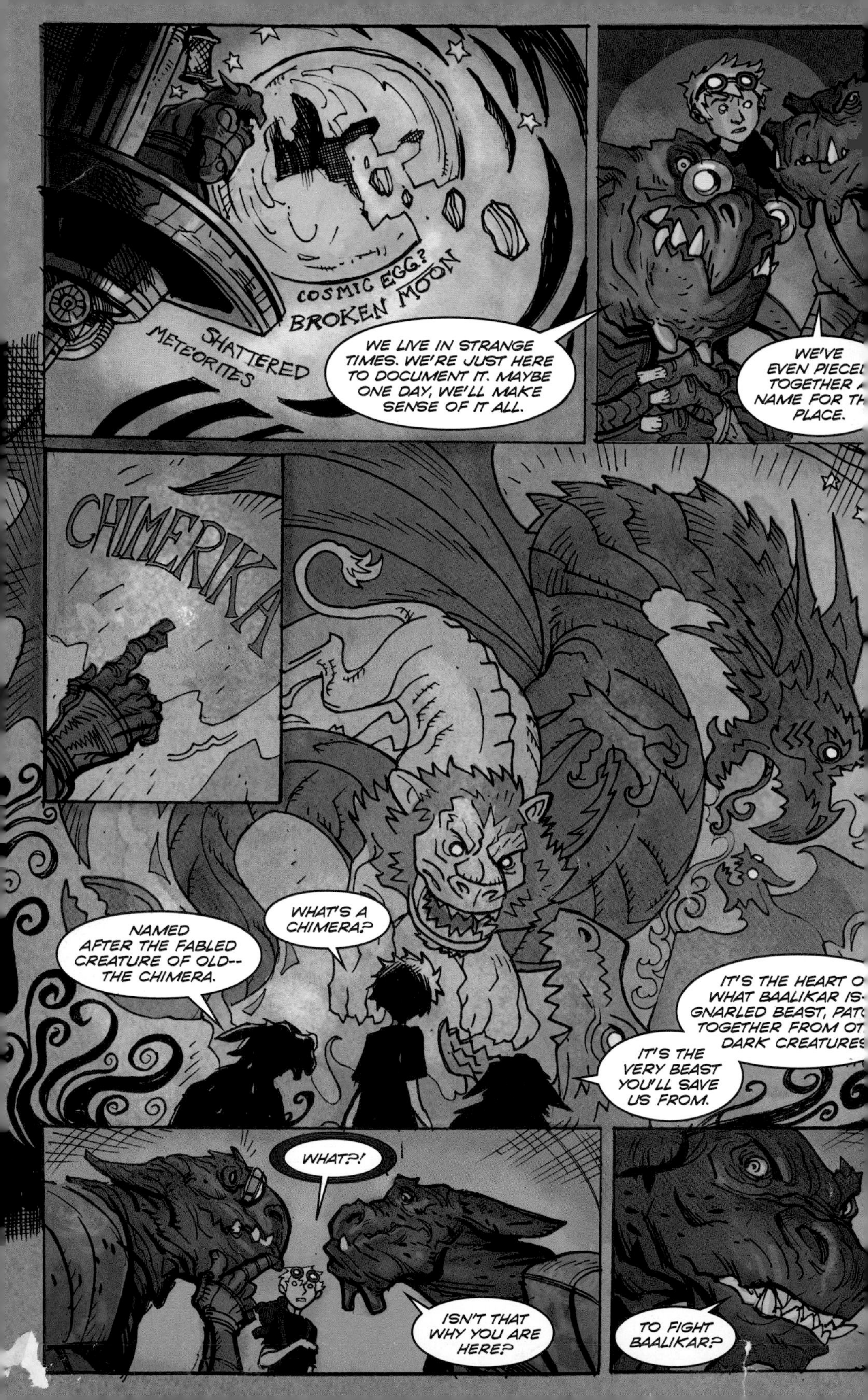
COSMIC EGG?
BROKEN MOON
SHATTERED METEORITES
WE LIVE IN STRANGE TIMES. WE'RE JUST HERE TO DOCUMENT IT. MAYBE ONE DAY, WE'LL MAKE SENSE OF IT ALL.
WE'VE EVEN PIECED TOGETHER A NAME FOR TH PLACE.
CHIMERIKA
NAMED AFTER THE FABLED CREATURE OF OLD-- THE CHIMERA.
WHAT'S A CHIMERA?
IT'S THE HEART O WHAT BAALIKAR IS- GNARLED BEAST, PAT TOGETHER FROM OT DARK CREATURES
IT'S THE VERY BEAST YOU'LL SAVE US FROM.
WHAT?!
ISN'T THAT WHY YOU ARE HERE?
TO FIGHT BAALIKAR?

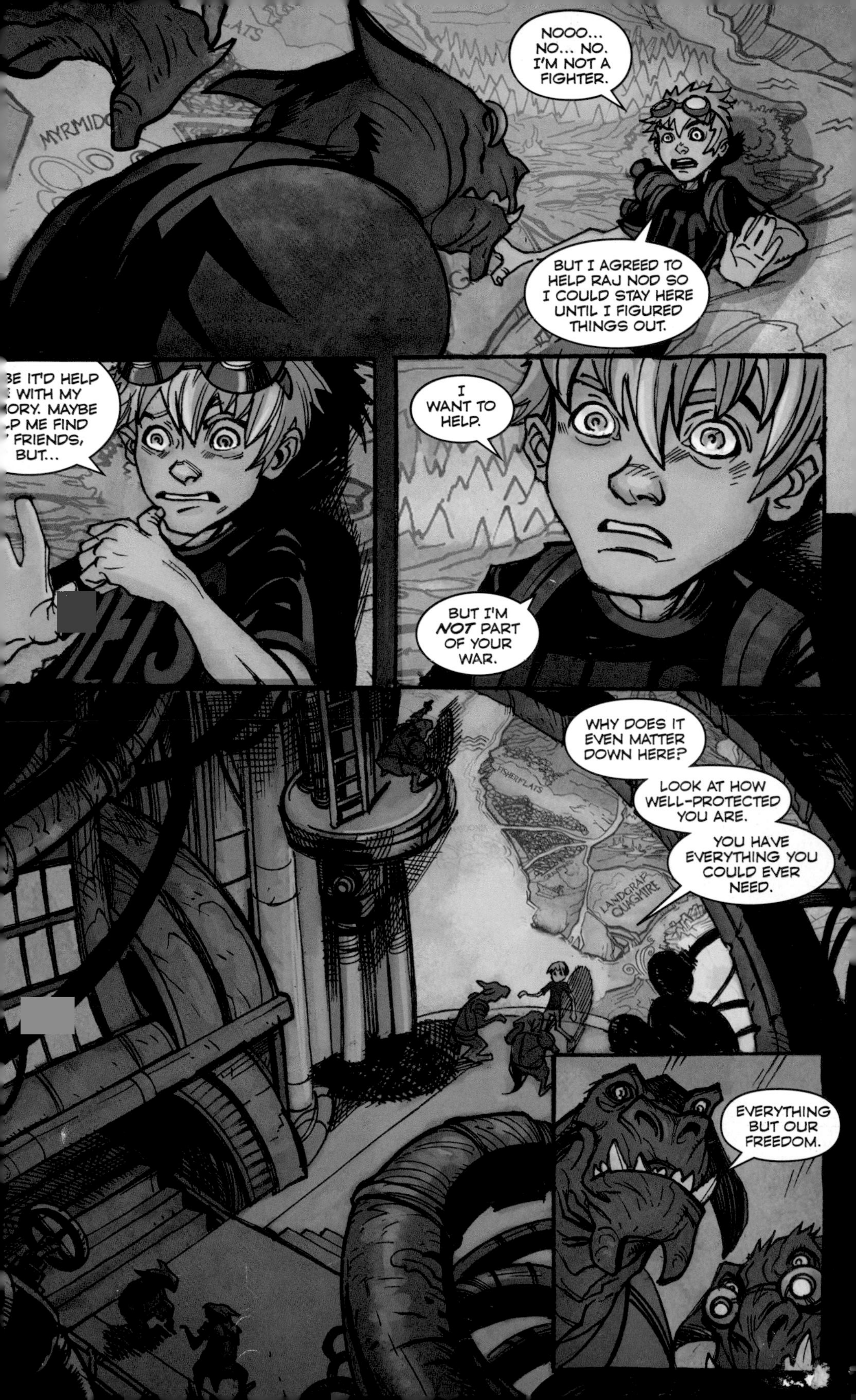
NOOO... NO... NO. I'M NOT A FIGHTER.
BUT I AGREED TO HELP RAJ NOD SO I COULD STAY HERE UNTIL I FIGURED THINGS OUT.
BE IT'D HELP WITH MY ORY. MAYBE P ME FIND FRIENDS, BUT...
I WANT TO HELP.
BUT I'M ***NOT*** PART OF YOUR WAR.
WHY DOES IT EVEN MATTER DOWN HERE?
LOOK AT HOW WELL-PROTECTED YOU ARE.
YOU HAVE EVERYTHING YOU COULD EVER NEED.
EVERYTHING BUT OUR FREEDOM.
MYRMIDO
FISHERFLATS
LANDGRAF QUAGMIRE

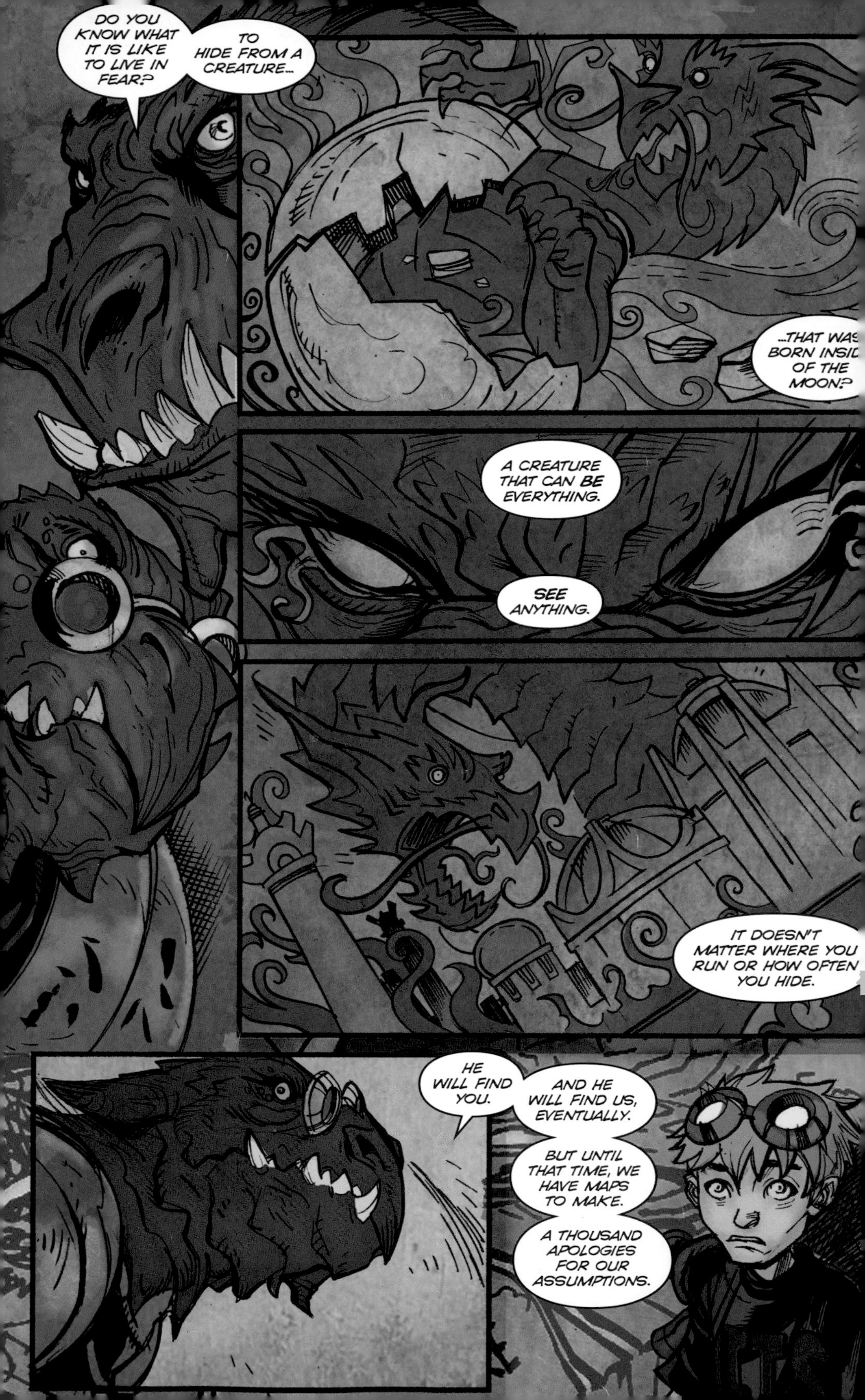

DO YOU KNOW WHAT IT IS LIKE TO LIVE IN FEAR?
TO HIDE FROM A CREATURE...
...THAT WAS BORN INSIDE OF THE MOON?
A CREATURE THAT CAN BE EVERYTHING.
SEE ANYTHING.
IT DOESN'T MATTER WHERE YOU RUN OR HOW OFTEN YOU HIDE.
HE WILL FIND YOU.
AND HE WILL FIND US, EVENTUALLY.
BUT UNTIL THAT TIME, WE HAVE MAPS TO MAKE.
A THOUSAND APOLOGIES FOR OUR ASSUMPTIONS.

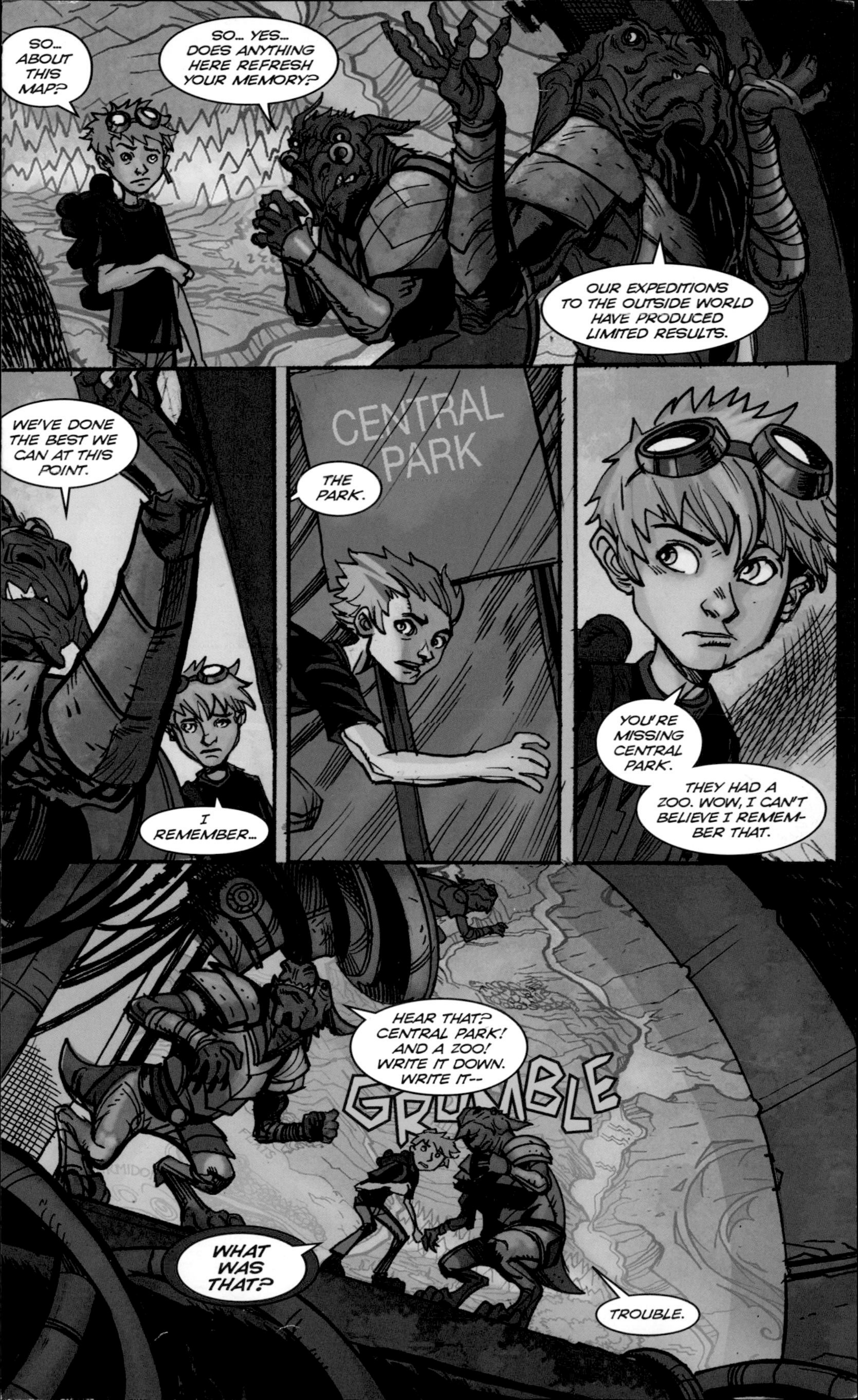
SO... ABOUT THIS MAP?
SO... YES... DOES ANYTHING HERE REFRESH YOUR MEMORY?
OUR EXPEDITIONS TO THE OUTSIDE WORLD HAVE PRODUCED LIMITED RESULTS.
WE'VE DONE THE BEST WE CAN AT THIS POINT.
I REMEMBER...
CENTRAL PARK
THE PARK.
YOU'RE MISSING CENTRAL PARK.
THEY HAD A ZOO. WOW, I CAN'T BELIEVE I REMEMBER THAT.
HEAR THAT? CENTRAL PARK! AND A ZOO! WRITE IT DOWN. WRITE IT--
GRUMBLE
WHAT WAS THAT?
TROUBLE.

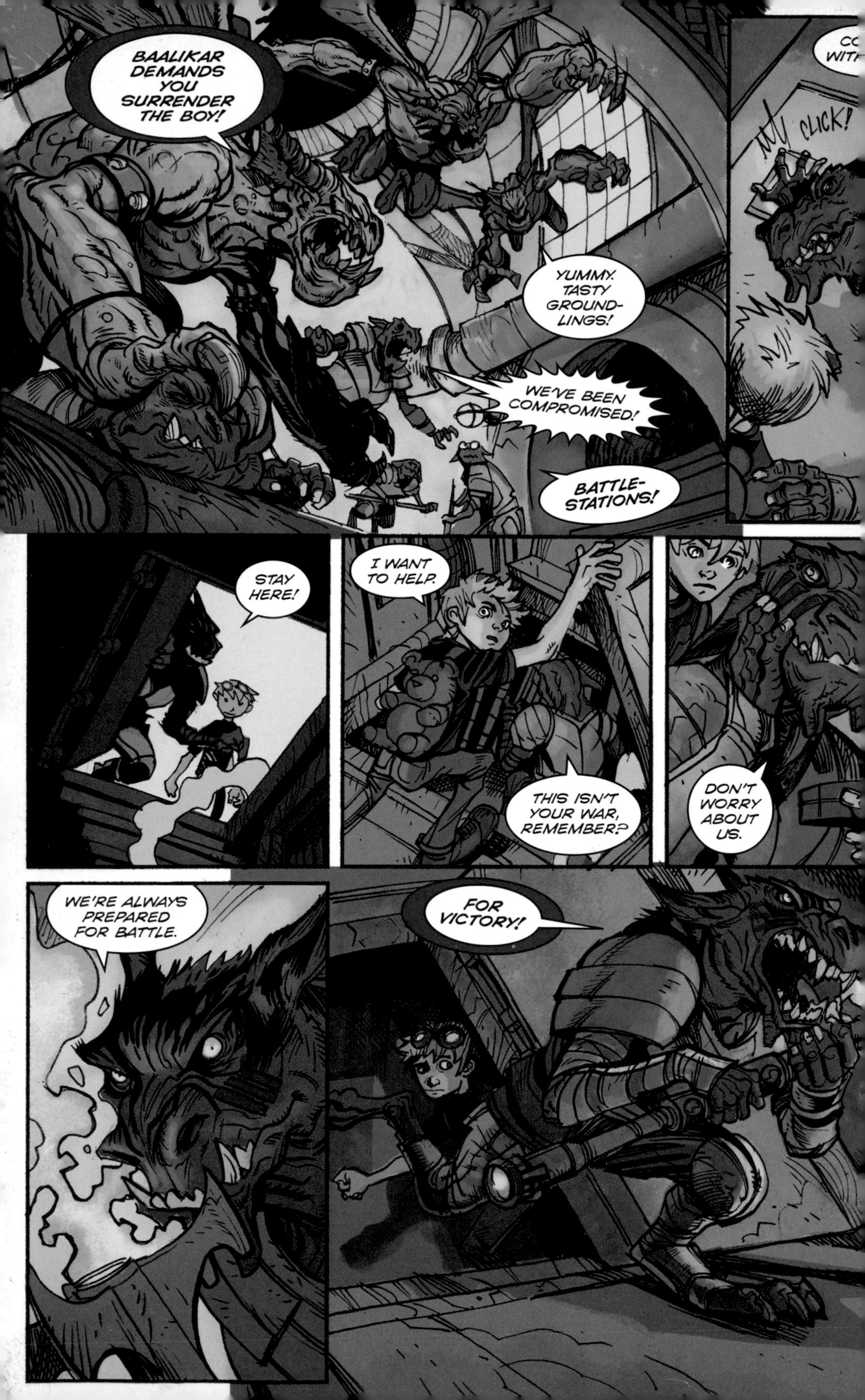
BAALIKAR DEMANDS YOU SURRENDER THE BOY!
YUMMY. TASTY GROUNDLINGS!
WE'VE BEEN COMPROMISED!
BATTLE-STATIONS!
CLICK!
STAY HERE!
I WANT TO HELP.
THIS ISN'T YOUR WAR, REMEMBER?
DON'T WORRY ABOUT US.
WE'RE ALWAYS PREPARED FOR BATTLE.
FOR VICTORY!

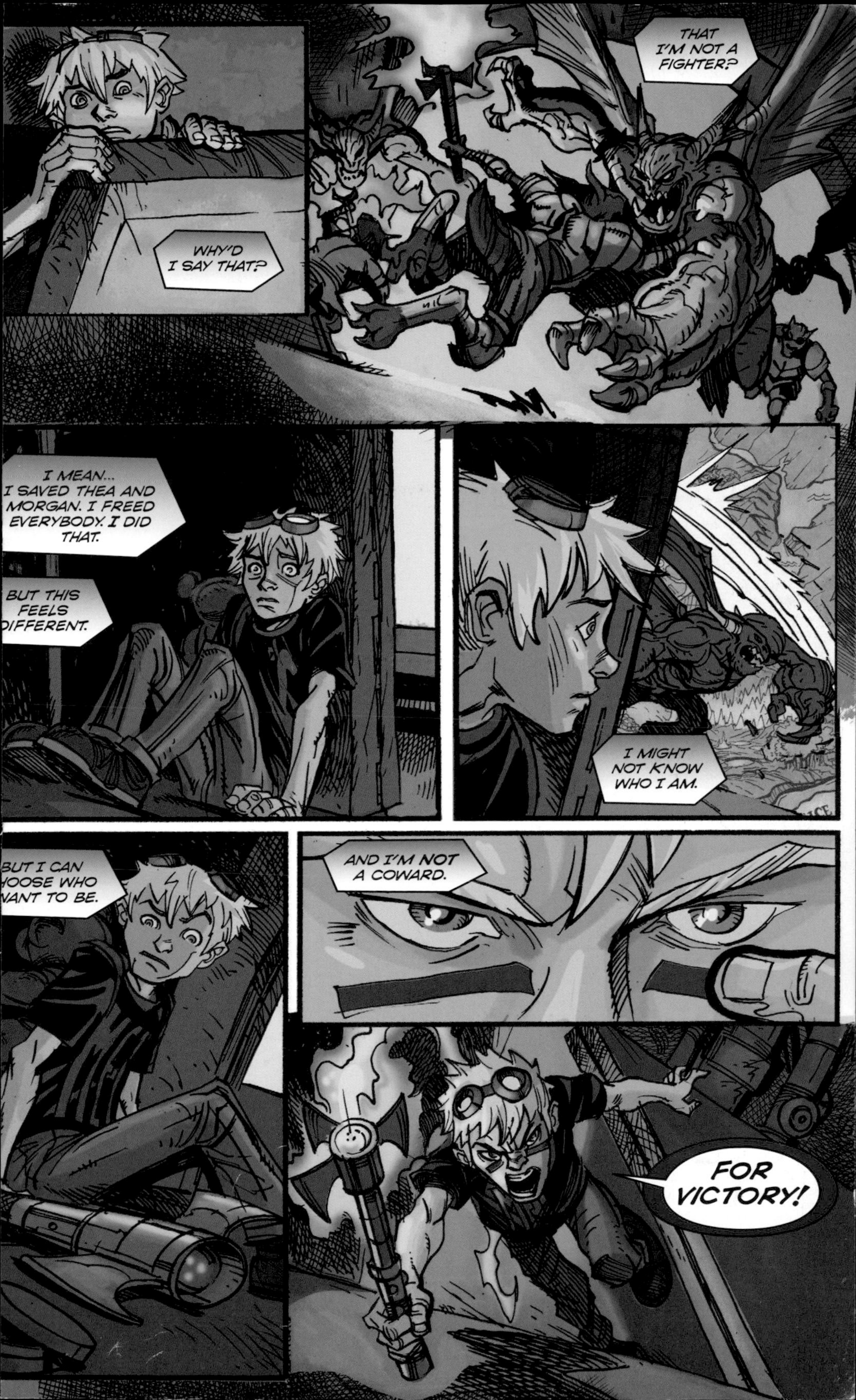
WHY'D I SAY THAT?
THAT I'M NOT A FIGHTER?
I MEAN... I SAVED THEA AND MORGAN. I FREED EVERYBODY. I DID THAT.
BUT THIS FEELS DIFFERENT.
I MIGHT NOT KNOW WHO I AM.
BUT I CAN HOOSE WHO WANT TO BE.
AND I'M NOT A COWARD.
FOR VICTORY!

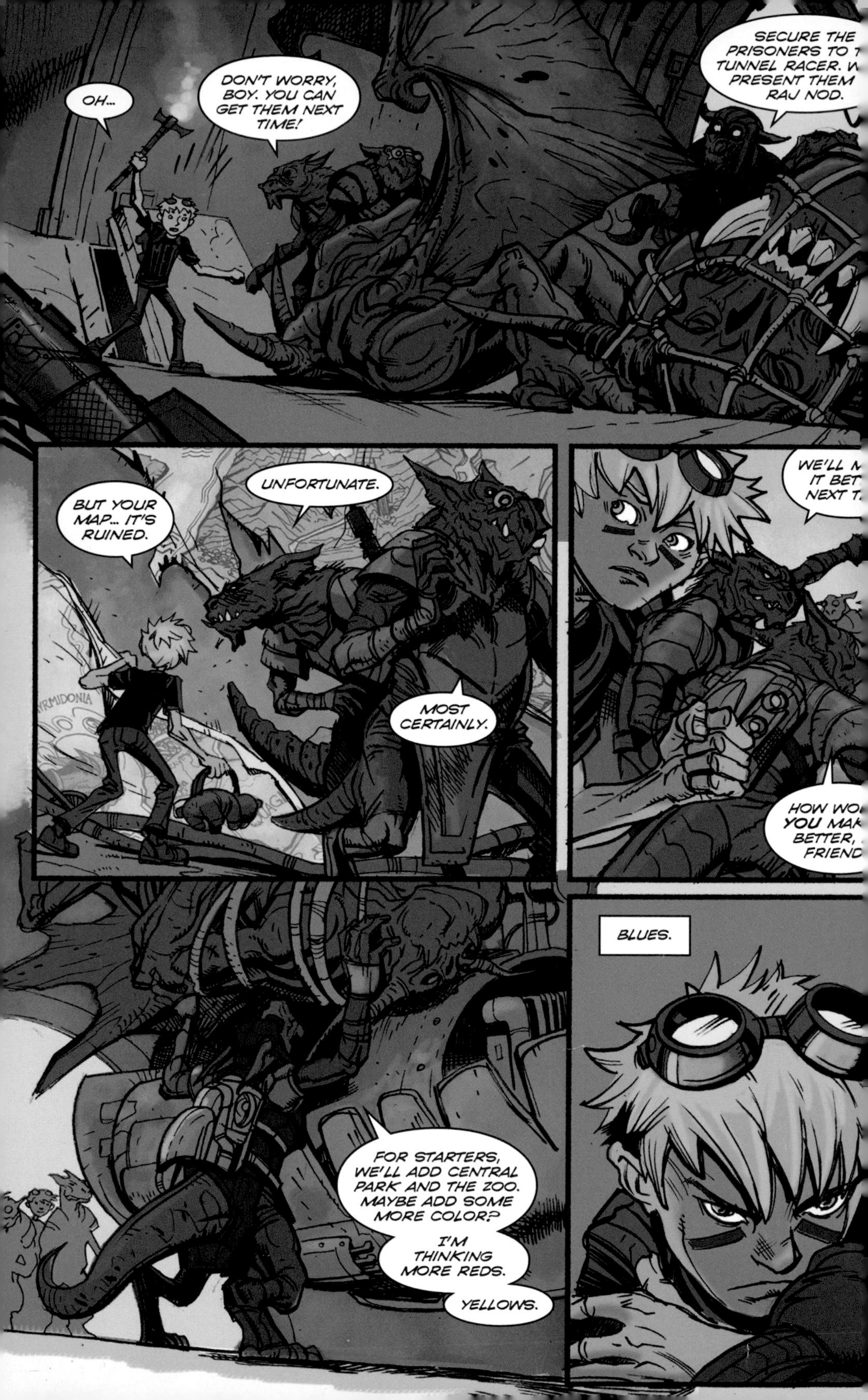
OH...
DON'T WORRY, BOY. YOU CAN GET THEM NEXT TIME!
BUT YOUR MAP... IT'S RUINED.
UNFORTUNATE.
MOST CERTAINLY.
FOR STARTERS, WE'LL ADD CENTRAL PARK AND THE ZOO. MAYBE ADD SOME MORE COLOR?
I'M THINKING MORE REDS.
YELLOWS.
BLUES.

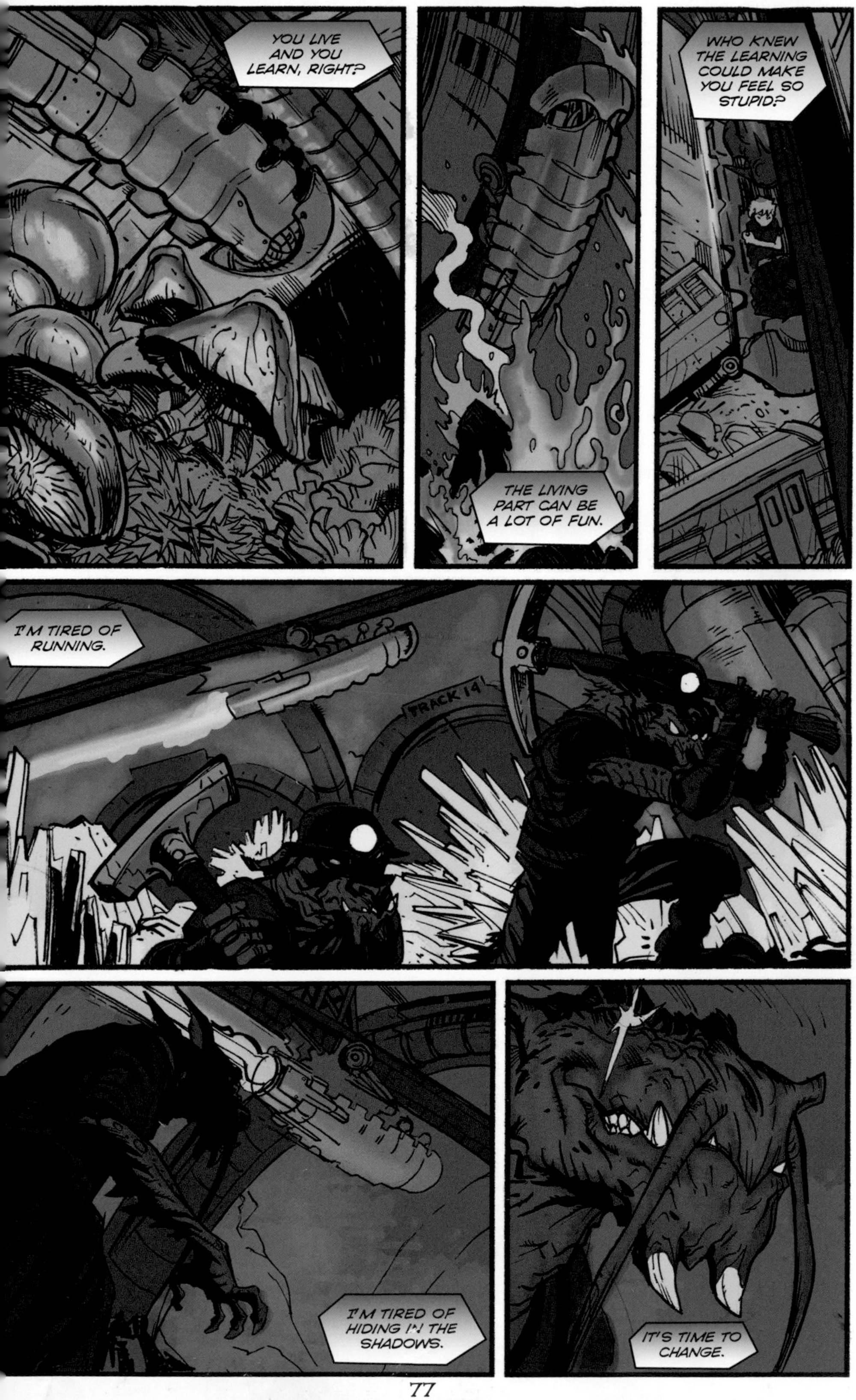
YOU LIVE AND YOU LEARN, RIGHT?
THE LIVING PART CAN BE A LOT OF FUN.
WHO KNEW THE LEARNING COULD MAKE YOU FEEL SO STUPID?
I'M TIRED OF RUNNING.
TRACK 14
I'M TIRED OF HIDING IN THE SHADOWS.
IT'S TIME TO CHANGE.

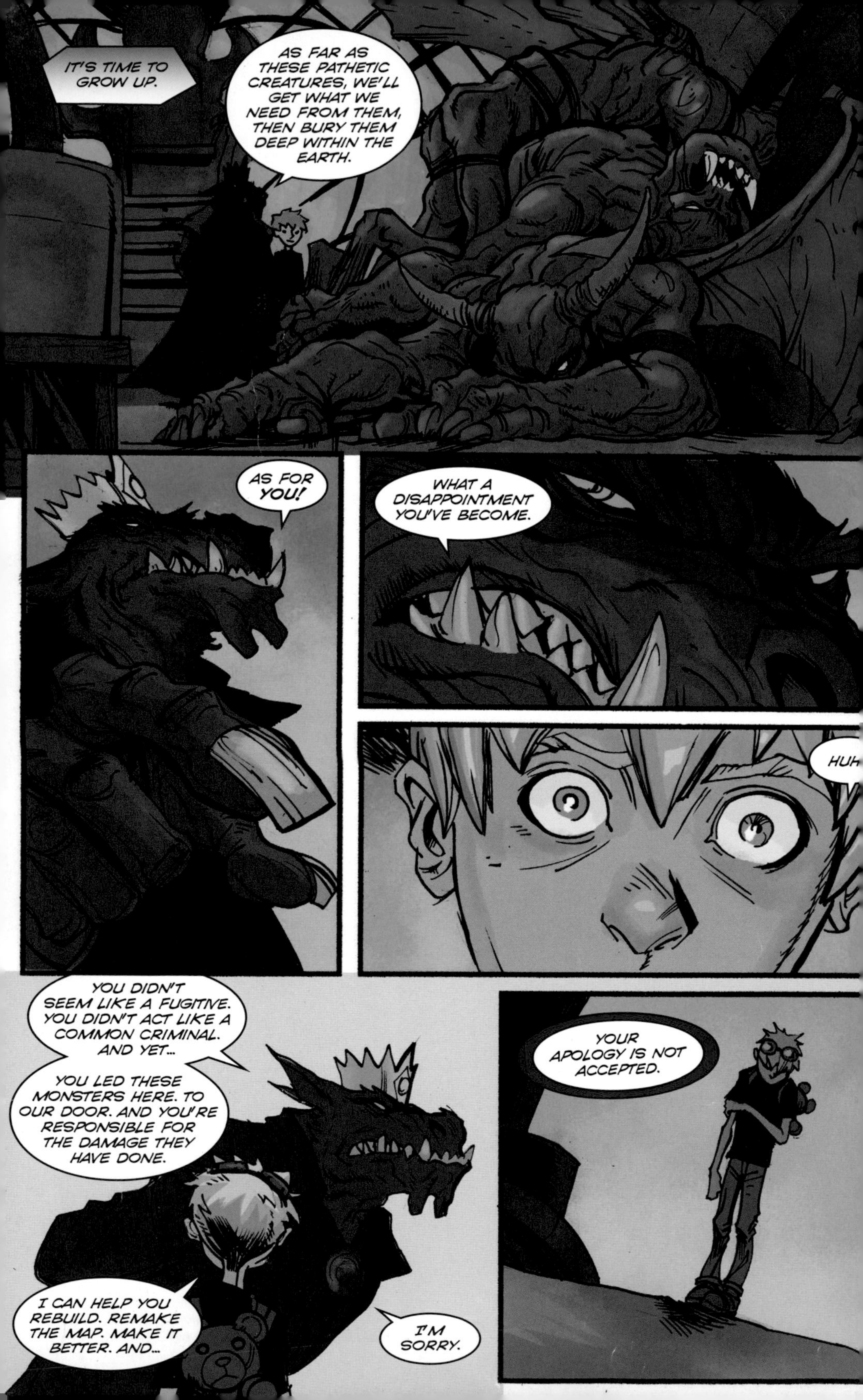
IT'S TIME TO GROW UP.
AS FAR AS THESE PATHETIC CREATURES, WE'LL GET WHAT WE NEED FROM THEM, THEN BURY THEM DEEP WITHIN THE EARTH.
AS FOR YOU!
WHAT A DISAPPOINTMENT YOU'VE BECOME.
HUH
YOU DIDN'T SEEM LIKE A FUGITIVE. YOU DIDN'T ACT LIKE A COMMON CRIMINAL. AND YET...
YOU LED THESE MONSTERS HERE. TO OUR DOOR. AND YOU'RE RESPONSIBLE FOR THE DAMAGE THEY HAVE DONE.
I CAN HELP YOU REBUILD. REMAKE THE MAP. MAKE IT BETTER. AND...
I'M SORRY.
YOUR APOLOGY IS NOT ACCEPTED.

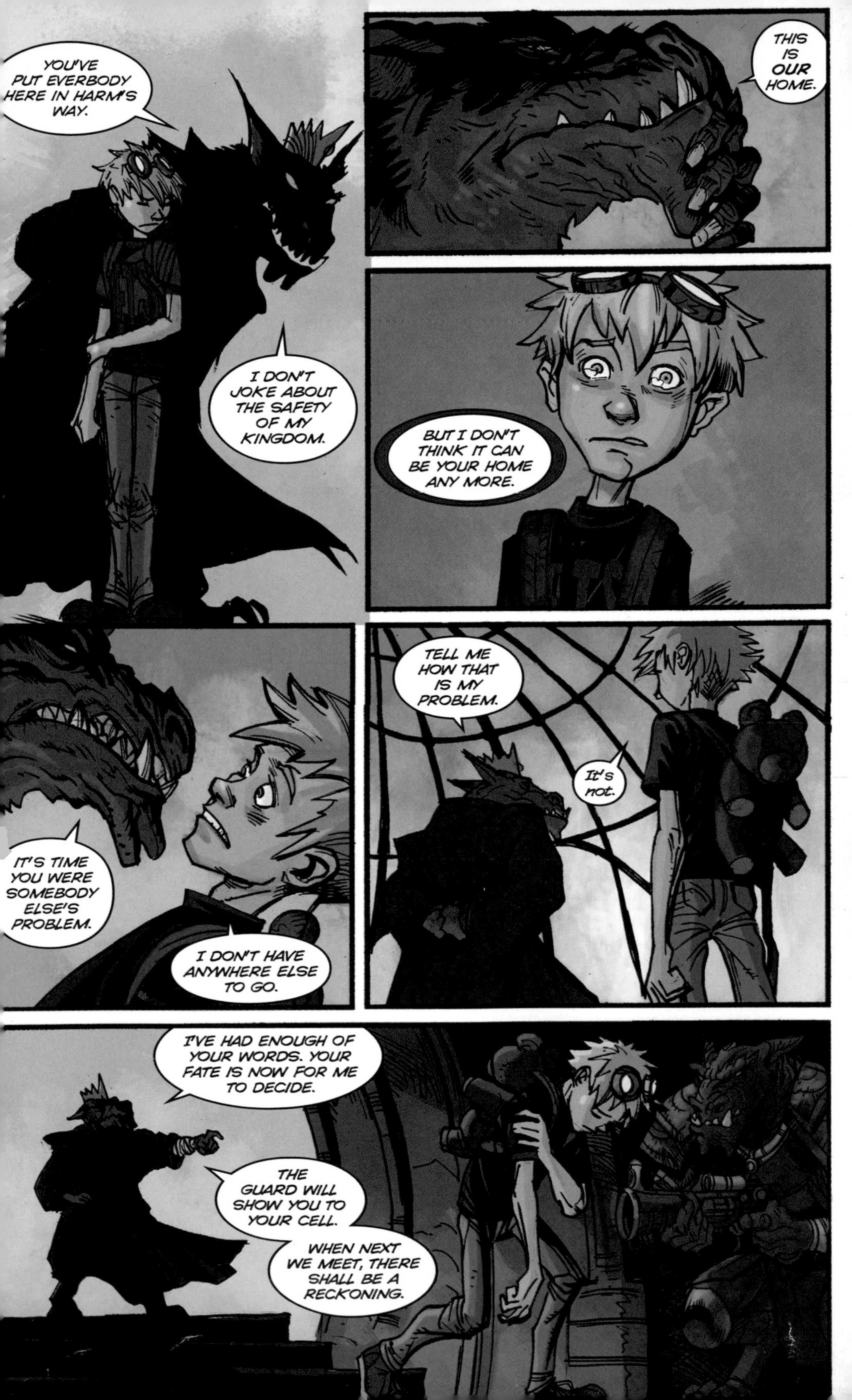
YOU'VE PUT EVERBODY HERE IN HARM'S WAY.
I DON'T JOKE ABOUT THE SAFETY OF MY KINGDOM.
THIS IS OUR HOME.
BUT I DON'T THINK IT CAN BE YOUR HOME ANY MORE.
IT'S TIME YOU WERE SOMEBODY ELSE'S PROBLEM.
I DON'T HAVE ANYWHERE ELSE TO GO.
TELL ME HOW THAT IS MY PROBLEM.
It's not.
I'VE HAD ENOUGH OF YOUR WORDS. YOUR FATE IS NOW FOR ME TO DECIDE.
THE GUARD WILL SHOW YOU TO YOUR CELL.
WHEN NEXT WE MEET, THERE SHALL BE A RECKONING.

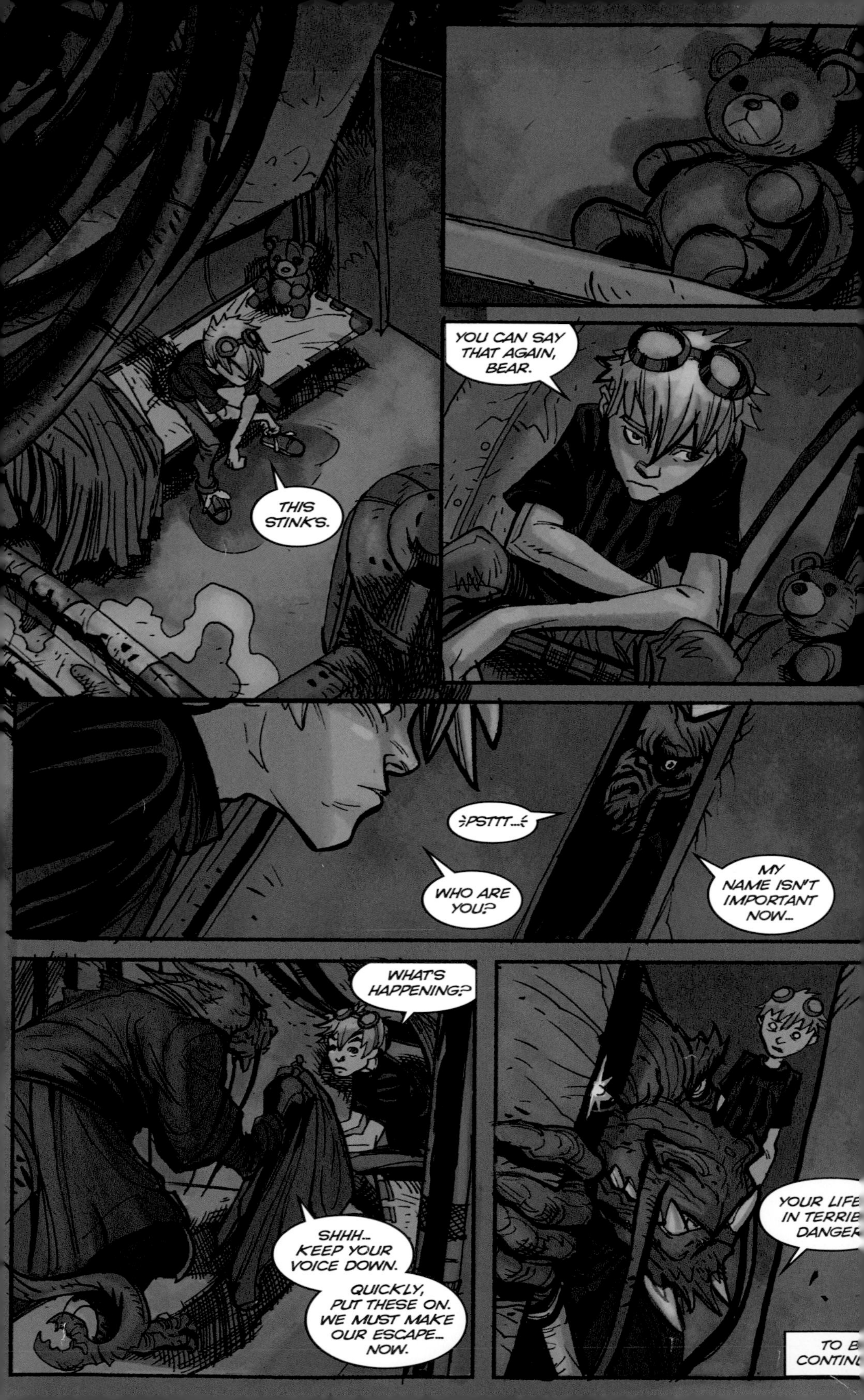
THIS STINKS.
YOU CAN SAY THAT AGAIN, BEAR.
PSTTT...
WHO ARE YOU?
MY NAME ISN'T IMPORTANT NOW...
WHAT'S HAPPENING?
SHHH... KEEP YOUR VOICE DOWN.
QUICKLY, PUT THESE ON. WE MUST MAKE OUR ESCAPE... NOW.

WATCH OUT FOR PAPERCUTZ™

elcome to the pulse-pounding, perplexing-problems-packed, premiere THE ONLY LIVING BOY graphic novel, by David llaher and Steve Ellis from Papercutz–those seemingly still alive comic-makers dedicated to publishing great graphic vels for all ages. I'm Jim Salicrup, the only sleeping Editor-in-Chief, and I'm here to take you behind the scenes–both Papercutz and the world of THE ONLY LIVING BOY.

t's start at the beginning. A little over ten years ago, Papercutz publisher Terry Nantier and I founded this little comicbook mpany to address a need–there just didn't seem to be enough comics and graphic novels for kids. That was incredibly nic, since most folks think of comics as being for kids. After ten years of producing all types of comics for all ages, we ade a great deal with the Dara Hyde at the Hill Nadell Agency, the agent for David and Steve, to publish the print version of eir popular online comics series THE ONLY LIVING BOY. This particular webcomic has already garnered three Harvey Award minations, including Best Original Graphic Publication for Younger Readers, but it was our erstwhile Production Coordinator th Scorzato who originally suggested that Papercutz should look into publishing it as a printed graphic novel series. Though ited-edition print editions have previously been sold by the creators at comic cons, Papercutz will proudly be offering our rsion–with all-new covers by Steve Ellis–through booksellers and comicbook stores, as well as through libraries.

r those of you not familiar with web comics, it's been quite the innovation. Theoretically, the Internet provides any would- comics-creator worldwide distribution. Back in the Old Days, if comicbook writers and artists wished to self-publish their aterial, it was taking quite a risk, especially if they printed up comics before getting actual orders. With comics online, eators can post pages one at a time on a daily or weekly basis, with their only financial risk being their investment of time eating the comics. Eventually, enough pages are accumulated that collections, such as ours, are possible.

any people wonder why a print edition is even necessary, and that's an excellent question. After all, why buy something uch as a book) when you can get the same material online for free? Makes sense, right? Yet one of the best-selling graphic vels series ever is *Diary of a Wimpy Kid* by Jeff Kinney (not to be confused with *Diary of Stinky Dead Kid*, which appeared TALES FROM THE CRYPT #8 and #9, from Papercutz!), which started as a web comic–so go figure!

nlike most Papercutz graphic novels which usually include self-contained stories, THE ONLY LIVING BOY is an ongoing series at's more in the tradition of ongoing comicbook series or ongoing TV series that tell stories that stretch out over several isodes. On the following pages, we're giving you a sneak peek at the second THE ONLY LIVING BOY graphic novel. We pe you enjoy it and return to find out what happens to Erik Farrell next in Beyond Sea and Sky"! Thanks,

Jim

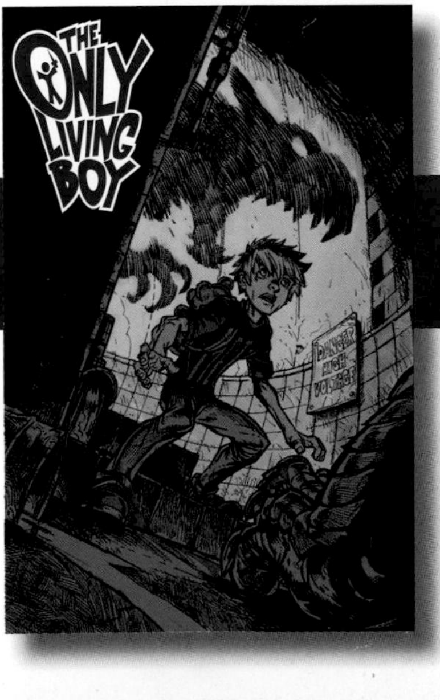
THE ONLY LIVING BOY

Cover of the second limited-edtion THE ONLY LIVING BOY ailable only at comic conventions from David Gallaher and Steve Ellis.

STAY IN TOUCH!

EMAIL: salicrup@papercutz.com
WEB: papercutz.com
TWITTER: @papercutzgn
FACEBOOK: PAPERCUTZGRAPHICNOVELS
FAN MAIL: Papercutz, 160 Broadway, Suite 700, East Wing, New York, NY 10038

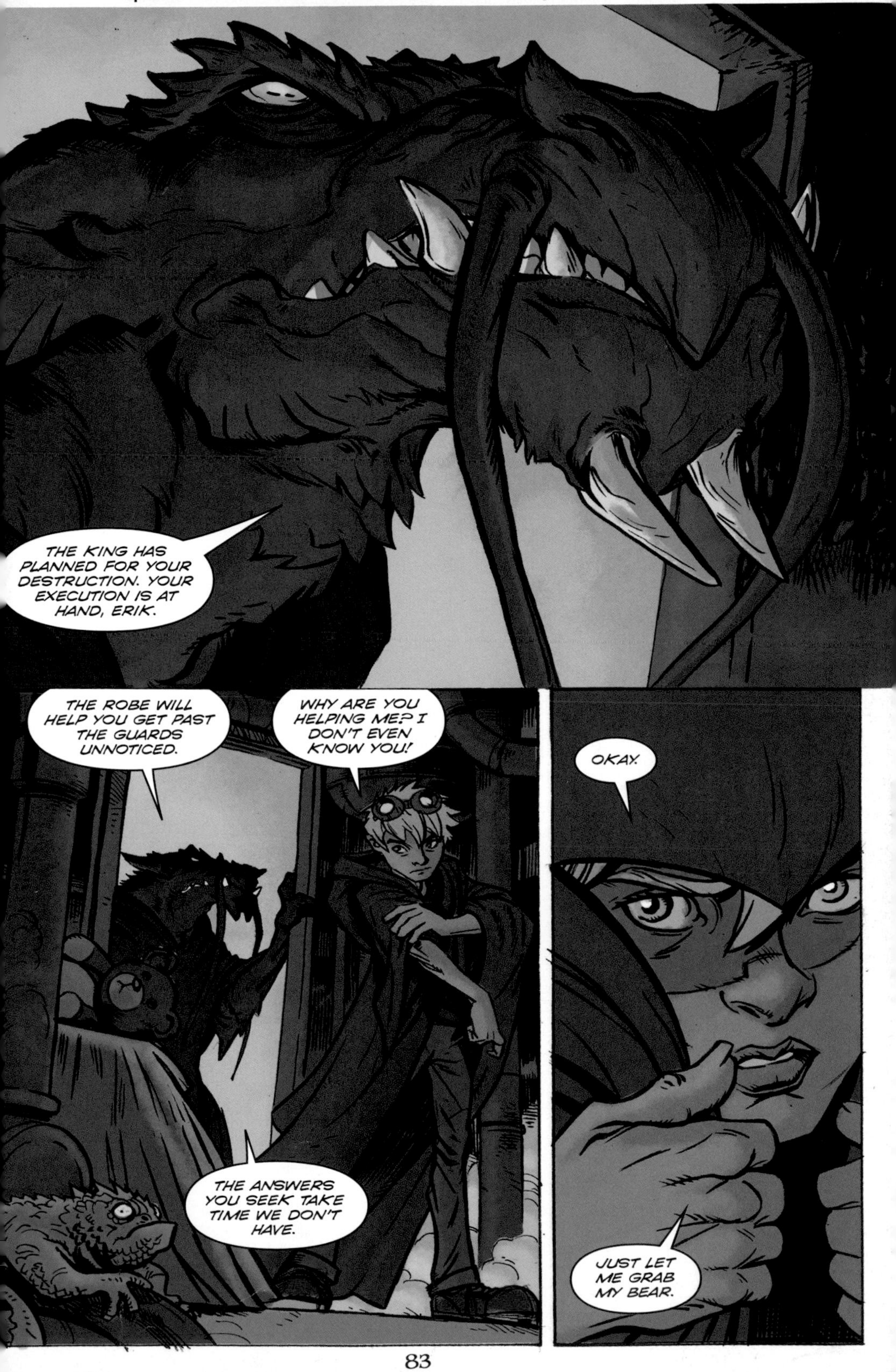
THE KING HAS PLANNED FOR YOUR DESTRUCTION. YOUR EXECUTION IS AT HAND, ERIK.
THE ROBE WILL HELP YOU GET PAST THE GUARDS UNNOTICED.
WHY ARE YOU HELPING ME? I DON'T EVEN KNOW YOU!
THE ANSWERS YOU SEEK TAKE TIME WE DON'T HAVE.
OKAY.
JUST LET ME GRAB MY BEAR.

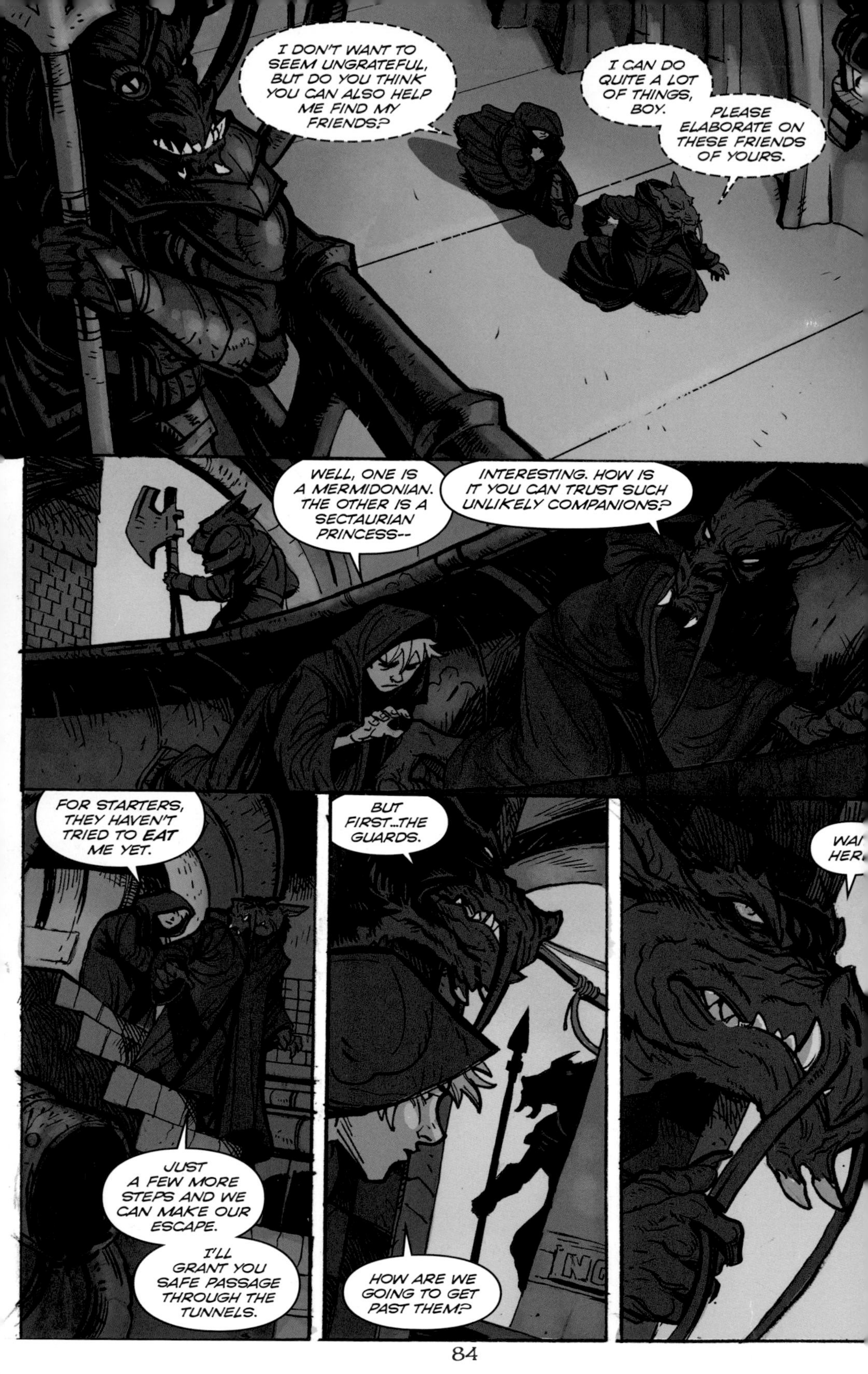

I DON'T WANT TO SEEM UNGRATEFUL, BUT DO YOU THINK YOU CAN ALSO HELP ME FIND MY FRIENDS?
I CAN DO QUITE A LOT OF THINGS, BOY.
PLEASE ELABORATE ON THESE FRIENDS OF YOURS.
WELL, ONE IS A MERMIDONIAN. THE OTHER IS A SECTAURIAN PRINCESS--
INTERESTING. HOW IS IT YOU CAN TRUST SUCH UNLIKELY COMPANIONS?
FOR STARTERS, THEY HAVEN'T TRIED TO EAT ME YET.
JUST A FEW MORE STEPS AND WE CAN MAKE OUR ESCAPE.
I'LL GRANT YOU SAFE PASSAGE THROUGH THE TUNNELS.
BUT FIRST...THE GUARDS.
HOW ARE WE GOING TO GET PAST THEM?

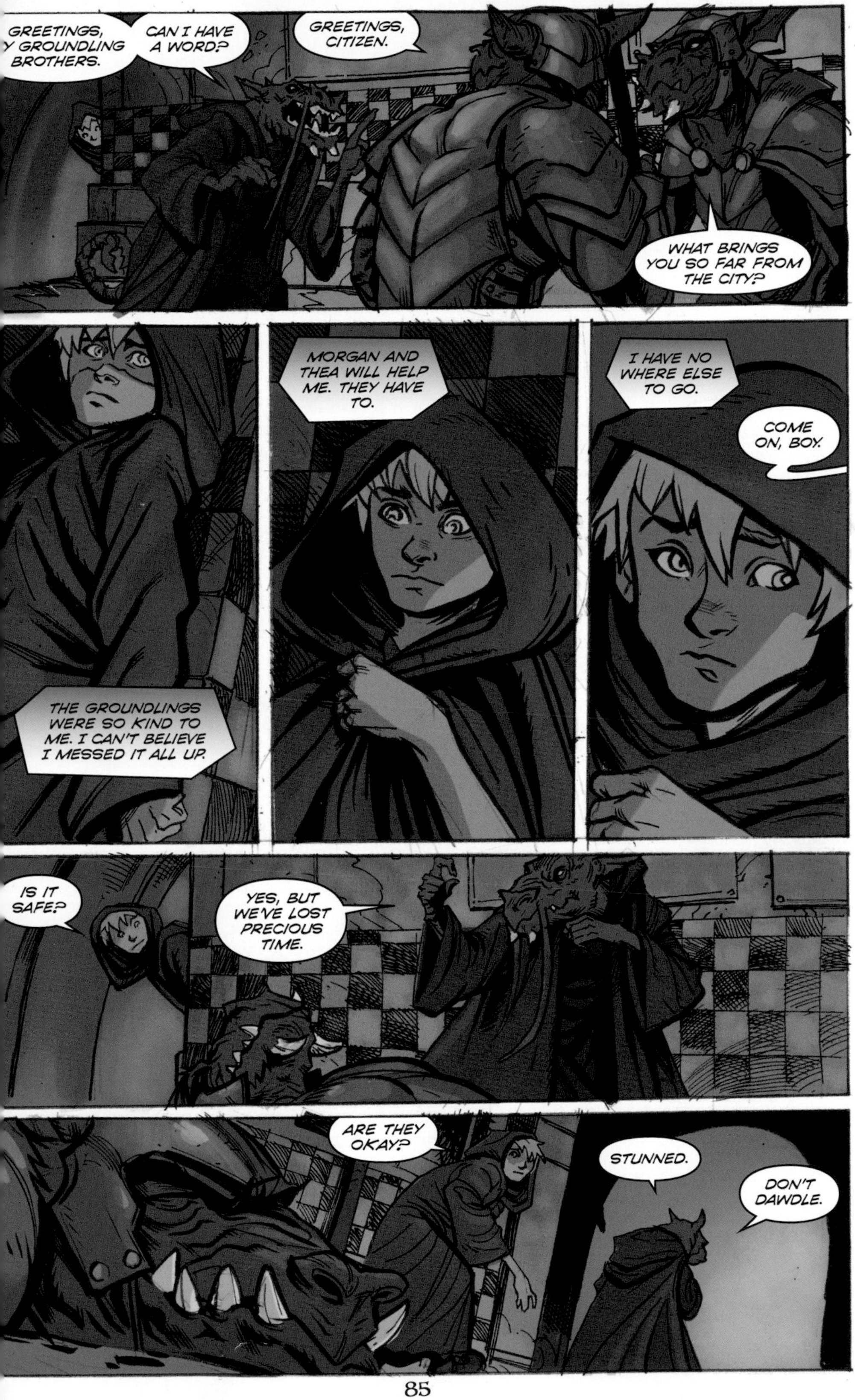
GREETINGS, Y GROUNDLING BROTHERS.
CAN I HAVE A WORD?
GREETINGS, CITIZEN.
WHAT BRINGS YOU SO FAR FROM THE CITY?
THE GROUNDLINGS WERE SO KIND TO ME. I CAN'T BELIEVE I MESSED IT ALL UP.
MORGAN AND THEA WILL HELP ME. THEY HAVE TO.
I HAVE NO WHERE ELSE TO GO.
COME ON, BOY.
IS IT SAFE?
YES, BUT WE'VE LOST PRECIOUS TIME.
ARE THEY OKAY?
STUNNED.
DON'T DAWDLE.

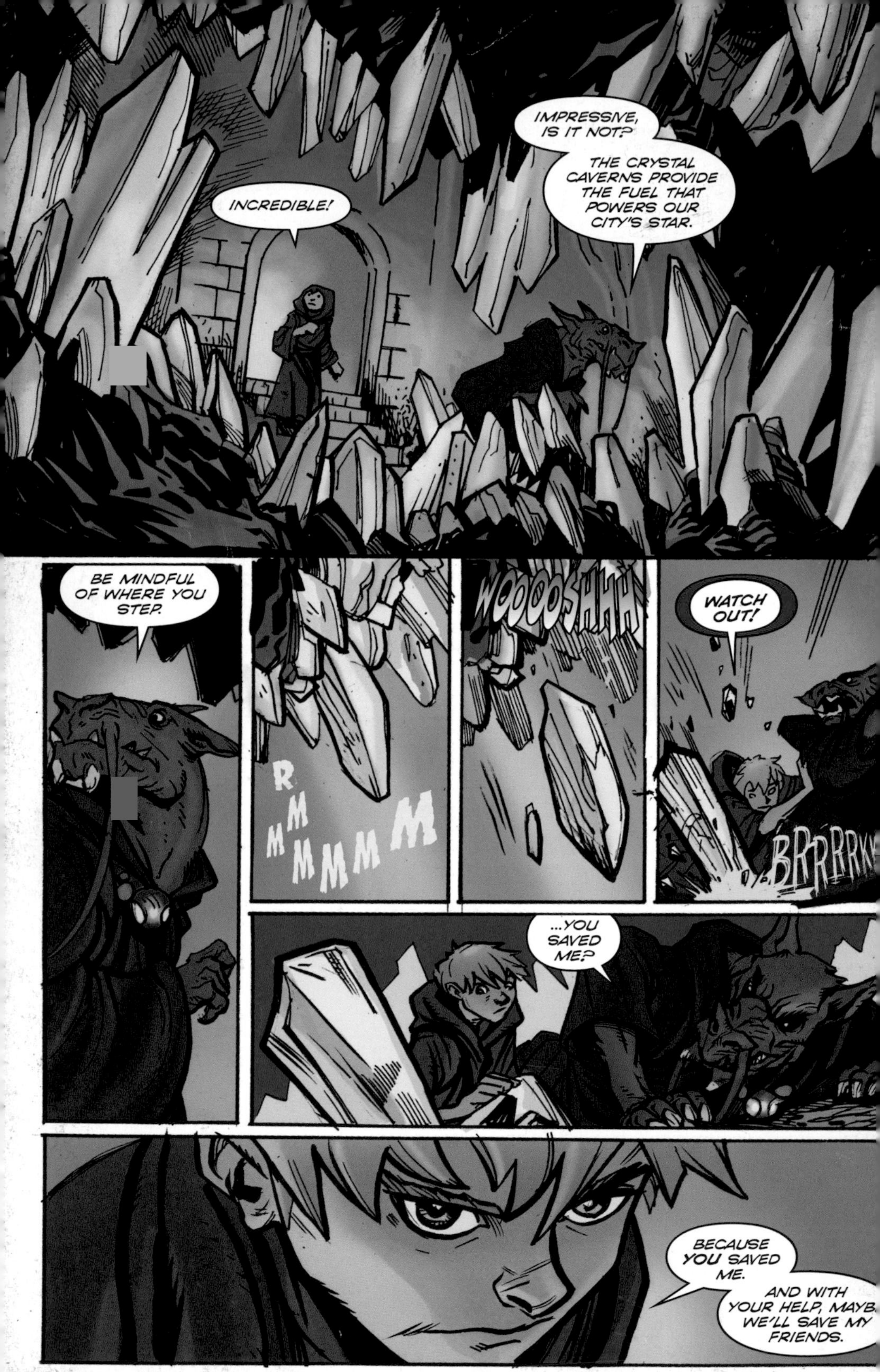
INCREDIBLE!
IMPRESSIVE, IS IT NOT?
THE CRYSTAL CAVERNS PROVIDE THE FUEL THAT POWERS OUR CITY'S STAR.
BE MINDFUL OF WHERE YOU STEP.
WATCH OUT!
...YOU SAVED ME?
BECAUSE YOU SAVED ME.
AND WITH YOUR HELP, MAYB WE'LL SAVE MY FRIENDS.

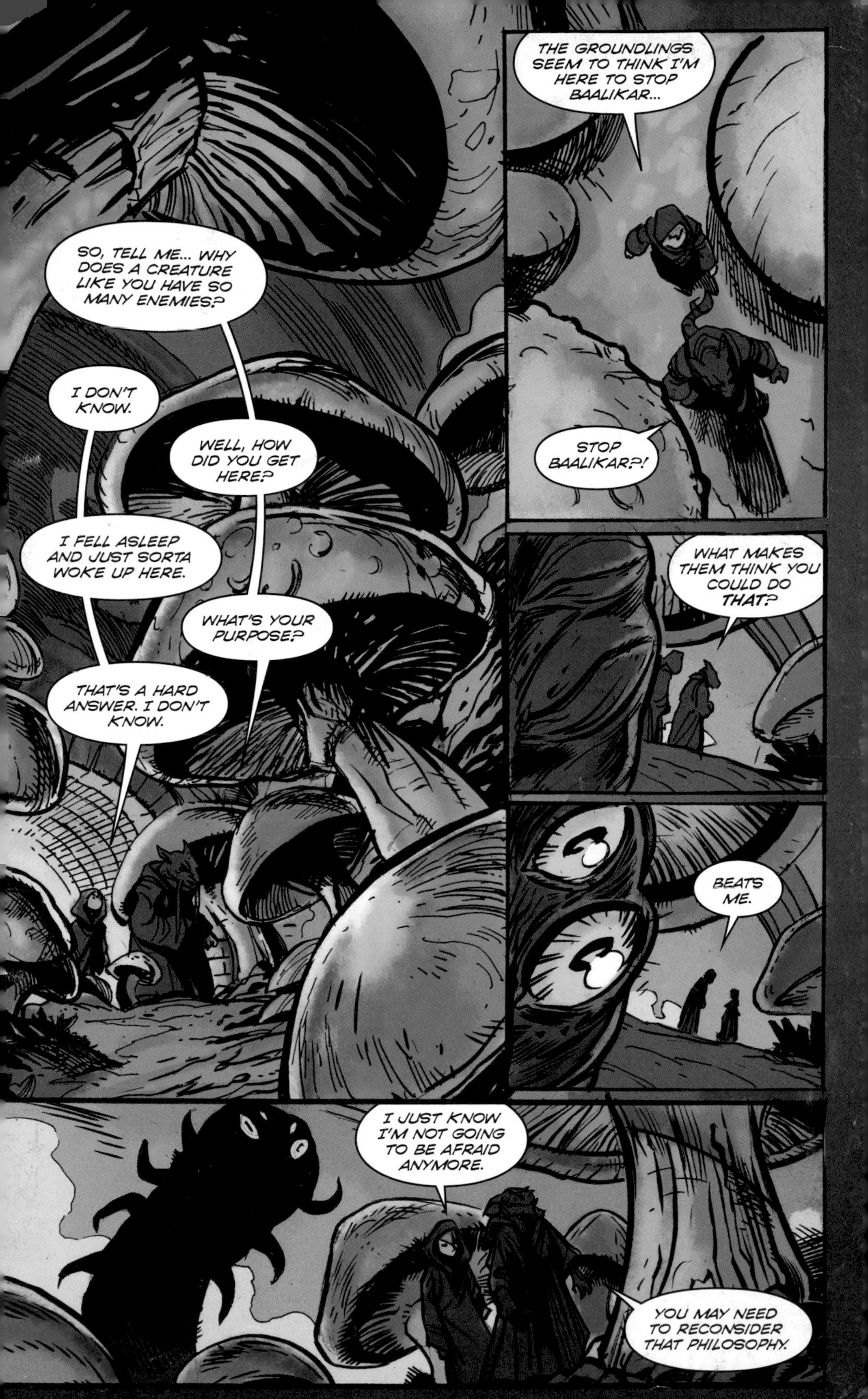
SO, TELL ME... WHY DOES A CREATURE LIKE YOU HAVE SO MANY ENEMIES?
I DON'T KNOW.
WELL, HOW DID YOU GET HERE?
I FELL ASLEEP AND JUST SORTA WOKE UP HERE.
WHAT'S YOUR PURPOSE?
THAT'S A HARD ANSWER. I DON'T KNOW.
THE GROUNDLINGS SEEM TO THINK I'M HERE TO STOP BAALIKAR...
STOP BAALIKAR?!
WHAT MAKES THEM THINK YOU COULD DO THAT?
BEATS ME.
I JUST KNOW I'M NOT GOING TO BE AFRAID ANYMORE.
YOU MAY NEED TO RECONSIDER THAT PHILOSOPHY.

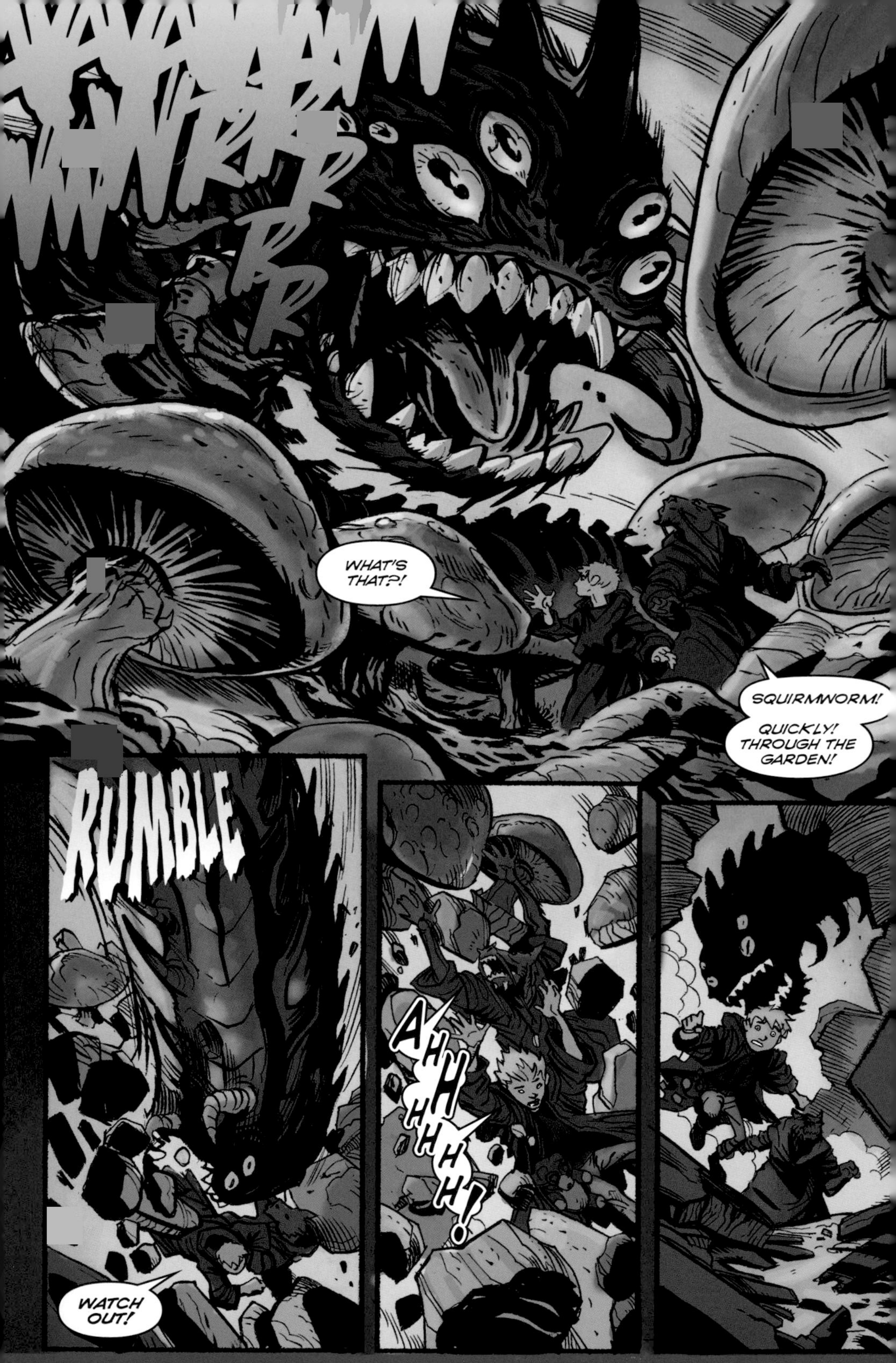
WHAT'S THAT?!
SQUIRMWORM!
QUICKLY! THROUGH THE GARDEN!
RUMBLE
WATCH OUT!
AHHHHHHH!